...CAN BE THE RISKIEST GAME IN TOWN

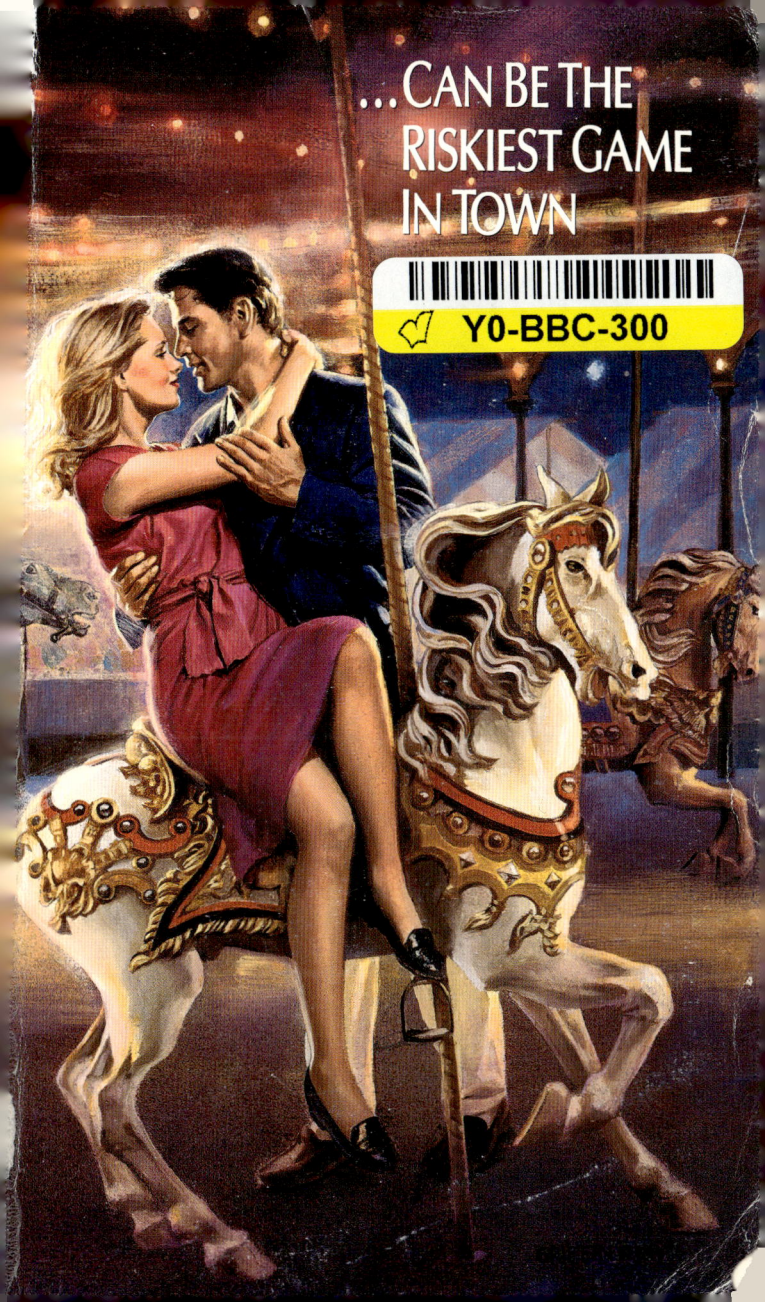

# THE WAGER

"Look, lady," he said, "I haven't done anything to you. I'm just here trying to do these people a favor . . ."

"A favor?" She laughed. "That's rich. You came here because you heard there was money here."

"Is that why you came here, Carny?"

She didn't ask how he knew her name. "It's none of your business why I came."

"Maybe it is," he said. "Maybe you're feeling threatened. Maybe you're the one with the scam, and you're afraid I'll horn in on it. You know what they say. You can't con a con."

"That's right," she said, standing up and starting to walk away. Then she looked over her shoulder and added, "And you can't con the daughter of a con, either. You've got your work cut out for you here, Brisco."

He didn't know whether that was meant as a threat or a casual warning, but something about it excited him more that anything had in years.

# Books by Terri Herrington

*Silena*
*Her Father's Daughter*
*One Good Man*
*Winner Take All*

Available from HarperPaperbacks

**Harper Monogram**

# WINNER TAKE ALL

*Terri Herrington*

**HarperPaperbacks**
*A Division of HarperCollinsPublishers*

If you purchased this book without a cover, you should be aware that this book is stolen property. It was reported as "unsold and destroyed" to the publisher and neither the author nor the publisher has received any payment for this "stripped book."

This is a work of fiction. The characters, incidents, and dialogues are products of the author's imagination and are not to be construed as real. Any resemblance to actual events or persons, living or dead, is entirely coincidental.

HarperPaperbacks  *A Division of* HarperCollins*Publishers*
10 East 53rd Street, New York, N.Y. 10022

Copyright © 1994 by Terri Herrington Blackstock
All rights reserved. No part of this book may be used or reproduced in any manner whatsoever without written permission of the publisher, except in the case of brief quotations embodied in critical articles and reviews. For information address HarperCollins*Publishers,*
10 East 53rd Street, New York, N.Y. 10022.

Front cover illustration by Paul Wright.
Stepback illustration by Jim Griffin.

First printing: February 1995

Printed in the United States of America

HarperPaperbacks, HarperMonogram, and colophon are trademarks of HarperCollins*Publishers*

❖ 10 9 8 7 6 5 4 3 2 1

# 1

*Logan Brisco had the* smile of an evangelical preacher, the confidence of a busy capitalist, the secrecy of a government spy, and the charisma of the pied piper. No one in the town of Serenity, Texas knew where he'd come from or why he was there, but they had gathered from his casually flung hints that he had come on a mission, and that it was something big.

From the moment he got off the train in his thousand-dollar suit and Italian shoes, carrying a briefcase in one hand and a duffel bag in the other, greeting strangers like a salesman, and flashing that Dennis Quaid smile to everyone he passed, he'd been the talk of the town. Two days later, when Larry Milford, the UPS man who made a daily run through Serenity from Odessa, delivered several large, heavy boxes marked "fragile" and addressed to "Brisco, c/o Welcome Inn," the gossip grew more frenzied.

Some said he was an IRS agent sent to spy on the moonshiners in the county. Others said he was with military intelligence and had come to investigate the UFOs that Sarah Jenkins claimed had abducted her fourteen times. Some of the men at Slade Hampton's Barber Shop decided he was a movie producer scouting talent for his latest picture. And the weekly patrons of the Curl Up & Dye Salon were sure he was a billionaire-in-hiding, looking for a wife.

In short, Logan Brisco had the townsfolk eating out of his hand, and that was just where he wanted them.

For three weeks, he fed this enigmatic image by keeping his mission clandestine. He talked to the people of the town, ate in its restaurants, shopped in its stores, bonded with its men, flirted with its women. When speculation had reached its height, and the town was ripe for the picking, Logan prepared to go in for the kill.

*This one,* he thought, *might be the biggest one yet.*

The first step would be to hold one of his seminars, the kind where people come in with a bundle of money and leave with empty pockets and heads full of dreams. That was what he was best at, he told himself. Building dreams, and taking money for them.

As if the universe were in cahoots with him, the

sun chose to shine brightly that Saturday after a week of rain. Serenity seemed to have come awake as its citizens came to town—which consisted mostly of four streets of shops, offices, and restaurants—to catch up on errands and chores. It was the perfect day to reach them, Logan thought.

His first stop that morning was at Peabody's print shop, where yesterday he had talked Julia Peabody into printing a thousand fliers for him on credit. "I'm not authorized to spend money on this project without the signatures of my major investors," he told her in a low voice, as if in confidence. "Can you just bill me at the Welcome Inn?"

Julia, the pretty daughter of the print-shop owner, glanced over her shoulder to see if her father was near. "Well, we're not supposed to give credit, Mr. Brisco."

"Logan, please," he said, leaning close to her across the counter.

"Logan," she said, blushing. "I mean . . . couldn't you just write a check and let them pay you back?"

"I'm in the process of opening a bank account here," he said with a hint of a grin sparkling in his eyes. "Thing is, I opened it yesterday, but they told me not to write any checks on it until my money is transferred from the Dallas bank where I've been doing business. Now if I were to write you a check and ask you to hold it, that would be exactly the same thing as your giving me credit, wouldn't it?"

"Well, yes, I guess it would," she said.

He smiled and paused for a moment, as though

he'd lost his train of thought. "You know, they sure do grow the women pretty in Serenity."

Julia breathed a laugh and rolled her eyes.

"Oh, I'm sorry," Logan said. "I changed the subject, didn't I?"

"That's okay."

"So . . . would you prefer a postdated check or credit?"

While she was thinking it over, he dropped the timbre of his voice and said, "By the way, are you planning to be at the bingo hall tonight?"

"I think so."

"Good," he said. "I was hoping you would."

Flustered, she handed him the fliers. "All right, Logan, I'll give you credit. You don't look like the type who would make me sorry."

Still grinning, he said, "Just look into these eyes, Julia. Tell me you don't see pure, grade-A honesty."

Laughing, she had to agree. "That's what I see."

"All right then." Standing straight, he glanced at the fliers. "They look good."

Julia looked over them, too, then cleared her throat. "Uh . . . I meant to ask you . . . what project is it that you're working on, Logan? I looked all over it, but the flier didn't say."

He shot her a you-devil grin and brought his index finger to his lips. "I can't tell you before I tell the rest of the townsfolk, now can I, Julia? It wouldn't be fair to cut you in before anybody else has had a chance."

"Oh, but I wouldn't tell anyone," she promised.

"Discretion is my middle name. Secrets come through this shop all the time, and I never say a word. Politicians, clergymen, whatnot. Everybody in town knows they can trust me."

Chuckling, he handed her back one of the fliers. "Come to the hall early tonight, in time for the meeting, and you'll hear everything you want to know. Now don't forget to send me that bill."

With a wink he was out the door, leaving her staring after him with a wistful look on her face.

Stepping out into the cool sunlight of the May day, he looked down at the box of fliers. *It shouldn't be too hard to pass all of them out by tonight,* he thought. And having the seminar at the bingo hall was a stroke of genius. That place drew hundreds of people on Saturday night, and tonight they'd just come a little early to hear him. By tomorrow, he'd be riding high.

He started to cross the street and head toward the hardware store, which seemed inordinately busy today. Easy marks there, he told himself. He'd hook every one of them.

He stopped, waited for a car to pass, then started to dart across, when he heard a Harley Hog growling its warning as it tore its way up the street, breaking the relative quiet that he had come to associate with the town. He stepped back as it passed, but as its wheel cut through a puddle on the street, it splashed mud onto the shins of his pants.

"Hey!" he yelled. But the driver apparently didn't hear, and as Logan stared after the bike, he realized it carried a woman and a little boy. Her shoulder-length baby-blonde hair stuck out from under the unlatched helmet she wore, softening the look of the potential Hell's Angel. As she went up the street, people looked her way and waved, apparently pleased to see her rather than annoyed at the disruption.

Logan tried to rein in his temper as she pulled into a parking space and cut off the loud engine. It wouldn't pay to ruin the image he'd so carefully cultivated here by throttling the first woman who had the gall to ruffle his feathers. It was an accident, he told himself. An accident she would, no doubt, be glad to apologize for.

As she got off the bike, he reached her. "Excuse me. You just splashed mud all over my pants."

The woman pulled off her helmet, revealing a head full of hair. First, she eyed him with curiosity, then glanced down at his pants. "Sure did. The street's full of puddles today. Jason and I have mud all over our legs, too, don't we, Jase?"

Logan saw that they did indeed, but they accepted the fact with determined nonchalance. Shifting the fliers from one arm to the other, Logan gaped at the little boy as he got off the bike, and then brought his gaze back to the woman. She didn't seem to have the stature to hold up a Harley, much less ride one.

"This is the only pair of dress pants I have with me."

Shrugging, she said, "Then you should have been more careful."

"Me?" He glanced down at the little boy pulling

his helmet off, then back to the woman standing there, looking at him with those big green eyes, oblivious to what she'd done wrong. "*You're* the one who did it."

Again, she eyed the mud on his pants. "You know, I bet it would come off with a little water, if you don't stand here and let them dry. A little mud never hurt anyone. Did it, Jason?"

"Nope. It washes right off. I get into it all the time." The child, who looked no more than seven, held up his own feet and showed him the caked mud on the bottoms of his shoes. "Hey, are you the movie producer guy?"

Still frowning, Logan nodded. "Yeah. I mean, no. Where'd you get that idea?"

"Everybody's talking," Jason said.

With decided effort, Logan let go of his ire and flashed him that political grin. "Well, I guess they are. Maybe I've been a little too secretive. My name's Logan Brisco." He reached out to shake the woman's hand, but she crossed her arms, refusing it. As an alternative, he settled for shaking the boy's.

"I'm Jason Sullivan. And this is my mom."

"Mrs. Sullivan," he said, nodding and searching those eyes for some sign of a crack in that seemingly hard facade. Women usually didn't like the formalities, he thought. They usually corrected him, and told him their first names. But this one seemed a little tougher than the usual women he ran across. "You know, if everybody's so curious, they'll be able to find out tonight what I'm doing in town. Six o'clock, at the bingo hall. Hope you'll both be there. And here . . . I'll give you a few of these fliers to pass out, if you wouldn't mind."

The woman didn't take the fliers, but the boy grabbed the stack he proffered.

"Me too? Do I get to come?" the kid asked.

"Sure. This affects everybody in town."

"What does?" the woman asked. She took one of the fliers out of her son's hand and scanned it. "It doesn't say here what your seminar is about."

Logan set his hand across her shoulders and dipping his head to her ear, said in his most conspiratorial voice, "It's about making all your dreams come true."

She shrugged his arm off her. "My dreams have already come true."

That was a new one, he thought, stepping back. No one had ever told him that. "Then let me show you how to make the most of them," he said in the mesmerizing tone that had made him such a success in his line of work. "Let me show you how to maximize your potential and minimize your risk, how to build your fortune the way everybody else in this town is going to, how to make your mark in the world and leave your signature on it."

As he spoke, instead of the starry-eyed wonder he usually encountered with that speech, he saw her expression hardening even more. "Let me give you a warning, mister. Not everyone in this town is fooled by that act. It only takes one person to blow your cover, and I'm the one who's going to do it."

He looked shocked. "Assuming there's a cover to blow."

Her cool smile told him there was no doubt in her mind. "I know your kind," she said. "I knew it the first time one of my neighbors started waxing poetic about the new man in town. You're a two-bit con artist, and you think you can come into Serenity and milk these people for everything they're worth. This town has enough problems, and I'm not gonna let you do it."

She started to walk away, but he couldn't let it go at that. Following her, he said, "You're pretty sure of yourself, aren't you?"

"That's right."

"What if you're wrong, and you miss out on your chance to get richer than you ever imagined?"

"I'm never wrong," she said. "Ask anybody." Then holding her helmet by the chin strap, she threw it over her shoulder and started up the sidewalk.

Logan watched her sashay away from him, walking like a woman who didn't care who admired her, or who didn't. She wasn't the kind who needed attention, but he would have staked everything on the fact that she got it wherever she went. When she reached the hardware store her son had gone into moments before, she glanced back, as if to make sure Logan was watching as she dropped his flier into a wastebasket.

Logan grinned. This was going to be even more fun than he thought. He might even have to stay longer than he'd planned, just to meet the challenge of the little lady whose first name he didn't know.

\* \* \*

The ladies of the Curl Up & Dye Salon cackled and fluttered as Logan stepped inside, breathing in the scent of hair spray and peroxide, and trying not to cough. "Hello, ladies," he said with that disarming grin.

A dozen women crooned back their hellos and preened with their rollers, their rods, and their teased tresses, as if he would see past them to the beauty that lay just moments away. Across the room, he saw Julia Peabody, the woman who'd done the fliers, sitting in front of the hair dryers where she had the attention of at least five women. *Perfect*, Logan thought.

"Mr. Brisco," Lahoma Kirtland called from the sink where she was dyeing the head of Mildred Smith. Abandoning her client, she held her gloved, red-dyed hands up like a surgeon, and made a bee-line across the shop.

"Please, darlin'. My daddy was Mr. Brisco. I'm just Logan." His grin was downright sinful as he looked around the room. "I was just strolling through town, wondering where all the prettiest ladies were. And lo and behold, I think I've found them all right here."

The women giggled and exchanged delighted looks. "It's so nice to see you," Lahoma said. "We were just talking about you, weren't we, girls?"

"Were you now? Nothing bad, I hope." He glanced through the arch that separated the main part of the salon from the room with the dryers.

"Julia, honey. You aren't giving away all my secrets now, are you?"

Julia stood up from her chair, looking embarrassed. "I was just spreading word about your seminar. Everyone's so excited."

"Well, good," he said, reaching into his box and pulling out a handful of fliers. "I hope you'll all tell your friends, and your friends' friends, and your enemies, and your lovers, and . . . "

A titter of giggles made its way around the shop as he put a flier into each lady's hand.

"Tell them all that this could be the most important meeting of their lives. Years from now, you'll all look back and remember how your lives were changed when Logan Brisco blew into town."

The door clanged open behind him and closed with a tinkling bell. He turned around and saw the blonde woman bouncing her son on her back as she cut across the first level of the salon and up the stairs to where Lahoma's station was, zigzagging and swaying, pretending she might drop him. Holding on for dear life, the boy giggled and shouted for her to stop.

Realizing Lahoma wasn't at her station, she spun around, inciting a scream from the child. "Lahoma," she shouted over his giggles when she spotted the proprietor, "have you got time to give Jason a haircut? Slade's too busy down at the barbershop."

"We can work him in, honey, as soon as one of the girls is finished," Lahoma said. "Come on over here and get one of Logan's fliers."

It was only then that she saw Logan standing behind Lahoma, grinning as if he'd manipulated the whole day to get her to this moment. Letting her son slide down her back, she blew her wispy bangs out of her eyes and came toward the beautician who held his flier with her rubber gloves still wet with red dye.

"Yeah, I got one," she said, coming toward them. "I put it in an appropriate place."

Grinning, he turned back to the patrons. "Now if you ladies wouldn't mind passing some out," he said, "I'll give you a few extra fliers."

"I'll take some," a woman from the dryer called.

The woman with the red dye forgotten in her hair sat up. "I'll take some, too."

"Anybody else?" Logan asked. "You won't regret it. Anybody you talk into coming is going to owe you a lifelong debt."

"Sold," his nemesis said, her eyes dancing. "Give me the whole stack. I'll be rid of them in five minutes."

He chuckled and withheld them from her. "I don't think so. Besides, you've got that haircut to wait for. And this place is chock-full of lovely young ladies who'd be more than willing to come to the aid of a newcomer to town."

"Oh, brother," she said, grabbing her son's hand and starting back to the door. "Come on, Jason, let's go."

"Aren't you going to get him his haircut?" Lahoma called after her.

"I think I'll go wait for Slade," she said. "The

air's a little hot in here. And Lahoma, you should really finish Mildred's hair before that peroxide eats through her scalp."

The door clanged shut behind her, and Lahoma slapped her red hands on her face. "Oh, my lord, I forgot!" She ran up to the second level, where Mildred still sat with dye dripping down her forehead, and hastily pushed Mildred's head back into the sink and turned the water on.

Logan grinned and watched out the window as the blonde woman sashayed up the sidewalk. "I don't think she likes me."

"Sure she does," Lahoma said. "Carny gets along with everybody. She has a way about her that you have to get used to, but she's been a breath of fresh air to this town."

"Carny?" he asked. "What kind of name is that?"

"She was brought up in the carnival," Lahoma replied.

Mildred's eyes rolled back in her head as Lahoma scrubbed her scalp, and in a voice just short of a groan, added, "Carny Sullivan. She moved here when she married Bev's boy Abe."

"Then she isn't a native of Serenity?"

"Carny?" Lahoma chuckled. "Heavens no. But she's sure brought a little color to it. Abe was no good, though. He lit out a year after he brought her here, hasn't been heard from since."

"And she stayed?"

"Of course she did. She's one of us now. We love her, even if she does do her own hair."

Laughing, Logan offered his good-byes to the

ladies, and went back outside. On the next block, he saw Carny and her son sitting on the bench outside the barbershop. He strolled toward them as if he were in no particular hurry.

He tried to calculate her age as he did and decided she was probably under twenty-five. But the kid was at least six . . . maybe seven. She'd been a child bride, he decided, and probably a teenaged mother. The confusing part was that savvy edge she had, that mature expression on her face, that lack of innocence that only came with age.

He should stay away from her, he told himself. That had been Montague's first rule. Never let a woman get under your skin—especially one who had the goods on you. It could be the kiss of death. Yet he couldn't seem to keep himself from confronting her again . . . just one more time.

"I saw you coming out of the print shop," she said as he approached her. "Twenty bucks says you didn't pay for those fliers."

He glanced down at her, surprised that she would know that. "Of course I did."

She laughed and pulled her foot up to the edge of the bench. "No, you didn't. You conned her into giving you credit, didn't you?"

"Mom!" the boy said, embarrassed.

"And you probably haven't let go of a cent at the Welcome Inn yet."

He set the fliers on the end of the bench. "How did you know where I'm staying?"

She smiled. "I'm a genius. That, and the fact that it's the only motel in town. So how are you gonna hoodwink the men in the barbershop? Can't flirt with them like you did the ladies. But you can still flatter them, can't you? Touch on their misfortune. Plant ideas in their minds. You've probably learned enough about the town after three weeks to know everybody's Achilles' heels."

His smile faded, and slowly, deliberately, he put his mud-splattered foot on the edge of the bench and leaned toward her. "I don't know yours."

"That's because I don't have one."

Why her comeback delighted him so, he wasn't sure, but he found himself grinning at her and wondering what made her so different from the other women he was usually able to charm. Was it that she stared back at him, undaunted and unflattered by his close scrutiny? Or that she had his number, or thought she did, and wasn't going to let him get away with a thing?

She glanced away when she heard Jason's name being called from inside and nodded for the boy to go in. "Tell him to cut it shorter around the ears. And I want to be able to see your eyebrows."

"Aw, Mom!"

"Go," she said, shooing him away.

When he was gone, she brought her gaze back to Logan, and stared at him as if waiting for him to explain why he was standing there with his foot on her bench.

"Look, I don't know what your vendetta is, but I haven't done anything to you. I'm just here trying to do these people a favor. . . ."

"A favor?" She laughed. "That's rich. You came

here because you heard there was money here. That the local oil boom back in the fifties left these people sitting pretty, and that the town was vulnerable, because the wells have played out, and the farms have been losing money, and everybody's waiting for a savior to show them how to get rich quick."

"Is that why you came here, Carny?"

She didn't ask how he knew her name. "It's none of your business why I came."

"Maybe it is," he said. "Maybe you're feeling threatened. Maybe you're the one with the scam, and you're afraid I'll horn in on it. You know what they say. You can't con a con."

"They're right, whoever they are," she said, standing up and starting toward the door of the barbershop. Just before she went in, she looked over her shoulder and added, "And you can't con the daughter of a con, either. You've got your work cut out for you here, Brisco."

Logan didn't know whether that was meant as a threat or a casual warning, but something about it excited him more than anything had in years.

As he picked up his fliers and started up the street, he told himself that he wasn't just going to get rich in Serenity. He was also going to have the time of his life, with this little fireball who called herself Carny.

# 2

*Jason got away from* Carny that night before she'd even had time to stop her truck completely. Sighing, she watched him catch up to his friends, who were going into the bingo hall en masse. This Logan fellow was good, she thought, cutting off her engine. She had to give him that. He had the town in a fever, and she supposed he could sell them Romania tonight, if she was right about their moods. The fact that it wasn't for sale wouldn't even cross their minds.

That's why she had come.

She got out of the pickup, glad she hadn't chosen to bring her Harley tonight. She'd rather not call attention to the fact that she had come to hear what he had to say. She slammed the door shut behind her.

"Hey, Carny," Paul Dillard called from his parking space across the street.

She waved and waited for the man who'd had his eye on her since Abe had brought her to Serenity. "Not you, too, Paul. You're not buying what this guy's selling, are you?"

"I don't *know* what he's selling," he said. "Never hurts to listen."

"Yeah, well, just don't give him any money tonight, okay? No matter what he says, don't give him any money."

"If you're so doggone sure he's up to no good, why are you here?"

"Somebody sane had to be here. I swear, I think I'm the only one in town who's thinking straight about this guy."

"You're just the suspicious type," Paul said, opening the door for her as they reached the aluminum building.

"There's a difference between suspicious and savvy," she said. "I've been around, Paul. I know when things aren't right."

"Just listen to the man," he said. "He might surprise you."

Carny caught Logan's eye as she entered the packed room, and when he flashed her that devil-may-care smile, she shook her head. "I don't think so, Paul. Nothing he does is going to surprise me."

She left Paul there and wove through the townspeople she had come to know well over the last seven years. She couldn't believe how many of them had turned out for this. They didn't get this

# WINNER TAKE ALL

big a crowd at church on Sunday mornings, or at the Fourth of July picnic, or at the Christmas pageant. And the nervous, excited hum over the crowd was something she hadn't experienced since she'd settled here.

But she had experienced it before.

It was the same anticipation that the marks had had at the carnival. The same fervor that her father and mother had inspired to set up their own little scams. Carny had even been a part of them. She'd picked her share of pockets, created her share of diversions, acted in her share of schemes. And the more excited the crowd became at whatever the grift happened to be, the more she told herself they deserved what they were getting.

But the people of Serenity didn't deserve anything of the kind.

A few of the men on the outskirts of the bingo hall offered her their seats, but she chose to stand. It made her feel more empowered. She suspected that it wouldn't pay ever to be caught sitting when Logan Brisco was around.

She watched as the man who had drawn this crowd, the enigma about whom there had been so much gossip in the last three weeks, walked up to the podium. That charm-packed grin gave him an ironic look of innocence as he scanned the room. "Well, now. It looks like there are more intelligent people in Serenity, Texas, than I thought there were."

His gaze landed on her as the crowd gave a light round of applause, and she knew what he was thinking. He was thinking that she had been too curious to stay away, that he was winning her over. He was thinking that she was just like all the other suckers in the room.

But soon enough he would see what she was made of. If he was going to run a scam through this town, he'd have hell to pay first.

"Ladies and gentlemen," he said in a soft accent that she guessed came from the Midwest somewhere, "I thank you all for coming. And I can promise you won't regret it. I've come to grow pretty fond of many of you over the last three weeks. Slade, who gives the best haircuts this side of the Mississippi. And Bonnie at the cafe, who makes the best lemon icebox pie I've ever put in my mouth. And Mildred and Tommy Slater at the hardware store, and the Sheaffers over at the post office . . . Well, I could go on and on. Suffice it to say that I've never met a warmer town. And because you've all touched me in such a personal way, I want to give something back now."

*Here it comes*, Carny thought as her stomach tightened. *Get the shovels ready.*

Logan cleared his throat. "Many of you have wondered why I've been so secretive over the last three weeks. Well, I suppose you have a right to be curious. But the truth is that I represent a venture that is being backed by some of the biggest banks in Texas, as well as some corporate investors I'm not at liberty to name just yet. But we're talking technological giants, with money to burn. I've spent the last several months scouting around in rural parts of the state, trying to find the best location for this venture. Serenity, while it wasn't at the top of our list of sites, looked like a good possibility. There's an awful lot of fallow land on the western side of Serenity. Acres and acres of land that's being used for absolutely nothing."

He leaned on the podium then, getting personal with the people of Serenity, meeting them one at a time with direct looks. He was good, Carny thought with a sick feeling. Too good.

"Now I'm a businessman, and I don't usually let personal feelings get in my way of sound decision making. But having gotten to know the people of Serenity, and this unique area, well, I have to tell you, I don't think I have to look any farther."

Applause erupted over the crowd, and Carny looked around, appalled. He hadn't even told them what he was doing, and already they'd given him full approval. Stiffening, she crossed her arms.

"There are a lot of citizens in Serenity who, through no fault of their own, have lost their farms. The banks own them now, and good farmers have had to turn to factory work in Odessa to support their families. Those of you who are more fortunate, the ones who've known what it is to have a lot of money from oil leases and the drilling that's taken place on your land, are discovering what it's like to do without. Your wells are playing out, and the money's not coming in like it used to. It's time for all of you, from both ends of the ladder, farmers, factory workers, business owners, sales clerks, secretaries and oil boomers, to find something else to put your hopes and dreams into, something else that can make Serenity a prosperous town again."

Again, thunderous applause filled the bingo hall, as if they knew their savior had come, and trusted whatever he would tell them.

"Here's the bottom line," he said, leaning on the podium again and gazing out into the crowd. "My investors are going to build a multimillion-dollar amusement park somewhere in Texas. It's going to make Astro World look like a state fair and put Six Flags out of business. Whatever community we choose is going to get . . . if you'll pardon the expression . . . sopping rich. It'll bring in a whole new industry in tourism. The citizens of Serenity who own their own businesses will see 500 percent increases in their profits, if not more, and there will be thousands of new jobs . . . I could just go on and on. But the best thing about this endeavor is that we're willing to cut the community in. You invest in this project and you'll get a percentage of the profits. No matter how much or how little you put in, you'll get your cut. And ladies and gentlemen, I think there'd have to be something wrong with anybody who'd pass up a chance like this. You just can't lose."

An amusement park, Carny thought as the crowd roared in approval. Perfect. He'd rake in his profits tonight, taking everything anyone would give him, and then he'd be on the first train out of town tomorrow.

An overwhelming rage came over her as she stood there, looking around at the excitement, the fever, on everyone's face. Without another thought, she pushed through those standing on the sides of the room and made her way to the front. When the applause died enough for her to be heard, she darted in front of Logan Brisco, grabbed the microphone, and shouted, "Wait a minute! I have something to say!"

For the first time that night, a look of dread passed over Logan's face, but he quickly pushed it away. "Be my guest," he said. "This is a big venture. It's going to require a little discussion. Carny . . ." He gestured toward the microphone, surrendering it completely.

"First of all," she said, "I think it's important that we think about what's going on here. This man has been in town for three weeks, and we know virtually nothing about him, yet most of you are already reaching for your checkbooks. What's wrong with this picture?"

A moan of argument swept over the crowd, and she raised her hand to stop them. "Second, if there really is a venture complete with investors, do we really *want* an amusement park ruining this town? I came here for the peace and stability the town offered me, and I love it just the way it is. If we were to build this here, nothing would ever be the same again. We'd have tourists coming through all the time, lowlifes and thieves. Crime would go up and the quality of life would go down. Are we willing to sell out our beautiful little town for that?"

Slade Hampton, one of the town's unofficial leaders, since he ran the barbershop, stepped into the aisle, his dog Jack following behind him. "Carny, the town's in trouble. We need something like this. This could be the answer to our prayers."

"If Logan Brisco is the answer to your prayers, Slade, then I'm Mother Teresa's long-lost daughter. Listen to me. I know what I'm talking about."

"Excuse me," Logan said, moving Carny aside and commandeering the microphone again. "I hope I didn't make any of you think that the policies of the park would be dictated to you. On the contrary, your own county government would make all the policies. If you build this park here, you can set all the limitations about how it's to be done. You can protect this town from the elements Carny is talking about, if you just put your heads together. The hotels you'd build could be put outside town. Set up gift shops, tourist areas, new restaurants. You could divert all the traffic from the main part of town, if you wanted. Ladies and gentlemen, it can be done to your satisfaction. Some of you will even be on the planning board. This will be your baby."

"How much can we invest, Logan?" someone asked from the back of the room.

"The more the better," he answered, "but there's no amount that's too small. I'll keep careful logs of every penny given to me, and you'll each be paid dividends based on your percentage. If we can get enough investors here, we may not have to offer it as public stock. That means more profit for all of you."

Carny gaped at her friends and neighbors as their excitement grew. Couples began conferring about how much to write their checks for; others wrote feverishly and began tearing out their checks, as if being the first would somehow give them the best portion of the park.

"Do we have time to go to the ATM down the street and get some money out?" someone shouted from the back of the room.

"Of course," Logan said. "I'll be here signing up investors for the next few hours. That is, if the bingo players don't mind me taking one table for that purpose."

B. C. Jenkins, the town's bingo caller, indicated that it would be just fine, and Carny snatched the microphone from Logan again. "Wait a minute! Please, everybody, just hold on."

People quieted down and cast irritated looks up at her.

"Look at yourselves! What's the big hurry? The biggest sign of a con artist is that he wants his money immediately. Trust me, people, I know. If this guy's legitimate, then he'll give you time to think about how much you can afford to lose, to check his credentials and those of his investors— who, by the way, he hasn't named yet. And if he won't give you that kind of time, or the information you need to make an informed decision, then you'd better kiss your money good-bye, because you'll never see it again."

A few people around the room began to nod and whisper in agreement, and Carny looked up at Logan, her eyes full of fire and vigor. The look he returned to her had no trace of his usual amusement. She had ruined it for him, and he didn't like it.

With his lips pressed together, he took the microphone back, and looked into the crowd. Slowly, that smile returned to his face. She thought he deserved an Oscar for the performance.

"You know, ladies and gentlemen, she's right. This is a big decision, probably one of the biggest you'll ever make. You do need to think about it, and lord knows, I don't want any regrets later on. Truth is, I don't even have the approval yet to put the park in Serenity. The number of investors I get here will indicate community support and swing things in your favor. But there's really no rush. Put your money away."

Titters waved over the crowd, and Carny gaped up at him, surprised at the new twist. She hadn't expected this.

"I'll be staying at the Welcome Inn, and starting tomorrow, anyone who wants to meet with me and discuss making an investment, can do that. But I'm not here to rob anyone. I don't want your grocery money or your kids' college fund. I don't want anybody making an investment they can't afford. Think about it, and if you think you want to be a part of an endeavor that will set your family up, and ensure generations of prosperity, then we'll talk. But I won't take your money tonight."

Then he set the mike back in its stand, flashed Carny that amused grin, and said, "You want the first appointment?"

She crossed her arms. "I'm impressed, I'll say that. But I'm still not fooled. Just be prepared. I'm going to fight you every inch of the way."

"I'll look forward to it," he said. "Changing your mind will be one of my top goals while I'm here."

"Second only to changing my town," she said, starting off the stage. "Don't let your guard down, Brisco. I'm watching every move you make."

Logan's motel room was cold when he went in that night. He'd left the air conditioner on to combat the damp muskiness of the room, and now it felt like an icebox. Locking the door behind him—mostly out of habit—he dropped his briefcase on one of the hard, tightly made beds, and flicked on the power to the computer he'd shipped before leaving the last town. It had been delivered here just a few days after his arrival. Pushing a few keys, he made the information he needed scroll across the screen, then sank onto the bed and looked dismally around the room.

It ought to feel like home, he thought, since motel rooms had been his only home for so long—except for the times when some pretty little lady had invited him to bunk with her for the duration of his stay in her town. Still, no matter how many times he came back to a room like this, it felt empty. But those kinds of feelings were counterproductive, he told himself. Montague wouldn't have stood for them.

Just as he wouldn't have stood for what had happened tonight. Montague would have jumped the first train out of town. He would have seen right away that the scam couldn't work, as long as there was one person standing in his way. It didn't pay to attract that kind of attention or to stay any longer than he had to. Montague would have accused him of letting Carny dupe him into staying when he knew the odds were against him already.

Maybe Montague would have been right.

Lying down, Logan stretched his arms back behind his head, and closed his eyes. "You're right, old buddy. But I'm not you. I never have been."

As many rules as Montague had taught him about the line of work he'd fallen into, there was one rule that had served him better than any other over the years. Follow your gut. And tonight, his gut said to stay in Serenity, play this one out, and face the challenge Carny Sullivan had thrown at him.

He didn't like being thought of as a two-bit con artist. He didn't like being called a liar. And he especially didn't like having his integrity questioned. Even if everything she suspected about him was true.

It wasn't as if he ever really hurt anyone. As Montague had always said, you can't cheat an honest man. Logan considered himself something of a teacher . . . a teacher of the hard lessons that people needed to learn. Better from him than from some mean-spirited criminal type who would leave them unable to recover.

Logan's scams were always clean and neat. He came, he squeezed, he left. End of story. No attachments, no regrets, and no real consequences.

He'd already paid his dues long ago.

# 3

*Logan Brisco had learned* the first of life's dirty lessons when he became a ward of the state of Iowa at the age of three. He had never known his father, and no one had explained to him that his mother had been killed in a careless car accident. Each night, after he was sent to a strange bed in a strange home, he would lie awake for hours, remembering bedtime stories and whispered prayers, songs his mother had sung while she bathed him, the laughter in the house where they'd lived. She had never left him before, except at a baby-sitter's while she worked, and he had always thought she would come back for him.

By the time he was four, he'd forgotten what she looked like. When he turned five, he stopped looking for her in crowds. At six, he learned to curse her for leaving him alone, and by the time he was seven, her memory was just a numbness in the center of his heart, and he had no more expectations than he had answers.

By the time he was eight he had learned that no one—especially his mother—really wanted him, and that he was nothing more than an unwelcome burden to the succession of families who took him in. He also realized, on some basic eight-year-old level, that the fact that he had a roof over his head at all boiled down to a question of money. The state paid people to feed and house him; otherwise, he would have grown up in an institution, which, he supposed, might even be worse.

It was that year that he had the idea to peruse his file the next time his social worker left him alone in her office, and find the answers that had plagued him for most of his young life. But the answers hadn't been what he wanted to find.

On the first page, under his parents, his mother was listed as deceased.

He never forgot the rage and despair that assaulted him that day in that barren office, or the dread as he turned the pages and learned that she had died when he was three, and that for five long years the state had searched for someone—anyone—to adopt him. But his file described him as a precocious, angry child, prone to trouble. And while he wasn't sure what those words meant, he did know that it wasn't a glowing advertisement for him.

The brightness he exhibited, rather than being an attractive trait, came across as sarcastic, stubborn, and smart-mouthed. His young inquiries into the workings of the world often landed him in the attic or basement for punishment, and on one particularly cruel occasion, in a broom closet for thirty-six hours. When his third foster mother withheld meals from him for an entire day because of what she considered a "sassy mouth," he stole a dollar from her purse, climbed out the bathroom window, and went to the corner convenience store where he bought a bag of potato chips and a soda.

It had been the perfect crime, until the worried store clerk, not accustomed to seeing children out so late, reported it to his foster father who was a regular in the store. When his punishment resulted in a concussion, Logan was moved once again.

As Logan grew older, he channeled his intelligence into surviving. He knew that he had been denied the blessings that other children his age took for granted and that things weren't likely to come his way unless he found a way to take them.

Taking those things landed him in more than his share of trouble and got him thrown out of every home he was dumped in. By the time he was ten, he'd given up on the idea that anyone would ever adopt him and begun to rely on his size and intellect to get him out of his scrapes. He looked at least three years older than he was, and that number seemed to multiply exponentially as he got older.

At the age of twelve, standing five feet eight inches tall, he went to live with the Millers, a couple who kept foster kids to supplement their meager income. Evelyn Miller, a small woman with a pallid complexion and a perpetual scowl on her face, embraced martyrdom and never failed to tell anyone in her path how miserable her existence was. Her husband Scotty was a foulmouthed veteran with such a bad back he couldn't hold a job, even though he managed to bend over a pool table at every opportunity.

That Scotty lived next door to the local pool hall was no coincidence, Logan discovered later. He spent every night there, drinking with his cronies and shooting pool, laying down bets that he usually won. It was the first time in his life Logan had found himself fascinated by anything, and as time went on, he found it increasingly difficult to stay away from the pool hall when Scotty was playing. But if the state had found out that he was spending time in such a place, Evelyn swore, they would close down their foster home and stop sending the checks they so badly needed.

So every night, Logan hung around the house, listening to Evelyn Miller stomp around quoting scripture under her breath and sweeping up cigarette butts, while alternately yelling at the five children in her care to get out of her way and go to bed. Logan was always the first to oblige and, when lights were turned out, he slipped out the window and crept over to the pool hall.

He was a quick study in dishonesty, and after

watching Scotty's techniques several times, he realized the man was a hustler. Scotty would catch every newcomer who entered the pool hall and challenge him to a game. The first game he would always lose, as his opponent expected, and then, just as the opponent was about to clean up, he would suggest a triple or nothing play-off. Inevitably, he'd sweep the table clean in his first few shots, and would always go home the richer for it.

As Logan got better at the game, he found he had an aptitude for it that rivaled Scotty's. Scotty used talent and precision, but Logan was better at the con, itself. If people continually underestimated Scotty's talent, they would certainly underestimate the talent of a kid.

He began to spend his afternoons going from one pool hall to another in the town, engaging other boys in games, the first few of which he lost, and then he would turn things around and blow them away in a winner-take-all coup. When he realized he had fleeced the area pool halls for everything he could, and that he was easily recognized in each of them now, he decided it was time to move on to greener pastures. Besides, there was no sense in being dependent on the Millers or the state of Iowa anymore. He was fourteen, had a pocketful of money, and a lucrative vocation.

For a while, Logan hustled his way from one town to another, stopping in every pool hall he could find and swindling the regulars for everything he could get out of them. Not accustomed to losing so much money on a kid, the players often got angry. Logan made many an escape out the men's room window, the fire-exit door, or down an alley with a posse of pool-cue-waving losers on his tail.

One night, when he was attempting a getaway from two irate opponents at a combination bowling alley/pool hall, a car screeched to a halt in front of the building, and a man threw open the passenger door and shouted, "Get in, son."

Since the only alternative was to be beaten senseless by the ruthless, and poorer, pool players he'd fleeced, Logan dove into the front seat without a moment's thought. The car skidded away, leaving the boys behind, cursing and vowing to get even.

Catching his breath, Logan sat up and glanced at his savior. He recognized the man immediately as one he'd noticed earlier, sitting at a table between the bowling alley and the pool tables, watching him hustle. Something about the man then had made him uneasy; he was always sucking on that pipe between his teeth as if he knew a hustle when he saw one. He'd worn a three-piece suit and a black derby, and he'd had a white handlebar mustache and a pocket watch on a gold chain that draped across his vest and into his pocket. In the bowling alley, he'd worn a monocle in one eye, and Logan remembered thinking that he looked like a nineteenth-century banker from one of those old movies he used to watch.

"I don't know who you are, mister," he said, breathless. "But you probably saved my life. Thanks."

"You have a few things yet to learn, my boy," the man told Logan in a heavy English accent. "Your technique is excellent, but your style needs a great deal of work. And your escape leaves quite a lot to be desired. How old are you, boy?"

"Nineteen," Logan lied. "I'll be twenty next month."

"You're twelve if you're a day," the man said.

"I am not!" Logan protested. "I'm fourteen!"

The man smiled. "That's more like it." He extended his hand across the seat. "My name's Montague Shelton. And yours?"

Logan briefly considered lying, but decided there was no purpose in it. "Logan Brisco."

"Logan Brisco," the man said, rolling the name over his tongue. "Sounds like a cowboy name. You Americans love cowboys, don't you? Outlaws and cutthroats and such?"

Logan shrugged. "It's just a name."

"Where are your parents?"

"Dead."

"How convenient," Montague said. "The parents of all runaways are dead."

"I'm not a runaway," Logan said, growing uneasy. "I'm not kidding. My parents are dead. I lived in a foster home, but it's time for me to go out on my own now. The state was about to release me, anyway."

"I don't know a great deal about your American laws," Montague said in a voice that had a polished sort of gruffness, but which was growing gentler by the moment. "But I do know that they don't throw children out in the street when they reach fourteen."

"Yeah, well, maybe I'm mature for my age. Maybe they knew I could support myself."

"Hustling pool? Yes, I can understand why they'd send you out on your own."

"Are you gonna turn me in or what?"

"Why shouldn't I?"

"Because I'll just run away again. I don't belong with the Millers. They probably haven't even noticed I'm gone yet. They'll be mad when the social worker cuts off what they were paying for them to keep me, but other than that it won't matter."

"Did they beat you?"

Logan almost laughed. "Scotty? No. He talked tough, but he has a bad back. He was scared that if he hit me, I'd hit him back. And Mrs. Miller gave me a good tongue-lashing every hour on the hour, but she wouldn't dare have raised her hand to a kid bigger than she was."

"Where are you sleeping tonight?" the man asked.

"I don't know. I have money. I could stay in a motel, if I wanted. But sometimes I just sleep in a parked car in an apartment complex or something."

Montague eyed him. "This is your lucky day, young man. I just happen to have a motel room myself. You're welcome to sleep in the extra bed."

Logan wasn't used to handouts, and he was suspicious of generosity. "What's in it for you?"

"Companionship," the man said. "And perhaps

partnership. We'll see how things look in the morning."

Logan didn't know what he meant by that, but he didn't question him further. All he wanted was a good night's sleep, and if the man tried anything funny, he was pretty sure he could hold him off. Montague was big, but he was old. At least fifty, Logan guessed.

Except for the man's snoring, which he found tolerable compared to Scotty Miller's, Logan found the sleeping conditions to be more than suitable that night. The next morning, as he was headed out the door, Montague stopped him.

"Young man, how would you like to go from making pocket change to real money?"

Logan shrugged. "Who wouldn't?"

Montague popped his monocle in his eye and stood up. Stroking his mustache, he strolled around Logan, studying him. "You have promise, boy. I think dressed in the right clothes, with the right haircut, and the right facial expressions, you could probably pass for twenty." He took out the monocle, wiped it on his lapel, and went on. "Not that I mind youngsters, you understand. They just have no place in my organization. But I could use a partner."

"What organization?" Logan asked.

"My traveling enterprises," he said. "I'm a businessman. I need someone of executive material, someone who looks fit and trim in a suit, someone who has a talent for making money."

"I don't have a suit," Logan said.

"We'll get you one, young man. If you stick with me, you'll wear the finest clothes, eat the finest meals, sleep in the finest hotels. I'll make you a rich man. Are you interested?"

"Yeah," Logan said. "I don't have anything better to do."

"Excellent," Montague said. "We'll have you fitted in St. Louis tomorrow. At which time, we'll get you a new birth certificate inflating your age just a wee bit, and perhaps a driver's license. You can drive, can't you?"

Logan nodded, though he'd never been behind the wheel. He'd worry about that later.

They loaded the car with Montague's belongings, which consisted of a computer, a small printing press, and several boxes of paper of various sizes and colors. "Where'd you get all this?" Logan asked. "This stuff must cost a mint. Are you in the printing business?"

"I once was," Montague said. "I consider myself something of an expert in the area of printing, and these machines help tremendously in my work. They are to be treated with the best of care. Without them, my business is greatly handicapped."

When they were on their way, Logan asked, "Are we heading for St. Louis today?"

"After one brief little stop by the bowling alley," the man said. "I was taking care of some business when I ran into you last night. I must conclude it this morning."

Logan worried that the same kids he'd hustled last night would be there this morning, but it was still early, so he decided he'd risk it. They pulled

# WINNER TAKE ALL 39 –

into the parking space near the door, and Montague sat still a moment. "Are you a man of honor?" he asked Logan.

"Well . . . sure, I guess."

"You must be, if you're to travel with me. Honor and loyalty. I expect you to support me in any of my endeavors, and I will do the same for you. Is that satisfactory?"

Logan nodded. "I guess so."

"No guessing, young man. You must be decisive. You must know what you want and how to get it. Indecision is the kiss of death in this business."

"What business did you say it was, again?"

"Moneymaking," Montague said, dropping his keys into his pocket. "Now, come along. You're my assistant, here to help me carry my load. I do the talking."

Logan nodded and shuffled behind Montague. The man walked with purpose, and the moment they were in the bowling alley, he went directly to an automatic teller machine against the wall. Putting his monocle in his eye, he punched a few numbers into the machine's computer, nodded his head at the string of numbers that filled the screen, and turned around as if looking for someone. Logan hung back as Montague cut across to the front desk.

"Hello, sir. My name is Sidney Moore, of the First Federal Bank of Des Moines. We installed this ATM machine late yesterday, but we had several complaints throughout the night on our twenty-four-hour line. I understand it isn't working properly."

"Yeah, it took a bunch of people's cards. Told 'em they had insufficient funds. One or two I could believe, but I doubt everybody who came in here was in the red. And on a Friday, too, when they just got paid."

"Hmmm," Montague said, fingering his mustache. "I'm going to have to remove it and take it in for repair. We'll make every effort to have a replacement here later today."

"Sure thing," the manager said. "We got along without it just fine until yesterday."

"Please tell your customers that their cards will be sent back to them in today's mail."

The man nodded and turned to one of the customers needing a pair of bowling shoes, and Montague strolled over to Logan and the ATM machine. "All right, son, let's load it up."

"Load it?" Logan asked. "Load it where?"

"In the back of my car," he said. "I assure you that it fits."

"But it's got to weigh a ton. And isn't it built into the wall or something?"

Montague winked, then slid it easily away from the wall. Unplugging it, he said, "It's no heavier than a small computer. But help me so that it looks heavier."

Logan lifted his side, and found that it didn't weigh more than twenty pounds. Together, they carried it out to his car, and slid it in behind his computer. Before closing the back door to the wagon, Montague leaned in, opened a compartment behind the ATM box, and retrieved two dozen or so ATM cards. Then, tearing off a printout at the back of the box, he nodded for Logan to get into the car.

As they slowly pulled out of the parking lot, Montague handed him the cards and the printout. "You see, my boy, having someone else's ATM card means nothing if you don't have their codes. But my friend here—" Reaching over the backseat, he patted the box affectionately—"just took care of that for us. Look for the account numbers and match them to the ID numbers the people punched in with them," he said. "The printout has it all. Then put the cards in order."

Quietly, Logan did as he was told.

"We'll have to hurry," Montague said. "Since it's Saturday, the banks aren't open, but it still doesn't pay to take chances."

"Hurry and do what?" Logan asked.

Montague pulled into a bank parking lot and idled the car for a moment. Logan watched, astounded, as he removed his derby, and replaced it with a big baseball cap, a pair of dark glasses, and a mouthpiece complete with a black mustache and beard. Tossing Logan a wig, he said, "Here, put this on. Just for the camera. We don't want to be identifiable."

Frowning, Logan pulled the wig on, and Montague pulled up to the drive-through ATM machine. "First card," he told him.

Logan handed him the top card. "ID number?"

"Three-two-nine-five," Logan read.

Montague slid the card into the machine, waited

for it to respond, then typed in the ID number. The computer asked him what amount he'd like to withdraw. Logan followed Montague's fingers as he punched in two hundred fifty dollars.

Holding his breath, he watched, amazed, as the machine rolled out two hundred fifty dollars. "One more," he said, reaching for another card.

They repeated the same steps, and got two hundred fifty dollars more, before they decided to move on.

That morning, they hit ten more banks, and drew two hundred fifty dollars out of twenty accounts. By the time they were on the highway toward St. Louis, they had five thousand dollars.

"Do you do this all the time?" Logan asked.

"Absolutely not," Montague said with a note of pride. "I have many other ventures. With my knowledge of computers and printing, I virtually have people handing me money wherever I go. Don't ever let anyone tell you that knowledge isn't a wonderful thing. It's your key, young man, to anywhere you want to go."

It was the first time Logan had believed that, and when Montague handed him his cut of one thousand dollars, Logan decided that he wanted to know everything Montague knew, and then some.

Over the next few months, Logan traveled with Montague and watched, ever amazed, as the man posed as an airline pilot, complete with a Delta uniform, and paraded around airports cashing counterfeit checks at the terminal desks. When he'd hit everyone, they went to the hotels that housed the pilots, checked in for the night on Delta's tab, cashed another check the next morning, and went on their merry way. Some of them were payroll checks on Delta's account, others were personal checks in the name of Lawrence Cartland, but they had all been created by Montague's hand on his printing press.

Several of his scams involved dressing in uniform as a bank security guard complete with unloaded guns—since Montague took pride in the fact that white-collar criminals did not carry loaded guns. In these guises he would padlock the night depository at airports, and collect all the receipts of the day from every enterprise at work in the building by simply standing beside the depository looking official, and explaining to everyone who came to make a deposit that there had been several break-ins at the depository, so he had been hired to collect the receipts personally.

For the most part, Logan just observed over the next year. Montague gave him a fake birth certificate, which enabled him to get a real driver's license in the state of Georgia, and Logan became his getaway-car driver, his assistant who helped him carry machines and bags of money, his diversion when it was needed. He also learned how to use the printing press almost as deftly as his teacher, until he, too, could counterfeit the most detailed documents.

But they both specialized in checks, with routing numbers at the bottom that would make the banks' computers send the rubber money to banks all over the country before anyone realized they weren't good. By then, he and Montague would be long gone.

They were victimless crimes, Montague always said, crimes that didn't hurt anyone. They were crimes against airlines, against corporations, against banks. In the few cases where actual individuals took the losses, such as in the ATM withdrawals, they kept their thefts to a minimum.

In one case, when the police had been close on their trail and Montague was desperate for an escape, he had convinced a stranger he had befriended in an airport bar to cash a check for five hundred dollars. The check was phony, but he'd saved the man's business card, and when they reached their next destination, he'd sent the man a money order for the full amount plus interest.

Montague's code of honor was a strict one, and by the time Logan was old enough to pull his own stings, he had his friend's unwritten "commandments" drilled into his mind.

The first was "Never hurt anyone." Honorable men only took from those who could afford to lose something or those who were insured. But after that rule always came the qualifying contradiction: "You can't cheat an honest man." Logan never questioned whether that particular philosophy made hurting someone all right, in the event that he couldn't keep rule number one.

Second, Montague taught him to "Never stay in one place too long." They had to assume that Feds were always on their spoor, just a town behind them. One day too long could make the difference between freedom and years of incarceration.

Montague's third rule was, "Never let your conscience slow you down." There was no room for guilt or regrets in this line of work, and on the few occasions when Logan expressed self-recriminations, Montague made it clear he had little patience for it.

Fourth, he warned "Never allow your picture to be taken, except in the case of counterfeit IDs or passports." All it would take was one photograph sent to the authorities by a suspicious mark, and shown to a past victim, to land them behind bars.

"Never fall in love" was the fifth rule. The moment a woman started to get under your skin, you were to leave town. There was nothing more dangerous to this "career," Montague maintained, than the brain damage a woman could inflict on a man. It caused him to take unnecessary chances and make serious mistakes that could jeopardize everything they'd worked for.

Sixth, "Never sleep with vulnerable women." Montague loved women, and he didn't for a moment suggest that they should remain celibate. However, he believed in pursuing only those who wouldn't be devastated when he disappeared from their lives.

The seventh rule was, "Always travel light." Accumulation could be fatal. In their business, one had to be able to leave things—and people— behind without regrets, and replace them when they could.

And eighth, "You can be forgiven any crime if you commit it with class." Once he'd outfitted Logan in a wardrobe fit for a Kennedy, forcing him to discard all of his jeans, tennis shoes, and T-shirts. They were only to dress with class, carry themselves with class, and if they happened to be in a town with a choice of restaurants and hotels, they slept in the finest accommodations and ate the richest food. "People will believe you are whatever you appear to be, my boy. Your life is a blank slate, and you must imagine your past and future to be as grand as you wish it," Montague said.

Armed with those rules, Logan concocted the first scam of his own at age fifteen. Posing as a twenty-one-year-old, which was believable since he now stood over six feet tall, he went into a tax filing office, carrying a fake W-2 form, as well as several counterfeit receipts, and had his tax return done. When it was finished and his sizable refund was calculated, he requested "Fast Cash," which was an immediate refund offered by the company at a nominal interest rate, much like a loan. Logan walked out with two thousand dollars in his pocket. When Montague tried the same scam, he netted even more.

The heady feeling Logan got from charming his way through his own scam was addictive, and soon, he had more ideas. For each one, he spent hours at the library, researching the ins and outs of the businesses he intended to sting, making phone calls and talking to people, and analyzing the ways that he could pull the most lucrative scams.

Montague was clearly pleased with his progress, and as Logan grew closer to adulthood, he counted him as a cherished companion. Montague became the closest thing Logan had ever had to a father. As the years passed, Logan realized he hadn't been that much help to Montague in the early days, and he came to the conclusion that the man had wanted him along to fill his loneliness. Their friendship had served both of them well.

As Logan grew older, he began to keep company with gorgeous women who worked as flight attendants or entertainers in hotel nightclubs. With them, he posed as either a furloughed airline pilot or a successful lawyer, and he spent money on the women as if he had a bottomless source. Montague surprised him one birthday—the first one he could remember that anyone had paid any heed to at all—with a Delta uniform of his own, which he'd had made at the same tailor that made many of the firm's other uniforms, and which he'd probably charged to Delta's employee account. After that Logan began dressing as a pilot to attract women. No one noticed that he was a teenager who barely needed to shave. Women flocked to him when he was in uniform, so he wore it every chance he got.

Montague, on the other hand, attracted women whether he wore his uniform or his banker's garb, for he looked successful no matter where he was or what grift he was pulling. As he always said, women liked men with class.

But it took considerably more than the average dose of class to make an escape on some occasions.

The days of climbing through bathroom windows weren't entirely behind him, only this time, if he was caught, he was likely to wind up in jail, rather than merely beaten up. And Logan was sure that jail would be a monumental step down.

The older he got, the higher he lived, and the more money he required for keeping his women happy and his libido satisfied. He began putting his mind to work on bigger endeavors, the kind where they could sweep a town of all its spare cash, and move on without looking back.

The idea came to him when he was lounging in a hot tub, watching television one Sunday afternoon, and he saw a documercial for a real-estate venture. "That's it," he said aloud.

Montague, who seemed to be sleeping in the bubbling tub, opened his eyes. "Did I miss something?"

"Seminars," Logan said. "We need to give some seminars. You know. On real estate, or investments . . . get-rich schemes that would draw the greediest people in a town. We could hold the seminar, get them all worked up, then tell them they have to invest that night, or it'll be too late. Then we tell them that we have to go to the site . . . you know, Brazil or somewhere, and that we'll be back with their deeds. Give them time to have their checks clear before they get suspicious."

"Seminars," Montague repeated, thinking it over. "My boy, I believe you may have something there."

They did their first real-estate scam in Picayune, Mississippi, a small town near the Gulf Coast, where the residents showed up at their seminar, checkbooks in hand, ready to make the investment of their lifetime.

Neither of them lacked a talent for charming people. Montague lent a touch of integrity and regality to the act, and Logan offered unabashed enthusiasm, along with a zealous passion for his product, whatever it might be. Together, they couldn't lose. The night of their first seminar, in which they sold property in Brazil that would allegedly be developed into one of the most sought-after resorts in the southern hemisphere, they walked away with fifty thousand dollars.

"This is the caper that could help us retire from this nefarious life we lead," Montague said with a grin one night as he stacked his money into bundles and packed them in a suitcase.

Logan laughed. "*You*, retire? What would you do?"

"Buy a ranch in the Southwest," Montague said without hesitation. "Find myself a nice little bride. Raise horses."

"I can't see you on a ranch, Montague," Logan said. "I've always seen you as more the type to usurp a prince or something, and take over his castle. Fergie and Di are both available now, you know."

"Much too high profile for me," Montague said. "When I retire, it will be quietly. I'll put it all behind me, and hope the hounds never catch up to me."

But the hounds were always there, inching ever closer, gathering more ammunition for the day they caught them. It kept them moving, and it kept them careful. Despite the danger or the possible consequences, though, Logan had never been happier in his life.

But those happy times were soon to end. On Logan's nineteenth birthday, just before they were to pull off one of the biggest scams of his career, Montague buckled over with a heart attack. He was dead before Logan could get him to a hospital.

He buried his friend in the town they had been about to sting, then disappeared into the night alone, not sure where he would go but eager to get there.

He couldn't remember another time in his life when he had cried, for crying hadn't been tolerated well in the foster homes that had taken him in. But that night, as he drove across the country, with no destination and no ties, he had wept like a baby. For years he had felt like an adult, been treated as an adult, been paid as an adult. But that night, he felt like a child who'd just been abandoned for the second time.

For a while, he lived off the money that he and Montague had acquired—money they had stashed in several safe-deposit boxes across the South—and when several months had passed and the grief was not so profound, he tried to formulate a plan. But try as he might, he couldn't make himself carry out any of the scams that came to mind.

Maybe this was his reprieve, he told himself. His chance to start over. He had a stake now, and he could do just about anything he wanted. Maybe he needed a legitimate line. Maybe he needed an education.

Since he hadn't actually finished school, he created a counterfeit diploma with Montague's computer, and enrolled in a small college in Virginia. He chose marketing as his major, for Montague had taught him that one should never forget one's assets, and his happened to be a handsome face and a wizard's tongue. He could sell anything put before him, con anyone in his way, and leave them all smiling, even when they found him out. With minimal study, he charmed all his teachers into thinking he had the IQ of a sales genius, and he wound up with a transcript full of A's and a degree that lent him his first and only legitimate credential.

Logan's first job in a computer sales position after he'd graduated had earned him phenomenal commissions, for he was the best salesman the company had ever had on staff. Always eager to find a new angle, he had researched every aspect of the products and his customers, and had used every legitimate resource available to move the merchandise.

But when his boss began cheating him out of the commissions he had earned, he realized that con artists existed even within the bounds of legitimate enterprise. If that was the case, he determined, he'd rather do things Montague's way.

It was comfortable slipping back into the old way of life that he and Montague had shared. Again, Logan traveled from one town to the next, meeting consistently greater challenges. He calculated the ways and weaknesses of the people, and created elaborate, custom-made deals that leached the greediest citizens of their savings. Montague's old motto that "You can't cheat an honest man" hung like a sanction in his mind, and for ten years he found himself able to justify almost anything he did, and never get caught. Indeed, he was rarely even questioned about his integrity, for he pulled off his scams with such finesse.

When his Texas research led him to the town of Serenity, with its big stretch of fallow farmland outside town and its dwindling surplus of oil money, he'd planned to spend three weeks laying the groundwork, hit them with the seminar, sweep up all the cash they gave him, and leave town before anyone had had second thoughts.

But then he met Carny Sullivan, and found that there was an even greater challenge than pulling off this scam. And success, to Logan, lay not in the money, but in the degree of challenge. Even if it broke all of his old friend's rules, he was going to stay until he met this one.

# 4

*Jason Sullivan always got* off the school bus with a smile on his face that suggested he had a secret. But today his smile was not secretive, but exuberant, as he bounded into the house, dropped his backpack on the floor, and ran to find his mother.

"Mom! Mom! We're gonna be rich! Did you hear?"

Carny came out of the back of the house and caught her son. "What?"

"That man. Logan Brisco. He came to school today." Pushing past her, he ran into his room. "He's gonna give us free passes. And there might be a TV show. We can be the stars!"

Carny watched as he grabbed his piggy bank

and started shaking it out, dumping pennies and nickels all over his dresser.

"Passes to what? What are you talking about?"

"If we invest," he said. "I'm gonna give him everything I've got, Mom! How much do you think I have?"

"Slow down!" Carny turned her son around and forced him to look at her. "Let's go over this, now. You're telling me that Logan Brisco came to your school today?"

"Yeah. And he said he's gonna hold a lot of workshops for us kids after school, so he can explain the whole park to us and get our ideas and stuff. And if we get our parents to invest, we'll be part owners!"

Carny let her son go, and he turned back to his pennies. "Jason, he's a crook. A thief. You can't give him your money."

"Mom! Everybody else believes him."

"Everybody else is going to get stung, Jason."

"Oh, yeah?" Jason swung around. "Then how come he didn't just do it the other night? Lots of people were ready to invest, until you stopped them. If he was a crook, he would have taken their money then. But he wanted it to be a wise investment."

"Is that what he told you?"

"Sure it is. And after he talked to us, when the kids were going back to class, he came up to me and remembered my name! He's a nice guy. I like him."

As he spoke, Jason arranged his pennies into little stacks of ten, and Carny grabbed his hand. "Jason, I don't want you talking to him anymore.

Do you hear me? And I won't let you give him one cent!"

"But Mom!"

"End of discussion." Making her oversize shirt into a catchall, she raked the pennies into it and started to the living room.

"But Mom! That's not fair! It's my money!"

She dumped the pennies into a bowl on the counter, then grabbed the phone book. "You'll keep your money, Jason," she said, flipping through for a number. "You can keep saving for that go-cart you want. I'm not taking it away from you. But neither is he." She picked up the phone.

"Who are you calling?"

"The school," she said. "I'm going to tell Mr. Anderson to keep that man away from our children. He's a low-down thief, and he shouldn't be on campus."

"But Mom! People will hate you if you keep messing him up! Mom, please! Don't you want us to have a park?"

"There isn't going to be a park," she said. "Don't you hear what I'm saying? It's a scam! He's a con artist!"

Sarah Jenkins, the school secretary, answered, and Carny took a deep breath. "Sarah, this is Carny Sullivan. Is Mr. Anderson there?"

"Sure he is, Carny, honey. But before I transfer you, let me tell you that I think your intentions were good last night with that Mr. Brisco fella, but you're wrong. I can just feel it. I have feelings like that, you know. Just sensations, but they're usually right. I can sometimes just see things, feel people's thoughts, that sort of thing. I think during my last abduction those aliens gave me some kind of psychic ability."

Carny closed her eyes and decided not to touch the subject of Sarah's infamous alien abduction. The townspeople believed that, too. "Then why haven't you won the lottery, Sarah?"

The woman gasped. "Well, I never said I knew everything."

"And how many con artists have you known in your life?"

"Well, certainly none. But I'm sure I'd know if—"

"I've known dozens," Carny cut in. "I know their lines, I know their techniques, I know how they smile and how they walk, I know that they promise the world, and I know how they make people believe them."

"Just because your parents are underhanded, doesn't mean that everyone else is."

"My parents are not underhanded," she returned, stung. "I'm referring to other people in the carnival. People I grew up watching. I moved to Serenity because the people here are honest and good, even if they are a little naive. I won't let him screw you or anyone else—we'll leave that to your aliens. Now may I please speak to Mr. Anderson?"

Mumbling something incoherent, Sarah transferred the call.

The moment the principal answered, Carny could tell he was in a good mood. The promise of instant wealth often did that to people. "Hello?"

"Mr. Anderson, this is Carny Sullivan. I understand that you allowed Logan Brisco to brainwash our children today. My son came home ready to give him every cent of his life savings, and mine, too."

"Now, now," Mr. Anderson began with a chuckle. "I didn't mean to offend anyone by letting him speak, but when Mr. Brisco came by this morning, he convinced me that he wanted to get the children involved with the planning of the park. He suggested several school projects that can come out of it. It's really going to be a wonderful community effort, and I think it'll be terrific for the children to get involved."

"He's a liar, Mr. Anderson. I don't want him within a hundred yards of my son."

"Come on, Carny. You're really overreacting. I for one don't intend to let you get in the way of my making this investment. Good things don't often come to Serenity, and when they do, I hope that we're all wise enough to take advantage of it."

"I can't believe you! Serenity has everything. It's the sweetest, cleanest, most peaceful town I've ever seen, and I've seen plenty. Mr. Anderson, even if you believe him, and there is going to be a park, which I'm absolutely positive there isn't, don't you realize that it would ruin this town?"

"This town could use a few changes," he said. "All the farmers who've lost their land are practically destitute, one of the two factories has already closed, and the oil has dried up. Mr. Brisco is bringing us hope. All he wants is a little cooperation."

"And a lot of money."

"He doesn't have to build the park here, Carny. If we give him too much trouble, he'll take his plans somewhere else. As far as I'm concerned, Carny, Mr. Brisco can talk to the kids *or* the adults in this school almost anytime he wants. And I intend to be one of his first investors! Why, Hugh Berkstrom even invested this morning, and he wouldn't have done it if he hadn't been dead sure."

"Oh, no." Carny groaned. Surely, he was mistaken. Hugh was the richest man in town, and she would have given him credit for more sense than that. "Why won't any of you listen? You all know where I came from. You know how I was raised." She took a calming breath, and tried again. "Look, Mr. Anderson, let's just be hypothetical here. What if . . . just what *if* I'm right, and Logan Brisco is a con artist? What if he got everybody in town, including the children, all worked up, and managed to walk out of here with all our money? It could ruin us. We'd never recover. Don't you see how high the stakes are in this?"

"And what if he's honest and can make us rich?" Anderson replied. "What if he gets impatient with us and goes somewhere else, and the next thing we know they're getting the park and everybody there is getting rich instead of us?"

"Then we'd still have this beautiful little town and all the good people in it, and our spirits would be intact, and so would our savings."

"That's not good enough for me," Anderson said. "And it's not good enough for most of us here. Please. Just stay out of it."

Frustrated, Carny hung up and threw herself back on the couch as her son came back through the room at a clipped pace, with his backpack on his back. "Where are you going?" she asked.

"To Nathan's."

"What's in the backpack?"

He gave her an exaggerated look of innocence, which appeared more than a little guilty. "What backpack?"

"The one on your back," she said. She got up and took the pack off. "This must weigh thirty pounds," she said, unzipping it. "What a surprise. Money. The same money I just poured into that bowl." Glancing toward the bowl, she slapped her forehead. "And now the bowl's empty."

"Mom! You're standing in my way of fame and fortune! I just want to be a part of it!"

"Over my dead body."

"Well, when the town lynches you, that may happen."

She took the backpack away from him and put it on top of the refrigerator. "I have to go somewhere for a few minutes. You stay at Nathan's until I get back."

"Mom, are you going to cause trouble for him?"

"You bet I am," she said, grabbing her keys. "Logan Brisco has met his match."


Carny brought her Harley to a halt outside the motel, and she ran her fingers through her windblown hair. She hated wearing a helmet, and only put the thing on when her son was riding with her. Someone from the sheriff's department pulled her over at least once a week and slapped her with a warning, but she hadn't yet gotten a ticket. The truth was that half of the deputies had a crush on her, and the other half considered her their little sister. None of them was about to get tough with her.

But Carny didn't take advantage of that often. It was sweet, she thought, and it was nice to know that so many nice guys lived in Serenity. If Abe Sullivan hadn't ruined her stomach for relationships, she might even start to take some of them seriously.

She sashayed into the office of "Doc" Carraway—so named not because he was a doctor, but because he'd flunked out of a South American med school. He'd chosen hotel management as an alternate occupation. Leaning on the counter, she said, "Hey, Doc. What room is Logan Brisco in?"

Doc looked up at her and instantly smoothed down his hair. "Uh . . . he's in 210. I ain't really supposed to tell you, in most cases, but since folks have been comin' in and out of there all day, I don't guess it's a secret."

If dread had a face, she wore it. "Don't tell me they've been bringing him money."

"If they're smart," Doc said. "Hugh Berkstrom got here at seven-thirty this morning."

"I heard he'd already invested," she said. "I thought he was smarter than that."

"Well, I'll tell you this much. Hugh didn't make his fortune with careless investments. If the richest man in town is trusting Logan Brisco, then as far as I'm concerned, there's no better investment. And some of the folks who've come by this morning have been trying to make deals with him to put shops and restaurants inside the park."

"Doc, there isn't going to be a park."

He just smiled. "We'll see, won't we?"

Sighing with exasperation, she headed back out and around to the stairwell. She found room 210 and knocked firmly on the door.

Logan came to the door wearing a clean pair of pants and a white shirt with the sleeves rolled up. It was the first time she'd seen him without his jacket.

He grinned as if he'd been expecting her. "Well, well."

"We have to talk," she said, pushing into his room. She stopped cold when she saw her in-laws, Bev and J. R. Sullivan, getting up from the table.

Her heart sank. "Oh, no. Not you, too."

"Don't start, Carny," J. R. said, stemming her outburst. "We know what we're doin'."

"Not if you gave him any money, you don't."

Bev shot a nervous glance to Logan. "Carny, please. We'll talk about it later."

For the first time in years, Carny felt the ache of tears behind her eyes. But she wouldn't cry in front of this man, she resolved. That would give him too much leverage.

"Look at me, Bev," she said, her voice shaking slightly. "You know me better than anybody else in this town. Have you ever known me to overreact?

Have you ever known me to say anything that wasn't true?"

"No, of course not," her mother-in-law replied.

J. R. looked up at her with weary eyes. "Honey, you can't suspect everybody that comes along, just because of your past."

"If I can't learn from my past, J. R., then I'd be pretty stupid, wouldn't I?"

Logan stepped between them, and from the amused look in his eyes, she knew that he was enjoying every minute of this. "I take it you know one another."

"She's our daughter-in-law," Bev said. "Look, we'll be going now. Honey, we can talk later."

Carny ground her teeth together and stared at Logan as the couple closed the door behind them. "Jail is too good for you. You should be shot."

He broadened that maddening smile. "Did you come to invest, too?"

"No, I did not," she said through her teeth. "I came to warn you to stay away from my son. Duping the adults of this town is bad enough, but when you start conning little kids . . . "

"Excuse me," he said, going to his table while she spoke and opening a logbook. "You don't mind if I make a few notations in here, do you? It's important that I log in every penny I get, so I can register the shares and get the profits paid out accordingly."

"Give me a break!" She jerked the logbook away from him, and caught her breath at the number of investments he'd already catalogued there. "Nice prop," she said. "Looks real legitimate."

He shook his head, still grinning. "You're determined to make me into a liar, aren't you?"

"No," she said, leaning over the table. "I'm determined to get you out of town. But first you're going to give back all the money you've already gotten. What was the take today, Logan? Ten thousand dollars? Twenty?"

Logan got up wearily, and crossing his arms, looked down at her. "What are you so hostile about?"

"You think this is hostility? Oh, no, this isn't hostility. You haven't seen hostility yet."

He dropped down onto the bed, and patted the spot next to him. "Sit down."

She gave a short laugh. "Yeah, right."

"No, really. If we're really going to talk, like two adults, then I'd prefer that you sit down."

"I don't really care what you prefer," she said. "I didn't come here to have a nice, cozy chat with you."

"No, you came to show me how tough you are." He stood up and leaned his hand against the wall. "So why didn't your husband come? Why does he let you fight these battles all alone?"

"Brisco, by now I'm pretty sure that you've found out everything there is to know about me. I'm your biggest stumbling block in this town. You've probably grilled everyone you've talked to about me, and they don't even realize it. So I'm sure you know that I'm divorced."

Logan grinned. It was true. He had asked everyone he'd met today about Carny. "Well, that explains how vulnerable your son is. He's hungry for a man's attention. I noticed that right away."

"Of course you did. It's your job to spot people's weaknesses. And right now you think Jason is mine. But it won't work. If you insist on staying here until you've stolen all their money, I'm going to make you sorry you ever took up crime as a profession."

He was getting aggravated, and he dropped his arms and glared at her. "What if I am legitimate? What if you're wrong about me?"

She faced off with him, her piercing look shooting straight through his lies, without the slightest hint of uncertainty. "I've seen more cons than you've ever dreamed of. I've even been part of some. I'm not wrong."

"Oh, so that's it," he said. "You want your cut. Join forces, as it were. Seeing how we have so much in common and all."

"We have nothing in common," she bit out. "I made something of my life in spite of my background. Something good because of this town. And by God, I'll fight tooth and nail to keep you from ruining it!"

His expression was serious as he stared at her, and for a moment she thought she might be getting through to him. Finally, he took a long breath, then said, "You're as sexy as hell when you have that look in your eye. Do you know that?"

He expected her to react, to blow up, to storm out. Instead, her face broke into a grin. Slowly, she sauntered toward him, until her breasts almost brushed his chest. "You bet I know it," she said.

"Eat your heart out. Because this is as close to me as you're ever going to get."

His eyes danced with the challenge. "Wanna lay odds on that?"

"Odds are the only thing that'll get laid tonight."

He laughed. "A hundred bucks says you'll come to me before the month is up."

"You're on," she said.

His eyes twinkled. "Winner take all."

For a moment, she stared at him and contemplated the arrogance that she was going to shoot down. It would be fun. Winner take all, indeed. Lock, stock, and ego.

Heading for the door, she looked back over her shoulder. "I know how to pick locks, Brisco. If you come near my son again, I'll come in here and castrate you while you sleep. That is, if someone hasn't already beat me to it."

Logan was grinning when she closed the door behind her. Slowly, he ambled to the window, watched her strut down the steps and across to her motorcycle, which she got on with an air of confidence that belied the absurdity of her driving such a beast.

Still chuckling, he went back to his logbook and flipped back until he came to the pages of notes he'd taken about her—the pages he was glad she hadn't seen. It was as complete as a dossier, and he was proud of it. He'd learned a lot about her today. Much more than he'd expected to. She was absolutely right about the citizens of Serenity not even knowing they were being pumped for information.

But Montague had taught him years ago that there was one difference between a successful huckster and one who wound up behind bars. And that was research.

That was why he'd wound up in Serenity in the first place. He had researched all of western Texas, soaked up information about the farms that had reverted to the banks, about the oil that had made some of the citizens rich, and about the people, most of whom had lived there all their lives.

He'd needed a town that was down on its luck, a town that needed a dream or two. But it had to be a town that still had resources. Preferably green resources . . . the kind that kept him in the lifestyle to which he was accustomed. He had researched the building of amusement parks, so that he would be able to speak on the subject with intelligence, and answer any questions from the most astute of the populace, without babbling or stumbling.

Then, after he'd come to the town, he researched the people, one at a time, deciding who would be the easiest marks, who had the most money, who were the entrepreneurs of the community, and who had the least to lose.

And today, he had researched Carny Sullivan.

Pulling out the chair at his desk, he sat down and went back over the things he'd learned about her. The facts about her—from her birth until today—still surprised him, and he couldn't help feeling an affinity with her. Whether she liked it or not, the two of them did have a lot in common.

Carny had been a con artist until she was seventeen. And it had been genetically inbred. According to Lahoma—whose brain he'd picked when she made her appointment this morning—Carny had been raised by two small-time con artists in a traveling carnival. Someone else had told him she was born in the back of a Winnebago in a carnival's convoy, somewhere between Shreveport and Monroe, Louisiana. She'd been named after her family's lifestyle and trained to follow in her parents' footsteps.

The citizens' accounts of Carny's past had been colorful and detailed, and he learned that she'd dazzled many of them with tales of her childhood over the seven years she'd lived in Serenity. Her in-laws had told him about Ruth, the carnival's fat lady and Carny's tutor, who had the IQ of a genius and a wall full of computers in her own RV, and spent every morning filling Carny's head with knowledge to such an extent that she probably knew more about a broader range of things than any college graduate.

From Blue Simpson, he'd learned how she'd spent afternoons with her parents, learning card tricks instead of ballet, rigging games instead of playing them, and creating diversions for their cons instead of getting attention from them. And from Eloise Trellis, whose deceased husband had launched Carny's current career, he'd seen the vision of the little girl walking alone each evening through the carnival while her father picked pockets and her mother guessed ages and weight.

He sat back, and tried to imagine the details he hadn't been told. His own childhood had left him with enough images to fill in the blanks of Carny's life. In his mind, he could see the little towheaded girl, with huge, beautiful eyes and dark circles under them from staying up too late and eating too much junk, trailing behind happy families with normal children who went to school and sang in choirs and had best friends. He knew without a doubt how it had been for her, for he'd experienced the same childhood wishes, before he'd grown too hardened to allow himself such indulgences.

He wondered if she'd imagined that, after the rides were broken down and the booths were loaded back onto their trailers, she would stay behind as one of those happy children. Leaning his head back on the seat, he rubbed his eyes, and wondered if, in her darkest hours, she had dreamed of starting over with normal parents who went to church and had barbecues and coached softball.

God knew, he had.

For a moment, he allowed himself to sink into the mire of self-pity, a luxury he rarely afforded himself. And for a split second, he was that little abandoned child, knowing his mother would return, and not understanding why she hadn't. For a split second, he knew intimately that little girl wandering down the midway, looking for a family to attach her imagination to.

Turning the page, he read through the rest of his notes. Not everything was there yet. He hadn't yet filled in the part about her escape from her old life and how she had come to Serenity. But he had it all in his head. Her in-laws, two people who loved her as if she were their own, had told him, almost in apology, everything else he needed to know.

Carny, at age seventeen, had met Abe Sullivan when the carnival came through Serenity. He'd been good-looking and soft-spoken, clean-cut, the apple-pie-and-mom type. After a weeklong romance, she had slipped out in the night with him and eloped, and the next morning when it was time for the carnival to tear down, she had informed her parents that she was staying behind.

She had been just a child, according to Abe's parents, but Logan knew better. You didn't get to be a child in that kind of environment. He suspected that she'd behaved in ways much older than her years, and that the marriage had had as much to do with her fascination for the sweet little town itself, as it had to do with the man she'd married. She had probably believed that, in the quiet little town of Serenity, she could have the kind of home she'd only dreamed of before. She had been old enough to know what she wanted out of life, but young enough to have illusions that such things existed.

He suspected that now, seven years later, she was much more savvy about the goodness that existed—or failed to exist—in the world. According to Abe's father—who'd seemed disgusted even to recount the tale, but couldn't seem to help himself to explain Carny's "rudeness"—Abe had taught Carny her first lesson about the grass being greener on the other side. Abe drank most of the time, had trouble holding a job, stayed out too late, and his mouth was even fouler than the worst mouths in the carnival. It amazed Logan now that two such sweet, kind people could have raised such a horror as a son. But as Bev Sullivan had said with a tear in her eye, "There's such a thing as loving too much. We spoiled him rotten. We blame ourselves. That's why we took Carny in at first. We felt so responsible."

According to Julia Peabody, who'd heard it at the Curl Up & Dye, when Carny caught her husband with a waitress from the diner on the same day she learned she was pregnant, she decided to leave him. Abe had made a mockery of her, telling his buddies at the bar that it was good riddance. A week later he'd left Serenity and joined the army, and he hadn't been heard from since.

Logan was surprised that she hadn't even considered going back to her parents' way of life, but had, instead, stayed with the Sullivans until her son was born. He suspected that they had given her the first nurturing love she'd ever known. The town had rallied around her, as well, something he found unusual for a community with relatively few newcomers. But the people he'd asked about her today had all voiced a deep love of the young woman, even if it was tinged with amusement.

She had a wild, unconventional streak, they said, and a free spirit that made them all smile. She was a little of what everyone in town wished they could be. And that she'd insulted and accused him publicly had been a reason for apology. She hadn't meant to be rude, they'd all said. She was just overly suspicious, because of her past. She was a passionate person, and sometimes she was overzealous. They loved her, but they apologized for her.

There was something about that—something he couldn't pinpoint—that he envied. Maybe it was that Carny had truly made herself a home here, and Logan was still running, looking for that pot of gold at the end of a self-made rainbow. Someday that rainbow would have to end, he thought, no matter how many times he painted extensions on it.

But he doubted that there was a Serenity waiting at the end of his.

# 5

*The Sullivans were waiting* on her front porch when Carny pulled her motorcycle up her gravel driveway. Cutting off the engine, she sat still for a moment.

"You guys are making a terrible mistake."

"Carny, honey, you don't have to worry," her mother-in-law said. "We're not giving him more than we can afford."

J. R. stood up from the rocker. "But the folks in town who have already invested are afraid that you'll talk Logan out of building the park here, and we'll lose out. You've got to stop it, Carny. We need this park in Serenity."

Groaning, she got off her bike and started up the porch steps. Sitting down on the top one, she leaned back against the post and looked up at them. "You just don't understand. He's got all the symptoms of a pigeon dropper. Why can't you listen?"

"What's a pigeon dropper?" J. R. asked, twisting his face at the image.

"A huckster. A shyster. A con man. J. R., if some big organization was considering building a park here the size of Six Flags, don't you think we'd have heard from the governor, the legislature, the bankers? Don't you think there would be some kind of competition among the towns? Don't you think there would be some sort of legal process involved?"

"We're in on the ground floor," J. R. returned. "All that will be later. But all Logan's doing is scouting around for the best place to build it. He's recommending us, and then I expect the governor will get involved."

Carny closed her eyes. "How you can be so naive and still have raised a low-down son like my ex-husband is a mystery to me."

"Carny!"

"I'm sorry, Bev," she said, raising her hands and starting into the house. "I didn't mean to say that. I'm just frustrated. Come on in, and I'll call Jason home."

"You do still have a class tonight, don't you?"

"Of course I do," she said. "I'm not gonna quit teaching just because there's a criminal wreaking havoc on my town."

J. R. shook his head. "Lands, how you do exaggerate." He walked to the television, grabbed the remote control, and plopped into his favorite chair, which she had bought just for him.

She paused for a moment and regarded J. R., who was already switching from *A Current Affair* to *911*, and back again. Bev was making herself at home in the adjoining kitchen, putting a pot of coffee on.

She loved them, and because she did, she couldn't just sit still and let him deceive them this way. Helplessness assailed her, and she stood still for a moment, wishing for the right thing to say to make them proceed more cautiously. But it was already too late.

"What would happen if he were a criminal?" she asked them softly. "I don't know how much you gave, but what would happen to the town if none of it worked out?"

They both looked at her, either unwilling or unable to answer. Finally, she got her keys to the pickup, slipped them into her pocket, and started for the door. "It took me seventeen years to find this place, and now that I'm here, I'm a little protective of it. I don't know what I'd do if I lost it." Her voice broke, and she looked down at her feet. "Maybe I'm fighting him out of selfishness. I want to keep things safe for me . . . and for Jason."

"Oh, honey." Bev came across the room and embraced her, the way her own mother had rarely done. "We know why you're doing it. And we can't even blame you. But that doesn't mean we have to agree with you."

"I'm gonna have to prove it to you, I guess," she

said. "Call Jason to come home, will you? The number's on the fridge. I'll be back around eight."

Then, before she lost control of her emotions, she hurried out to the truck.

She had driven two miles before the tears came to her eyes, but quickly, she wiped them away. It was going to be all right. She would stop Logan before he did too much damage. Her only hope was that he didn't skip town tomorrow with the money.

Taking in a deep breath, she turned onto the road that would take her out to her small airport, just on the outskirts of Serenity. Texas's Best Aviation School was her stake in this community. It was how she made her living, how she contributed to the town, and how she lent credibility to the wild streak she'd been born with. It hadn't been easy to settle in this tight little town, to become a part of it, to be trusted and loved.

In fact, there had been a lot of head shaking when Abe Sullivan had brought her home as his wife. Part of it had been because she was just a child, and another part was because they all knew that Abe was a low-down snake. But the other part, the part she had never quite forgotten, was because she had a checkered past. She had made it her business to get to know everyone in town, from Jed who cleaned the factory after hours, to Mayor Norman who said she looked like his daughter who had moved to California.

At first she'd struggled with the dichotomy of her strong desire to settle down, live a normal, peaceful, decent life for the first time, and her hungry spirit that craved adventure. Rather than moving on to satisfy that yearning, she had opted to take flying lessons. That way, she reasoned, she could feed the gypsy lust she had always denied before, but have a safe home to which she could always return.

To support herself and finance her flight lessons at the aviation school—which was nothing more than a concrete airstrip, a small tarmac, and a prefabricated building that housed the planes on one side and an office and classroom area on the other—she took a job as teller in the only bank in town. As her pregnancy progressed, she got to know the townspeople and feel like a part of the town. The moment she got her pilot's license, Wendell Trellis, owner of the Aviation School, as well as the air service that carried crucial deliveries from Serenity to wherever they needed to go, had offered her a flying job. It paid considerably more than she had made at the bank, allowing her, three years later, to venture away from the Sullivans' home and get a place of her own for Jason and her.

She had never forgotten the lump she'd had in her throat the day she'd brought Jason to the old house she'd bought for them, the first home she'd ever known. It had two bedrooms, and a huge kitchen that adjoined to an open den. And it had a garage. And a white picket fence around the backyard.

Jason was thrilled that there was a tire swing already in the yard, but the tiny child wasn't able to grasp how much this home meant to his mother. Her unsavory childhood didn't matter anymore.

What mattered now was that she was a good mother, making a good life for her son.

And it was no small feat that she'd gone from answering the phone for Wendell and making an occasional jaunt across the state, to actually buying the freight service when he retired and running it herself. She was proud of the fact that the bank where she had worked had approved her loan as a vote of confidence in her character. She was also proud of the fact that her aviation classes were always full, and her freight schedule was always busy. People needed her here, and they enjoyed her. And she had never felt so good about herself.

She pulled up to her hangar, threw the truck into park, and grabbed her bag full of papers. Already, there was a car here, a silver Mercedes with blackened windows. Had Jess Stevens traded in his Plymouth Belvedere? She chuckled at the picture of the old retired farmer letting go of a nickel he didn't absolutely have to. It could belong to Cass or Jacob Jordan, but they were both more the sports-car type. And it couldn't be either Bro Gillian's or Wayne Cash's, since they were union men and wouldn't be caught dead driving a foreign car. Since that ruled out all five of her students, she got out of the truck with a feeling of apprehension.

The Mercedes door opened, and she watched Logan Brisco get out.

"What are you doing here?"

Logan's grin piqued her as he stepped toward her. "I wanted to see your facilities. I thought I might need your services for some emergency deliveries."

"Deliveries of what?" she asked. "Large bundles of cash?"

He laughed. "No. One of the banks in Dallas will be spearheading the operation, and sending contracts, payroll, that kind of thing."

"Save it, Brisco." She went inside, dropped her papers down on her desk, and leaned back against it. "You're wasting your breath carrying out this scam on me. How did you know where I work?"

"Everybody knows," he said. "I must have gotten ten different versions of your life story today."

"Good," she said. "Then you know I can't be suckered."

"Oh, I knew that already."

"And that I don't give up."

"I'd suspected." He turned a chair around and sat down. "Tell me something, Carny. What would it take for us to call a truce?"

"For you to be on the next train out of town."

He laughed. "No, I mean what would it take for you to give me some peace while I'm here?"

Crossing her arms, she cocked her head and affected a thoughtful expression. "Well, let's see . . . Atlantis rising from the ocean floor, the Bermuda Triangle spitting out Amelia Earhart, Jimmy Hoffa being discovered on an island paradise with Elvis . . ."

"Okay, I get the point," he said, still amused. "Maybe you and I just need to get to know each other a little better. How long's it been since you've had a relationship with a man?"

It was her turn to laugh. "I have lots of relationships with men. But the odds of my ever having one with you are pretty much as likely as all the scenarios I just mentioned."

He tried to look wounded, but she wasn't buying. "Carny, I could have walked into town in a priest's collar waving a Bible and you still wouldn't have trusted me."

"You're right," she said. "My father posed as a priest once and made three thousand dollars a night 'healing' people. I was the little crippled girl he made walk. My mother was blind, until he mumbled a really loud prayer and made her see. I'm a tough sell, Brisco."

Logan was genuinely appalled. "And you think *I'm* low-down? Your father sounds like a real prince, and if that's the kind of thing you grew up watching, I don't blame you for being paranoid now."

"I'm not paranoid, Brisco. I'm realistic. And my father wasn't low-down. He was a desperate man trying to feed his family. What's your excuse?"

"Come on, Carny. You don't believe that. There's not much class in selling fake miracles to sick people, so stop kidding yourself. He did it because he was greedy."

Her face reddened as he made his speech and, through compressed lips, she said, "You'd better be careful, Logan. Someone might think you're the voice of experience. What's your point, anyway? That you're better than my father because your scams are cleaner?"

She'd hit a nerve, and for a moment Logan only

looked at her. "Carny, I realize that nothing short of my own miracle is going to persuade you to trust me," he said in a soft, almost convincing tone, "but I really want to do this for your town, because I think Serenity needs what I'm bringing it. And I think *you* need it. You're a woman who needs something she can trust . . . something to believe in."

"If that's what you think, then your conversations about me today weren't very productive. I happen to believe in a lot. I believe in God, and I believe in this town, and I believe in the goodness and purity that I've found here. And I believe in my instincts."

"Have your instincts ever been wrong?"

"Nope. Never."

He walked toward her, his face serious, and said, "Do some research on me, Carny. Check me out. Write for my college transcript. Talk to my teachers. I have a degree in marketing at Virginia State. Call A & T Marketing in Marietta, Georgia. Check out my employment records."

Doubt altered her expression. Con artists didn't often have college degrees, and they rarely had job histories. She whipped out a pad and pen, jotted down the two places, then looked up at him. "I'll call them tomorrow," she said. "What other jobs could I verify?"

He smiled. "None. Since I left A & T, I've been self-employed. I contract with corporations and banks to execute deals they're working on."

"Then give me the names of some of the bankers who are supposedly in on this deal."

He smiled calmly and shook his head. "I can't do that. It's still in the initial stages. If you were to start calling them and drilling them about the park, they'd get scared and pull out. It's my job to make everybody feel confident that this is going to work. Including my investors."

Smiling, she dropped her pen. "What else did I expect?"

He sighed and rubbed his hand through his dark hair, leaving it ruffled. "Look, I'm just curious. If you did trust me . . . if you had known me all your life and knew I had a sterling character, would you still be fighting me on this?"

"I sure would," she said.

He nodded. "I thought so. Why?"

"I told you. I don't want my town ruined by a flow of tourists, criminals, and carnies."

"Tourists, I can understand. But what makes you think either criminals or carnies will come here?"

"Because they will." She heard a car drive up, and glanced out the window. Her students, Cass and Jacob, were getting out of their car. "The criminals will come to rip off the tourists, and who do you think you'll get to run the park? Carnies, that's who!"

"Then work with me on this," he said. "Help me plan it so that we can avoid that. We can put a police station on the grounds, and somehow divert the traffic from the main town. We can build hotels way out and some malls near the park, so no one ever has cause to come into town. Carny, if this works, your airport could expand drastically. We'd need a bigger airport for planes to fly into. My investors could finance the expansion."

She lowered her voice as Cass and Jacob came closer. "Is that how you usually manage to pull off the gaff, Brisco? By making it personal? Telling each person in Serenity how they'll wake up rich one day, if they just give you all their money now? Gosh, Brisco, you're wasted in this line of work. With those talents you could have run for president."

He stared at her, for a moment feeling truly offended. Why wouldn't she listen?

She looked out as another of her students drove up, and finally said, "Well, I've enjoyed this little conversation, Brisco, but I have a class to teach."

He stood there, motionless.

"Did you hear me? You have to leave."

"Where do I sign up?" he asked suddenly.

She gaped at him. "Sign up for what?"

"For the class," he said. "I want to learn to fly."

The people coming in the back door and settling in her classroom heard her laughter ring out over the building. "You've got to be kidding."

"Why?" he asked. "I'm gonna need to know how to fly once this park gets off the ground."

"My class is full."

"You can fit one more in."

"I don't want you here!"

He smiled. "I know you don't. But if you think about it, it would be the smart thing to do. That way you could keep your eye on me. Make sure I don't skip town."

"There's nothing that says you can't skip town just because you're taking a class."

"No, I guess you're right. But I really do want to learn to fly, Carny. It's always been a dream of mine. I've just always been too busy."

He smiled at the truth in his words and recalled all the times he'd posed as a pilot to cash Montague's homemade Delta payroll checks at the airport terminals. He'd professed to a degree from Embry-Riddle Aeronautical University in Daytona Beach then, the leading school for commercial pilots. And he'd deadheaded on many a flight, posing as a pilot catching a ride between airports, listening to the talk in the cockpit, and watching the captains and first officers work. Now he'd have the chance to find out how actually to get the plane off the ground.

"Come on, Carny. I'll pay you in advance. Cash. And I'm a quick learner."

She looked at her students assembling in her classroom, and finally realized that he was right about at least one thing. It would be wise to keep her eye on him. Maybe he would slip up, and she'd find something to expose him . . . something to make everyone believe her. And the more money she could take from him, the better. After all, his cash had come from the people of her town.

"All right, Brisco," she said. "I charge fifty dollars an hour. To get a private pilot's license, you'll need flight school plus at least twenty dual-hours in the plane, and at least twenty solo-hours."

He smiled and pulled out his wallet. "And you call me a con artist."

"Cash in advance for you," she said. "And frankly, I wouldn't be comfortable letting you solo in my plane."

He looked insulted. "What am I gonna do, Carny? It's kind of hard to steal a plane."

"Yeah, well, I'd rather not take any chances. You can get your solo hours somewhere else."

He pulled out ten one-hundred-dollar bills and dropped them down in front of her. "How's that?"

Something tightened in her chest. Was she really going to have to teach him how to fly? Snatching the money up, as if the whole process made her more angry, she started into the classroom. "You still can't start tonight," she said. "I only have enough materials for five students at a time, and besides, these people are halfway through the course already."

"Then when do you have another class?"

"Well, I have one for kids after school on Tuesdays and two adult classes on Saturday. But they're all in progress."

"Then I guess you'll have to start a new class just for me."

"The price I gave you wasn't for private lessons," she said.

He laughed and reached into his wallet. "Damn, your daddy taught you well."

Something in her expression snapped, and she took a step closer, glaring into his eyes. "There's a difference between a con artist and a business person, Brisco, and you know it. If you don't like my rates, then find another instructor."

He pulled out the rest of what he had in his wallet and said, "Why don't you just take what you need, and give me back what's left over?"

"Fine." Snatching the money out of his hand, she counted out the bills she needed, wondering if it added up to what her in-laws had given him. "That ought to do it."

He looked down at the few bills she gave back to him. "This better be good."

"Oh, it will be," she said. "I have a delivery to make in Sherman tomorrow morning, but I should be back by midmorning. Meet me here at ten for your first lesson, Brisco."

"I'll be here."

Without another word, she left him standing there and disappeared into the classroom at the other side of the building.

Logan was right on time to her classroom the next day, and Carny began the first lesson that she always taught new students. But Logan already knew most of the parts of the plane, what their uses were, and many other aviation terms. Some of his knowledge applied more to commercial jets than to small single-engine planes, however, and she wondered where in the world he came up with such knowledge.

"I fly a lot," he told her.

"You don't pick this stuff up riding as a passenger," she said. "You already know how to fly, don't you? This is just another con."

"Well, if it is, it's a stupid one. I'm the one who paid you an arm and a leg, remember?" He raised his right hand. "I swear I don't know how to fly. But I know a lot of pilots. And I read a lot. There was a time when I thought I might want to be one, so I did some research. I told you, I'm a quick learner."

She bristled. "Don't waste my time, okay?"

"I won't. When you check me out, see if I have a pilot's license."

Carny leaned back on her desk. "You know, I do intend to check you out, but I have no illusions that you're even using your real name. You could have the name and history of some other poor soul."

Logan had, indeed, used aliases before, and the FBI was quite possibly looking for them now. His real name, however, was Logan Brisco. Because he did have a couple of legitimate credentials under that name, he'd decided to use it this time. "Now, how would I get identification with someone else's name?"

She laughed then. "All it takes is a computer and a laser printer, and a little ingenuity. My father once got the birth certificate of a contemporary of his who died, and with it, he was able to get a driver's license and a passport. But I would imagine you know all the tricks."

"You're the one with all the expertise. I should take notes."

"Yeah, but I don't make any bones about it. I was raised to be a hawker, but you might say I departed from the ways of my kin. Were you raised to be a con artist, Brisco, or did you leave your parents to answer to the cops every time you pulled off a new scam?"

His face sobered, and she could tell she had hit a nerve. "Nobody answers for me."

"Well, there must be somebody back there in Virginia . . . isn't that where you said you were from?"

"No. I didn't say."

"Oh, excuse me. I should have known that would have been a secret."

Wearily, he stood up and began to gather his notes. "It's no secret, Carny. I was born in Des Moines, Iowa."

"And went to school in Virginia? Interesting."

"People go away to school all the time."

"Yes, they sure do." She could see she was getting to him, and it empowered her. "Logan Brisco. Logan's an interesting name. Is it a family name? Your mother's maiden name, maybe?"

He didn't smile as he usually did when he knew she was pushing. "My mother never married. Brisco was her maiden name."

"Oh." Something about the way he said it rang true, and she almost wanted to back off, leave him alone. But she couldn't. "So where did the name Logan come from?"

"I don't know," he said. "I never got the chance to ask her."

"What do you mean, you never got the chance?"

He slammed the cover of his textbook shut.

"You tell me. You're the one with all the answers. Her name was Melissa Brisco, Carny, and you can find her death records in Des Moines, Iowa. Happy Hunting."

It was a bluff, she thought, but it didn't look like one. His eyes were intense, explosive, yet they dared her to make the call.

"When's the next lesson?" he asked in a clipped voice.

"Monday? Same time?"

"What's wrong with tomorrow?"

"Tomorrow's Sunday," she said. "I don't work on Sundays."

"Oh? Then what do you do on Sundays?"

"I go to church," she replied. "Have you ever gone to church, Brisco?"

The anger on his face cooled a degree. "Not without being dragged."

"You should give it another shot," she said. "Lord knows, a man like you could probably use a little spirituality. It might change your life."

The hint of a smile returned to his eyes. "Are you trying to convert me?"

She smiled. "Heavens, no. I'll leave that to Brother Tommy. He's worked miracles before. The real kind."

"With you, maybe?"

"Yeah," she said, lifting her chin. "With me. And with a lot of others in this town. You want to really get to know the people of Serenity, Brisco, you have to go to their church."

"And what church is that?"

"Ninety percent of Serenity goes to First Baptist Church. We're Southern Baptists, Brisco. Of the 'turn-the-other-cheek' ilk. Of the belief that 'if a man asks for your shirt, you should give him your cloak also.' That's why we make easy targets for people like you."

He gave a defeated laugh and started for the door. "Why on earth would you want a lowlife like me in your church?"

"Because," she said, ignoring the sarcasm, "if I can't stop you myself, maybe I can at least reactivate that conscience of yours. Maybe seeing the goodness in these people will make you back off. But beware, Brisco. You might decide you like them too much to fleece them. It could cost you a huge score."

With his hand on the knob, he turned around. "You never give up, do you?"

"Nope." But her smile was less condemning, and he saw the slightest trace of warmth in it.

"Do the Southern Baptists go to the town dances?" he asked.

She shrugged. "Of course we do. Everybody goes."

"Really? I thought Baptists were against dancing."

"Dancing, yes," she said with a grin, "but when you call it 'foot fellowship,' it's something altogether different."

He laughed, and when she joined him, she found that it relieved the pressure in her chest.

"You want to start a scandal and show up with me next Saturday night?" he asked.

Her grin almost disarmed him. "No, Brisco. I don't think so."

"Just thought I'd ask," he said.

He closed the door behind him, and through the window, she saw him getting into his rented Mercedes. He wasn't smiling.

Slowly, she walked to the window and reflected on the anger and pain she'd seen flash across his face when she'd mentioned his mother. In spite of her efforts not to be moved by him, something about his reaction had touched her.

*I never got the chance to ask her . . . Melissa Brisco . . . her death records . . .*

She went into her office and sat down behind her desk and tried to run what he'd told her through her mind. Some of it sounded true, and her instincts were often right. But there was so much that didn't add up.

She flicked on her computer, pulled up her communications network, and saw that she had a message waiting. It was from Ruth, the fat lady in the carnival, who sat on a stool by night while people ogled her and in front of her computer by day, where she designed software and fed her genius IQ while communicating with people all across the world.

She retrieved the message and smiled as she read it. "Hey, baby," it said. "Haven't heard from you in a week. How's Jason? When are you bringing him to see us again?"

Carny responded quickly, knowing that since it was morning and the carnival wasn't yet open, Ruth would see it within moments.

"Ruth, sorry I haven't written. I've been busy. Why don't you give me a call? I'll be at the hangar all afternoon. Jason's getting off the bus here at three. While you're at it, get Mama and Pop to call me, too. I need to talk to all of you."

She sent the message, then waited for the phone to ring. In moments, it did.

"Texas's Best Aviation," she said.

"Hi, baby," Ruth said in her voice that sounded so sultry on the phone that one would have never dreamed the speaker weighed almost five hundred pounds. "I got your message."

"I'm sorry I haven't E-mailed this week," Carny said. "It's just that this guy came to town, and I'm pretty sure he's trying to run a scam . . . and I've been a little distracted trying to expose him."

"Anybody I'd know?"

"Well, I don't know," she said. "That's why I wanted to talk to Mama and Pop. I thought they might have run into him."

"They're right here, darlin'. I'm gonna put on the speaker phone so we can all talk." She switched over, and Carny heard her mother. "Hi, sweetheart. How's it going?"

"Hi, Mama. Pop, are you there?"

"Right here, Carny. So how's that grandbaby of ours?"

"Growing like a weed. You wouldn't recognize him."

"When are you ever going to bring him to see us?" her mother asked. "You know we can't get away. We have carnivals booked up all through the state for the next six months."

"I'll come soon, Mom. But I have to ask you

something. There's a guy here who's trying to sell the town on building a huge amusement park. My instincts tell me it's a scam. He's taking money from all the people, telling them they'll get rich."

"Good line. Are you in on it with him?" her father asked.

Carny wilted. "No, Pop, I'm not. I told you, I'm living a clean life here. And I don't want him messing up this town. I wondered if you might know him. The name he's going by here is Logan Brisco."

"Brisco," her mother repeated. "I don't believe I've ever heard that name."

"Don't know him," her father assured her. "What's he look like?"

"Tall, dark hair, relatively handsome, but not as good-looking as he thinks he is. Of course, all the women here practically swoon every time he walks by. It's downright sickening. And he's got an unusual smile. Real big, and real contagious."

"Are you sure you're not swooning, too?" Ruth asked with a laugh.

"I'd rather be hung up by my toenails in the town square," Carny said, chagrined. "Does he sound familiar to any of you? He tells me he's from Iowa and went to school in Virginia, and he's also mentioned Marietta, Georgia. Have you ever run into him before?"

"Was he a carny?" her mother asked.

"No, I don't think so. My gut tells me his are white-collar scams."

"I'm sorry, honey, but none of what you've told us rings a bell."

She sighed. "All right, I just thought I'd ask."

"By the way, Carny," her father said. "If it turns out not to be a scam, and there really is a park, I'd like to meet him and talk to him. I could set him up with some rides, and your mother and I, and a bunch of our carnies, could come and set up some flat stores."

*Over my dead body,* Carny thought, but instead, she said, "It's not going to happen, Pop. And as soon as he realizes what a hard time I'm gonna give him, I'm sure he'll head out."

"So what's his line again?" he asked. "Building an amusement park? Telling them to invest and they'll get rich?"

She dropped her forehead into her palm at the thought that her father was taking notes. "Pop, don't you have enough scams already?"

"I was just asking, darling. That's all. Now when can I see my grandson?"

"Soon," she said, but the weak promise held no more weight than it ever had.

When they had finished catching up, she hung up, then called the operator and got the numbers for all the places Logan had told her to call. Within a few days, she thought, she would have something more to go on. And Logan Brisco would be exposed for exactly what he was.

# 6

*Logan hadn't expected to* be an honored guest at the First Baptist Church of Serenity, but when Brother Tommy, the preacher, spotted him before the service, he'd taken him under his wing and introduced him to the dozen or so deacons he hadn't yet met.

It was the damnedest thing, Logan thought, that the whole town actually set their alarms on Sunday mornings and showed up early enough for Sunday school. As they milled in to find their places before the service, he was hit with the strange and unexpected feeling that they actually enjoyed being here. It was a social gathering, where people smiled and laughed and encouraged one another, where they wore their Sunday best and fixed their hair, and men who rarely shaved during the week were spit-polished on that day.

He didn't know what Montague would have said about his being here, but he suspected he would have enjoyed it, too. As mercenary as he was, his old friend had always admired honor and decency, traits he vowed to adopt as soon as he made enough money. He would have loved the idea of Logan coming here—even though it had been Carny's idea. After all, what better place for him to get to know people than in their church?

Someone tapped Logan on the shoulder, and he turned around to find Slade Hampton, smiling like an old friend and waiting to shake his hand. Jack, his dog, was at his side.

Logan stood and shook Slade's hand, then bent to pet Jack. "They let you bring him in here?"

"Nobody's ever said anything about it," Slade said. "I guess they're so used to seeing us together, they've mostly forgotten he's not human. Besides, he enjoys it."

He could see that the dog did, indeed, enjoy it, for every child that came by stopped to "speak" to him. Slade slipped into the pew next to Logan, and Jack followed, curling up at his feet. As he and Slade talked, Logan told himself that he watched the crowds coming in the doors from Sunday school to see if there were others here he knew, and not because he anticipated seeing Carny Sullivan in a dress. But the moment he spotted her, he had to admit to the real reason he had come. And it was worth it.

She wore an outfit that would have changed his whole image of her, had he not already decided that she was a woman of complexities. It was a silky white blouse, buttoned to the top, with a man's tie knotted at her throat. A green vest that tapered to her small waist gave it a feminine touch, and the skirt that stopped just above her knee showed enough leg to make him remember how long it had been since he'd had a woman. Why he hadn't taken advantage of any of the opportunities he'd had with the little beauties of Serenity was beyond him.

Logan tore his gaze away as Julia Peabody approached him, and grinning his most flirtatious grin, he told her how handsome she looked, complimented the hat she wore, then glanced back at Carny. Her eyes met his, and then she looked down at Jason who was walking in at her side. It was almost as if she didn't care that Logan was there, almost as if she'd expected to see him and it didn't move her a bit.

Mildred Smith, with her hair glowing neon-red from the dye job Lahoma had given her, started to play the piano, and Logan watched Carny and Jason move through the people still coming in. Her hair was pulled up in a loose chignon, with tiny wisps around her face. He swallowed. *Man, she was beautiful,* he thought. She made every other woman in the room look like a poor imitation of femininity. Only she was the real thing.

Carny came up the aisle and stopped when she reached him.

"So you decided to come, did you, Brisco?"

Like the gentleman Montague had taught him to be, Logan stood up. He smiled. "A man has to worship somewhere."

"Right," she said. "I guess it depends on what he worships. Money, power, himself . . . Or all the above."

"You're an awful cynic for someone with such great legs. Just reminded me of that bet we had going."

She smiled, undaunted. "Do yourself a favor and listen to Brother Tommy, Brisco. You might learn something." Then she slipped into the aisle across from him.

He couldn't see her face as she settled in, but when he leaned slightly forward, he could see her crossing her legs. The high heels she wore only made her legs look longer, feeding his imagination and making him wish he wasn't in church.

Leaning back, he smiled, and wondered if she'd ridden her motorcycle today. The image of her revving that bike in her bare legs and high heels took him through the introductory hymn and the welcome to the visitors, and didn't leave him until after the offering plate had been passed. It wasn't until Brother Tommy took the pulpit and started talking about salvation that he finally let the vision go.

Logan didn't believe in God, and he rarely believed in goodness. And even if the people of this town were mostly Laura-Ingalls, John-Boy-Walton, and Opie-Taylor types, he didn't believe in heaven. There was one unspoken, yet crowning philosophy in Montague's life, and Logan had taken it for his own. And that was to look out for number one, because no one else was going to.

Still, as the preacher spoke in his mesmerizing voice about the insidious practices of the devil, of deceit and corruption, of greed and self-centeredness, he couldn't help listening. The man had a way of driving the point home, of relating it to the most distant of souls. He had a way of making one think.

By the time the service was over, Logan realized that it was the first time he'd ever sat through a church service without nodding off. And he thought that if he was still in town next Sunday, he might try it again.

Monday afternoon, Carny sighed, almost disappointed, as she hung up from the last of the phone calls she'd made about Logan. Something was wrong. All the sources he'd told her to call had checked out, and the rest of what she'd discovered, while it had been disturbing, hadn't indicted him at all.

Carny had spoken to the secretary at A & T, who still remembered him, and described him in an awestruck voice, leaving little doubt that they were talking about the same man. She'd related that he was the best salesperson they'd ever had, and in a voice that bordered on a whisper, told Carny he'd been cheated out of his pay, and she hadn't blamed him for leaving. When Carny spoke to those of his professors who were still at the college, they'd described him to a T. Charming, with a devilish grin. Smart. Charismatic.

But it was the call to the county clerk's office that had started her on the best track. Just as he'd said, his mother's death certificate was on file there, dated thirty years ago. When she'd asked the clerk how to find out what had become of the woman's child, she'd been directed to Human Services.

Posing as a detective looking for information on a case, she persuaded the woman to find Brisco's file. The woman read bits and pieces to her, enough to tell her that, from the age of three, Logan Brisco had been shuffled from one foster home to another, until he'd run away at the age of fourteen.

That was the source of the pain in his eyes when she'd mentioned his mother, she thought, feeling a little ashamed of herself. That kind of pain never went away. It had the power to mold a person into something he might never have been. It had the power to drive him toward the kind of life where he was in control and created his own destiny. Where close attachments were rare, and abandonment was impossible.

Something about his childhood made her see him in a different light, and for the first time, she allowed herself to wonder if he really was the grifter she believed him to be. Nothing she had discovered about him suggested that he'd ever been on the wrong side of the law. At least not before he was fourteen.

But there were giant holes in his life between the time he'd run away at fourteen until he'd gone to school, and between when he'd quit working for

A & T and now. All con artists had to start somewhere.

It didn't matter that she hadn't found any evidence of Brisco's duplicity, she thought as she gazed out her hangar window and saw Jason washing her Cessna. She still didn't trust the man, and she couldn't let her sympathy for his difficult childhood color her thinking now. She rarely doubted her instincts, and she wasn't about to give up on them now.

Again, her gaze wandered out the hangar window. Jason was almost finished washing the plane. She smiled at the serious way he went about it, talking to himself the whole time, as his imagination rambled. She wondered what part he was playing today. Was it fighter pilot with his guns aimed at the enemy? Was it firefighter, putting out a monstrous blaze?

She went outside and ran toward him. When he saw her he aimed the hose in her direction. Ducking, she reached for another hose coiled beside the hangar, turned on the water, and brought her own spray up to him.

Screaming and laughing, he ran behind the plane and sprayed at her over it. She ducked under it, and got him good from behind. Squealing with laughter, he reciprocated by drenching her.

"I got you first!" he shouted. "If those had been bullets, you'd have been dead before you reached for your hose!"

"Flesh wounds, my boy," she said in a bad English accent. "Mere flesh wounds. But your wounds were fatal."

"I don't think so," he said. "I can take a few bullets without even feeling them."

"Good," she said, and pulled her hose back up into his face, spraying him at point-blank range. He screamed and wrestled with the nozzle, and by the time they collapsed on the tarmac laughing, they were both sopping wet.

"Tell me two things," she said, finally. "Tell me how I could have raised a little boy without guns, without toys that look like guns, and without allowing television shows or video games with guns, and he can still manage to play war with a couple of hoses."

"You can make a pretend gun out of anything, Mom," he said matter-of-factly. "It's a guy thing."

"I guess so," she sighed. Around them, the hoses kept running, making a little river that puddled under them. But neither of them moved.

"What's the second thing you want me to tell you?"

"How we're going to get home on that motorcycle soaking wet. We'll freeze to death."

"Nah. It's 80 degrees. Almost summer. Hey, you know what, Mom? This summer, Nathan's dad said he'd buy us the lumber and stuff, and we can build a fort between our houses. Won't that be cool?"

"It sure will. Can I help?"

"No, Mom," he said, aggravated. "Girls don't know anything about building stuff."

"Sure we do," Carny said. "When I was growing up, we used to have to tear down everything everywhere we went, then put them back up when we got where we were going. I know a few things about construction. Come on," she said, tickling him. "Let your old mom help!"

He squirmed and held back. "Sure, if you don't mind my fort looking like a carnival booth. I don't think so."

"How'd you get to be such a male chauvinist at seven?"

"What's a male chauvinist?" He giggled, defending himself from her tickles.

"It's a guy who thinks building a fort is a guy thing. And I suppose if I don't get to help build it, I won't get to play in it, either, huh?"

Jason held her hands to stop the tickling, and tried to catch his breath. "That about sums it up. It's a boy's fort, Mom. No girls allowed."

"That's it," she said. "I'm suing."

"Mom!" he said. "You'd bump your head on the ceiling, anyway. It's for kids."

"Keep going. I've got two counts of discrimination, so far. I can get you for everything you're worth. I can probably even get the fort. I'll paint it pink and turn it into a doll house."

"Mom! That would be gross! Besides, you can't sue us for something that isn't even built!"

"Oh, yeah," she said. She got up, pulled her shirttail out of her jeans, and wrung it out. "And if I die of pneumonia, I probably can't sue, either. This was all a clever ploy to intimidate me out of taking you to court, wasn't it?"

He laughed and popped his wet shirt away from his skin, then let it stick back. "Hey, Mom. Are we going to the dance Friday night?"

"Why? You got a date?"

"I sorta told Amber I'd meet her there. I might dance with her this time."

Carny made a horrible face. "But she's a *girl*!"

"Girls are okay once in a while," he said, skipping behind her in the puddles as she turned off the hoses. "I mean, you can't have 'em coming in your forts and stuff, but they're okay to dance with. Are you going with Mr. Joey?"

Still chuckling at his perceptions of girls, she shook her head. "Nope."

"He said you were. He told me you were his girlfriend."

"Joey's got a lot to learn. I never told him I'd go with him to the dance."

"Then who are you going with? Mr. Paul? Mr. Sam?"

"None of the above. I thought I'd just go as your date."

His face sobered. "Okay, Mom. I think that would be okay. Amber probably wouldn't mind if it was just you."

She smiled and started into the hangar. "Come on. We'd better get home so we can change out of these wet clothes."

"I like them," he said, slapping his wet jeans.

"You would," she said. "But we're changing, anyway."

Thursday, Logan swung around in his chair at the Curl Up & Dye, where he spent as much of his spare time as he could buttering up the ladies, and grinned at the proprietor. "Tell me, Lahoma," he said, "do you consider yourself single-handedly responsible for the overabundance of beauty in this town?"

Her laughter had a sweet kind of ring to it, and it was infectious. Eliza Martin, whose hair she was working on, hooted right along with her, and the ladies under the dryers, who he didn't think had heard, chuckled, as well.

"You're such a talker," Lahoma said in her deep southern drawl. "By the way, have you heard about the dance tomorrow night? Down at the bingo hall?"

"I sure have," he said, "and I intend to be there."

"And have you got a date?" Lahoma asked with a wink.

He grinned. "You got somebody in mind?"

He saw her blush, but then, recovering, she said, "Well, if I was fifteen years younger, I'd snap you up myself. Might anyway, now that I think about it."

The other ladies guffawed, and Lahoma preened in the mirror, proud of herself. "No, Logan, I had someone more your age in mind. My daughter, Mary Beth, doesn't have a date yet. Or there's Jean Miller, who works at the drugstore. Or Bonnie . . . you know, the little waitress in the diner? Take your pick. There's plenty of women in Serenity who wouldn't mind going on your arm."

Grinning, he swung around in his chair again. "Well, you see, that's just the problem. There's so many I'd love to go with. It's hard to decide. I think I might just go stag so I can dance and flirt with all of them."

The women laughed again, as if that suited them just fine. Logan pulled up out of the seat, and sighed. "Well, ladies, I've sure enjoyed shooting the breeze with you. And like I said, if any of you wants an appointment with me, you know where you can find me. Time's running out, though. I have to have all my investors registered pretty soon. You know how those bankers can be. They don't much like being kept waiting. And the idea, of course, is to get the park finished and open by next summer. It'll take over a year to build it, so we're really under the gun here."

"My husband's gonna be calling you today, Logan," one of the ladies under the dryer said. "His name's Jess. When you hear from Jess, you'll know who he is. My husband."

Logan leaned down and took her hand. Kissing it, he said, "I sure will, ma'am. And if he's half as delightful as you, it'll be a pleasure going into partnership with him." He went to the next lady under the dryer, kissed her hand, then reached for the third. Every one of them tittered like little birds.

Then he grabbed Lahoma, pulled her into a waltz, and spun her. "Tomorrow night, you save a dance for me," he said, kissing her cheek.

"I will," she said, almost swooning. "Bye, Logan."

A hush seemed to fall over the beauty shop as Logan made his exit. After a moment, Lahoma turned back to Eliza Martin. "I don't think I've ever run across a nicer man," she said.

"I know," Eliza Martin answered. "He'd be some

catch for some nice young girl. We've got to find a wife for him."

"Find, nothing," Lahoma said. "If I could hook him, I'd marry him myself. In a minute. And he could eat crackers in my bed *every* night!"

The women howled with laughter.

Logan checked his watch and decided he had enough time before his lesson with Carny to stop by the barbershop and shoot the breeze some more. It was these intimate little gab sessions, unscheduled and relaxed, that seemed to inspire the kind of trust he needed to make them give him their money.

He came to the red-and-white peppermint sign outside, and looked in the window. Slade was cutting the mayor's hair, and Cecil was cutting that of a farmer Logan didn't know yet. There was one other man waiting, and they were all laughing.

Friendship. Camaraderie. It was something he'd missed terribly since Montague died. But he couldn't break Montague's rule of getting too close now, just because it felt good. A lot of things felt good, but they could also land him in jail. The goal now was to get to know the folk as well as he could while still holding himself aloof. That was a trick, but he was good at it. That was why it had always been easy to leave the towns behind.

But he might as well be in Mayberry, for Pete's sake. And this was Floyd's Barber Shop, and the men in the chairs could have been Andy and Barney. He hadn't really believed such towns existed. He couldn't blame Carny for being protective of it. But that couldn't matter to him now. A man had to make a living, after all.

Logan slid his hands into his pockets, and strolled inside. He felt like Norm in the *Cheers* bar, for everyone turned and greeted him. "Logan!"

Slade and Cecil shook his hand, and the mayor, strapped in by his cape, found his hand and shook it, too. As if he was the town celebrity, the other men introduced themselves and told him they had been at his town meeting.

Slade looked over at the chair where his dog sat, and said, "Jack, get up and let Logan sit down." The dog jumped down immediately and went to lie beside Slade's chair.

Laughing, Logan sat down and patted his leg. Answering the invitation, Jack waddled over and licked Logan's hand. "I don't need a haircut, Slade," he said as he stroked the dog. "I just had a few minutes to kill before my next meeting and thought I'd see what you fellows are up to."

*Fellows. Wasn't that how they would have said it in Mayberry?* He grinned at his own resourcefulness.

"Well, oddly enough, we were just talking about you."

"Oh yeah?" He looked up at them and saw that they were smiling, so he assumed they hadn't been raking him over the coals. "I came just in time to defend myself then, didn't I?"

"Oh, you don't need defending. Not from us, anyways. From Carny Sullivan, maybe."

"Yeah, I figured she was still at it. She's not so

bad, though. I'm taking flying lessons from her, you know. I figure when the park gets under way, I probably ought to buy a plane. Better know how to fly it."

"Carny's teaching you?" The man who'd introduced himself as Joey, a younger man than the others, who had an enviable beard and was as big as a bear, gave him a surprised look.

"Well, sure, she is. She's a good lady. Just a little suspicious, and from what I've heard about her, you can't blame her. It's a shame about her childhood."

"So which class are you in?" Joey asked. "Her Tuesday night class?"

"No. She's teaching me privately. All the other classes were already in progress."

Joey got quiet, and Logan noted that there was something behind the man's eyes. Was it jealousy? He couldn't afford to make any enemies in this town, so he tried to rally. "You're not the Joey she keeps mentioning, are you?"

The man's eyes lit up. "She talks about me?"

"Well, I guess it's you."

"What did she say?"

Logan laughed and bent down low to let the dog lick his face. "Well, now, I can't divulge that kind of information to you. Whatever she said, it was in confidence. But I will tell you that she thinks a lot of you."

Joey smiled and looked off into space, as if trying to conjure up circumstances under which she would have been talking about him.

"How long have you had Jack, Slade?"

Slade put the finishing touches on the mayor's hair. "Fifteen years. He's been by my side almost every minute of that time. Goes everywhere I go, don't you, boy?" Slade went over to pat the dog's head, then resumed his cutting.

"He looks like a loyal pal," Logan said. He patted the dog's coat one last time, and, as if he knew that meant a dismissal, Jack wandered back over to his corner.

"So how are the plans for the park shaping up?" Mayor Norman asked.

Logan crossed his arms and looked him straight in the eye. "Well, sir, I'm going to give the people of the town another week or two to get their investments in. Then I'm supposed to meet back with my big investors with my recommendation. I'm pretty sure that, if we can get enough support from the town, they'll choose this site for the park. In fact, I'd bet on it."

The mayor laughed. "The best thing to happen in this town in forty years, and it's during my administration. Who would have thought?"

"You're not gonna try to get credit for it, are you, Mayor?" Cecil asked.

The mayor shook his head. "Oh, no. No one would believe me. It's just kind of nice to be in office when so many good things are happening."

Slade took off his cape and shook it out, and the mayor got to his feet. "I'm going to need an appointment with you myself, Logan," he said as he fished through his wallet for Slade's fee, then dusted his shirt. "I'll call you later."

"I'm going your way, Mayor," Logan said, standing up and stretching. "I'll walk with you and we can nail down a time."

As if he had lived there all his life, and knew them each as well as they knew one another, they all waved him good-bye.

Logan's lesson with Carny that afternoon went well, and he noticed an ever so slight change in her attitude. "So did you check on me, yet? Have you discovered I'm legit?"

"I checked, Brisco," she said, looking at her appointment book for a good time for the next lesson.

"Good. Then I should be cleared. You want me to make *you* an appointment so you can talk about investing?"

She shot him a look. "Your stories may have checked out, Brisco, but I'm still not convinced you're on the level."

Not convinced, he thought. Wasn't that better than before, when she'd been absolutely certain he wasn't? Still, it aggravated him that she hadn't considered his references positive enough to clear him. Damn, she was smart.

"What did I ever do to you?"

"Nothing," she said with a flip smile. "You never did anything to me. I just don't intend to sign my soul and my bank account over to you like my friends and neighbors have. Don't get too secure, Brisco. I haven't given up trying to expose you."

"Carny, you have got to be the most stubborn woman I've ever met."

"I'll buy that," she said. "You've probably never met anyone like me."

"You've got that right."

"Good. Then you won't quite know how to handle me, will you? It looks like I'm the one who has the advantage here. I know exactly how to handle you."

"What if I'm one of the good guys, Carny? What if you're completely, absolutely wrong?"

"I'm not," she said simply. "Now, if you'll excuse me, I have a delivery to make. I have to hurry if I want to get back in time for Jason to get out of school."

"You still going to the dance tomorrow night?"

Jotting down the time for his class Saturday afternoon, she said, "Yep."

"Going with Joey?"

She stopped writing and looked up. "Boy, you don't miss anything, do you? No, I'm not going with Joey. I'm going alone."

"Oh, yeah?" He took the paper from her, looked at it, and put it into his pocket. "Me, too."

She slapped her hand against her forehead. "Say it isn't so. Logan Brisco, celebrity among us, has not got a date to the dance?"

"Oh, I could have gone with Lahoma's daughter, or Jean Miller, or Bonnie. . . . "

"Then why didn't you?"

"Because, I wanted to be free to dance every dance with you."

She laughed, and went to stack the boxes that needed loading onto the plane. "You'll have to stand in line."

He liked that spunk, and grinning, he started to the door. "I will," he said. "See you tonight."

She was still smiling when he closed the door behind him.

# 7

*High Five was the* town's country-music band that played at all the local gatherings, and consisted of the postmaster, one of the grocers, a traffic engineer from Odessa, and the twins who ran the railroad depot.

As usual, the makeshift dance floor in the bingo hall was full. Logan had never seen anything like it, and as he stepped into the room, smiling in answer to all the greetings he was immediately barraged with, he thought again that this surely was Mayberry. The dream town, where little boys named Opie grew up to be wholesome and good. Or little boys named Jason.

He caught Jason's wave across the crowd and saw that he was juking with a pretty little girl in a frilly dress. He winked and flashed him a thumbs-up, and Jason blushed. Logan laughed, and tried to remember being that age. Where had he been at age seven? With the Clements or the Legates? That was the year he'd been passed around three different times. The sobering thought killed his smile, and he glanced away. His gaze immediately collided with Carny's. He might have known she'd be on the dance floor, too, dancing with the confidence of a Fly Girl, while a group of men on the edge of the crowd watched her, probably waiting for their turn.

Damn, she was cute. That was the thing about her. A lot of women were pretty—in fact, a lot of the women right here in Serenity were pretty—but it was that cute quality, that bounciness and playfulness, juxtaposed against that serious side of her that made her capable of skewering a man while she flirted with him, that made her impossible to purge from his mind. And he'd tried. He'd tried hard.

He watched as she strayed from her partner and found her son dancing with his friend. Tapping him on the shoulder, she got him to turn her way, and he took her hand. The two of them began to dance, and Logan couldn't escape the look of pleasure in her eyes or the look of delight in the boy's.

Someone tapped on her back—Logan recognized him as Joey from the barbershop yesterday—and Jason deferred to him. Without batting an eye, Carny fell into step with him. She wasn't a tease, Logan thought, and she didn't care how many men would heap attention on her tonight. She didn't *need* that attention, but it was obvious that she enjoyed it. And he enjoyed watching her.

Something tugged at his leg, stealing his attention, and Logan looked down to see Jack, Slade Hampton's dog, looking up at him. "Hey, boy," Logan said, stooping down and petting the dog. "What's a nice boy like you doing in a place like this?"

The dog closed his eyes and rolled his head into Logan's hand, urging him to scratch. "Where's your old man, boy? Where's Slade?" Jack's ears perked up, and he looked to where Slade stood with a group of men. "Not far, huh, boy? I didn't think so."

Having gotten enough of Logan's ministrations, the dog went back to his master's side, and Slade bent down and unconsciously rubbed the dog's head while he talked.

Logan thought of joining them, but he couldn't seem to get his mind off the dance floor. Carny seemed to have boundless energy, and he looked around at the other women dancing around her, and realized they all paled in comparison. It was too bad that the only woman he was interested in in Serenity was the one who saw right through him.

Strolling along the outskirts of the crowd, he ran into Jean Miller, a pretty little redheaded woman with adoring eyes and a body that screamed "Take me," even though he had heard she was training to be a missionary. There was no doubt in his mind that, if he wanted to, he could make her forget her calling. But he wasn't that kind of man. He had always been diligent at keeping Montague's rule not to pursue innocent women.

Still, he asked Jean to dance and led her into the

crowd. She felt nice against him, and she smelled like an adolescent's fantasy, but his eyes kept straying to Carny. She had stopped dancing, finally, and was pouring punch for herself and Jason. Jason was rambling about something, and she was laughing as she listened.

"You've made quite an impression in this town," Jean told Logan, snatching his attention away. "I hope you plan to stay, even after the park is built."

"I sure do," he said with his most flirtatious grin. "I'm kind of getting attached to Serenity." Though it rolled off his tongue with the fluidity of the rest of his spiel, he had to admit it carried a lot of truth. There had never been a town he'd be sorrier to say good-bye to.

"Don't let folks like Carny run you off," Jean said. "Carny marches to her own drummer. Everybody loves her, but we don't put a lot of stock in anything she says or does."

"She's the flighty type, huh?" he asked. Jean, catching his lame attempt at a pun, burst into giggles.

The band ended the last song in their set and announced that they'd be back in fifteen minutes. Logan was relieved to let Jean go. Even though it had been too long since he'd been with a woman, he couldn't escape the fact that the only woman in the bingo hall he was interested in was Carny Sullivan.

Montague would have told him to pack his bags this very moment and leave town. There was nothing worse to cloud a man's judgment than to get tangled up with the wrong woman. And bad judgment meant making mistakes, and mistakes led to jail.

But he couldn't go. Not yet.

He watched as Jason went to play a video game against the wall with some of his friends, and Carny stepped outside the bingo hall alone. It didn't take more than seconds for him to follow her.

The moon was full, lighting the main street through town in silvery hues, and the lights from the windows and doorway spilled out, breaking up the darkness. He watched her walk up the sidewalk, fanning herself with her hand, then stop to get a soda out of the machine in front of the barbershop.

Logan stayed close to the buildings, not wanting to be seen just yet, and watched her lean against the wall, take a long sip of the soda, then stare off into space.

What was she thinking? Was she dreaming about one of those men in there, or thinking about where she would go tomorrow in that plane of hers, or was she remembering the days of her youth, when every night had been a party, and every day had been a reminder that this was not how life was supposed to be?

Finally, he pushed away from the wall and strolled up the sidewalk. She saw him coming before he reached her, and flashed him a knowing grin.

"Well, well. You never know what might be lurking in the dark," she said.

He didn't grin, as he often did, and he realized that, for maybe the first time in his life, he wanted to be sincere with her. But he wasn't sure how, for he'd been faking it for so long. "I've been watching you," he said.

She smiled. "Oh, yeah? You must be pretty bored."

"Not at all." He braced his hand on the wall, just above her head, and leaned down over her. "There's nothing boring about you, Carny."

She laughed. "You can say that again. I've been accused of a lot of things, but never of being boring. You either, I'd imagine."

He shrugged. "I know you don't like to admit it, Carny, but we have a lot in common."

Her smile faded, and she looked up at him, her eyes soft and vulnerable, but still so savvy that he didn't fear breaking her heart. "And what do you think we have in common?"

He breathed a laugh at the flipness of her question, but quickly, his smile faded. "Loneliness."

The laughter that burst from her mouth took him by surprise. "What? What's so funny?"

"That's pretty good, Brisco," she said. "But you can do better than that."

He bristled. "What do you mean?"

"Oh, you know." She walked a few steps away, still grinning, and when she turned back to him, he saw that she was genuinely amused. "Touch on the struggles I've had as a single parent. Tell me you have an empty house in the Midwest with five bedrooms you dream of filling up. Or my divorce. Tell me you think my ex was the world's biggest fool.

Or my disillusionment. Tell me you've had your share of the same, but that a woman like me could restore your faith...."

"What the hell are you talking about?"

"Cons, Brisco," she said, stepping closer to him and grinning up at him. "Let's face it. The usual ones won't work on me. You'll have to be more creative."

"Damn, you're as hard as nails. It wasn't a con, Carny. It was a statement of fact. You're a lonely woman. It's written all over you."

Again, she laughed. "You think you can read me? Gosh, you're arrogant. You don't know the first thing about me. If you did, you'd know that I don't need a man to be content."

"But a woman like you needs one to be happy. And you deserve to be happy, Carny."

"And you think happiness is rolling around in bed with the likes of you?"

Suddenly, he realized he was enjoying this, and that demon smile crept across his face. "No, I think happiness is rolling around in bed with the likes of you."

Again, she laughed, but this time it was a little more strained. She turned away from him, took a drink of her soda, and kicked at a rock. "Let me tell you something, Brisco. There are at least a dozen eligible men in town who are attractive, productive, and decent. Why on earth would I choose to sleep with you?"

"Because I'm different," he said. "Just like you. And for what it's worth, I do think your husband was a fool. If I'd ever caught a woman like you, I'd spend the rest of my life trying to keep her happy."

"No, you wouldn't," she said. "You probably wouldn't even wait two days before you'd withdraw every cent from her bank accounts and take the next train out of town."

His grin went from arrogant to rueful. "You sure don't give me much credit, do you?"

"No, Brisco," she said, starting back toward the bingo hall. "I've been around."

Logan watched as she went back in, and for a moment he listened to the sounds of the town, the sounds of friendship and family, the sounds of laughter and lightness, the sounds of somebody's home. Her home. But not his.

And the worst thing he could fault her with was that she was right. This wasn't going to be as easy as he thought. The only way he'd ever convince her that he was legitimate was if he *became* legitimate. And even then it would be questionable.

But he couldn't go to such lengths, not for a woman. He could already feel Montague's unrest, and that distant voice telling him to get out of there, that he'd stayed too long already, that no man could carry out a scam for more than a couple of weeks. It was dangerous. It was ludicrous. It was suicide. With every day that he stayed, his position—and his freedom—would be jeopardized more.

But for some reason, he couldn't make himself leave. There were challenges here he had yet to meet, and few of them had anything to do with money.

\* \* \*

Carny wandered back into the dance, and saw that Jason was still at the video games. High Five was just about to crank up again, and she glanced around the room. Her in-laws were clustered in a circle of friends, and she strolled toward them.

But someone grabbed her arm from behind, and she turned around. Joey stood over her, his eyes looking wounded, and she gave an inward groan. "Hey, Joey."

"Were you out there with him?" He gestured toward the door, where Logan was standing.

Carny noted the two women that had already spotted him and were giggling and preening around him. His grin told her he ate it all up. *Nothing lonely about that man,* she thought. "I was out there and he was out there, Joey."

"I thought you hated him."

"Well, I don't much approve of him, but that doesn't mean I can't breathe the same fresh air."

"I heard he was taking private lessons from you," Joey said. "Is he coming on to you?"

She chuckled then and looked back at Logan as the band struck up a new tune. He had swept one of the women into his arms, and was tangoing his way to the dance floor with her. "Look at him, Joey. He comes on to everybody. It's part of the con. Blow into town, dazzle everybody he meets, make the women fall in love with him, take all their money, then cut out. You haven't given him any, have you?"

Joey shook his head. "I don't think I like him."

"Well, good," she said, her eyes lighting up. "I'm proud of you. Come on, let's dance."

He seemed pleased that it was her idea, and he pulled her against him. As always, she enjoyed dancing with him. He felt good, like a big teddy bear, and he had a good sense of rhythm. But not for the first time, she wished he was more her type.

Her gaze strayed to Logan, and she watched as he dipped his partner dramatically, making her squeal, then swept her up and spun her around. The dancers around them were all watching, impressed. She looked away.

"I really wanted to bring you to the dance tonight, Carny. Why wouldn't you come with me?"

She sighed. "Because, I told you, you're getting too serious. We need to cool it a little."

"I don't want to cool it," Joey said. "I want to know when you're gonna marry me."

"I'm not marrying anybody. I've been there. I've done that."

"With the wrong guy."

"They're all the wrong guy once they get a ring on your finger."

He gazed down at her, and she had to look back up at him. He had sweet, sincere eyes, but they failed to move her. "Carny, what have I done wrong?"

"It's not you, Joey. It's me. I'm not your type. You deserve someone who is."

"You are my type, Carny. I love you."

She smiled, and whispered, "I love you, too. You're one of my best friends. But I'm not *in* love with you, or anybody else. Look at me, Joey. I ride a motorcycle. I fly planes for a living. I grew up in a carnival. You and I have different perspectives on life. I could never make you happy."

"No, I don't think that's it," he said. "Maybe it's more like I could never make *you* happy."

She knew that was true, but she would never have said it. Joey was the nice, quiet, settle-down type, and she knew he would make someone a terrific husband. But married to him, she would have been bored to death. And she had to admit, she didn't like that about herself.

"Who are you attracted to, Carny? Seriously. You're a hopeless flirt. Is there anybody in this town you're really attracted to?"

She laughed. "Oh, Joey. Why are you doing this?"

"I can take it," he said, though she knew better. "I've watched you shoot men down one at a time, politely and very sweetly, but I've never seen one that had a chance with you since Abe left. Who would, Carny? Him?"

She followed his eyes and saw that he referred to Logan, and suddenly she stopped dancing. "You know how I feel about him."

"I know how you're telling yourself to feel. But maybe that suspicion you have of him is just the excitement you need."

She broke free of him and stepped back. "You're making me mad, Joey. I know how I feel, and I don't need any amateur analysis."

"I'm sorry," he said quickly, reaching for her again. "I didn't mean it. You've just got me all bumfuzzled."

"I never meant to bumfuzzle you, Joey."

Finally, he smiled and fell back into the rhythm of the song. "I know you didn't, Carny. I think you just can't help yourself."

As the song ended, her gaze strayed to Logan again. He was holding the woman too close, looking too deeply into her eyes. She had a sudden surge of rage, and thought of jerking the girl away and telling her to run while she still had a clear head. He was poison. He was trouble. He was dangerous.

His eyes met hers across the girl's head, and his irreverent grin blossomed across his face. He was taunting her, daring her to step in, teasing her into reacting.

With all the strength she could muster, she excused herself from Joey and went to find her son.

The moment Carny left the dance, Logan lost interest in being there. And even though he could have taken the blonde woman back to the motel and vented all his frustrations with a few hours of unadulterated pleasure, he found that it wasn't what he really wanted to do.

And that disturbed him terribly.

It wasn't like him, to walk away from an available woman, or to ignore the flirtations of a dozen others who had approached him tonight. Why he couldn't keep his mind off Carny Sullivan was a mystery to him.

He slipped out of the party, leaving behind the people who accepted him so readily and made him feel like their friend, when he didn't dare call any of them friend. They were marks and that was all. He could never forget that. And the women were marks, too, the kind who threw themselves at him because they thought he was their dream bachelor, then kicked themselves when they were left holding bounced checks and empty bank accounts. Carny did have his number. And for the first time in a long time, he wished it was the wrong number.

But as he strolled down the lonely street, looking in the windows of stores closed up for the night, he realized that the irony of the whole thing was that, just maybe, he was the biggest mark of all.

He could feel Montague rolling over in his grave.

# 8

*Ever intent on completing* his mission, Logan made more money the Saturday morning after the dance than he'd ever made in one day. He imagined the couples had seen him horsing around like one of the citizens, fitting in and all that, and had decided that he was a man to be trusted with their investments.

The Trents had even invited him over for lunch, and he decided to take them up on it. The fact that they lived next door to Carny had something to do with his enthusiasm, for he hoped to have the chance to run into her again. Any woman that could keep him awake all night, without even being in the same room with him, deserved whatever hell he could give her.

He was just finishing lunch and waiting for the Trents to write out their sizable check to him, when

Jason ran in. "Nathan! Come on! The fish are biting like crazy. Papa caught six this morning!"

David Trent intercepted Jason before he reached the kitchen. "Whoa, there, boy! Nathan's not here. He's at his grandmother's today."

"His grandmother's?" Jason asked, as if the idea was ludicrous. "What did he want to go there for?"

David shot Logan an amused look. "He was helping his grandpa bathe the dogs."

Jason wilted. "And the fish are biting. Papa caught—"

"Six. I heard," David said. "Jason, you know Mr. Brisco, don't you?"

As if he only noticed him now, Jason looked at him directly. "Yeah. Hi, Logan. You fish?"

Logan laughed. "I've been known to." The truth, however, was that the only pole he'd ever held as a boy was a pool cue.

David handed him the check, and Logan pocketed it as he got to his feet. "Where do you fish?"

"I have a secret place over at the lake," Jason said. "Only Nathan and I know where it is."

"Well, you can go without him, can't you?"

"Nah, that's no fun," Jason said. "Hey, Logan, why don't you go with me? Please? You'd like it, I promise. And I know you'll catch some fish. This morning my papa caught . . ."

"Six," David and Logan said simultaneously, and they both laughed.

"Well, I guess I could go with you for a little while," Logan said, "not that I'm dressed for it."

Jason regarded his khaki pants and short-sleeved shirt, and the Italian shoes that weren't made for trekking through the woods. "That'll be fine," he said. "Honest. There's hardly any mud up there at all."

Something about the boy's exuberance was contagious. "You know I don't have a pole."

"He can use Nathan's, can't he Mr. David? Please?"

"Sure, Logan," David said, feigning seriousness. "I'll get it if you want. There really is practically no mud at all."

Logan chuckled. "Well, okay. I think we've got a deal."

He thanked Janice for the meal, underscoring it with the most flattery he could pack into a sincere-sounding statement, and followed David out to the garage. The pole David got for him was his own, instead of Nathan's, and Logan took it and thanked him. He'd bring it back when he came to get his car, he told him. Then, after tapping his pocket where he'd placed the check, he followed Jason through the woods behind the Trents' house.

"Shouldn't you tell your mother you're going?" Logan asked him.

"She knows," Jason said. "I told her I was going with Nathan."

"She might not like that you're going with me."

Jason shrugged. "She doesn't want me talking about the park with you, but she didn't say I couldn't go *fishing* with you. Besides, I don't tell her *everything*. There are some things a guy just has to keep to himself."

Logan couldn't help grinning at the boy's rationale. It sounded much like his when he'd sneaked out the Millers' window to go to the pool hall. There were, indeed, some things a boy had to keep to himself.

Logan felt like Andy walking with Opie in the opening credits of the *Andy Griffith Show*. As they came to the edge of the woods behind the house and the lake came into view, he stopped for a moment. A summer breeze whispered through the leaves on the trees and swept across his face, and the water circled in gentle ripples where a fish jumped or a turtle swam.

It wasn't real life, he told himself as some distant, hollow memory rose inside him. It was only a script that he played out, just like all of his life. It was no more real than a television show.

But the television show it reminded him of was the only semblance of true family life, or innocent childhood, that he had ever known. And something about that disturbed him now.

He watched Jason, who had gotten ahead of him, and the boy turned back. "Come on. I'll take you to my secret place. But you can't tell anyone."

"A secret, huh? I won't tell."

"You have to swear," Jason said. "Because it's real important."

"Okay, I swear," Logan said, holding up his right hand. "Scout's honor."

Jason regarded him a moment, considering whether he could trust him, then finally said, "Okay. It's this way."

They wove through trees skirting the edge of the lake, and as they walked, Jason pointed out where he and Nathan liked to swing from the vines in the summer and swim in the lake, and where they had once found a dead bobcat, and where they'd caught the snapping turtle that Jason kept in his room. The boy rambled on as if he'd known Logan all his life. Finally, they came to a small clearing with a stump where a tree had fallen adjacent to the lake, and Jason set his fishing gear down, stepped up on the log, and held his arms out. "Well, whadda ya think?"

Logan looked around, envying the boy for having a place like this. If he'd had one as a kid, rather than the smoky pool hall, things might have turned out differently. With someplace to go to find peace, someplace that could have been his own, maybe he would have felt less of the turmoil he'd known in his childhood. Maybe he would have grown into someone who followed the law-abiding path, settled down into a hometown of his own, and become a respectable member of society.

*That's a poisonous way to think,* came the voice from way back in his subconscious. It was Montague's voice, reminding him who he was, keeping him in focus, and keeping him out of trouble.

"This is the best hangout any guy ever had," Logan said. "Look. You've even got a place for me to sit." He sat down on the stump that had obviously been sawed down to form a comfortable fishing seat.

"Yeah, me and Nathan worked for a long time sawing that down. Before if you sat on it, you got splinters in your rump. I like to sit here on the log. One time we found a rabbit in the log, and we took it home, but Mom made us bring it back and let it go. Its mother was probably looking for it and stuff. Did you ever have a rabbit?"

"Nope. I never had a pet of any kind."

Jason picked up his pole and the small bucket he carried, and started digging through the dirt in it for some worms. He pulled a long one out, and handed it to Logan. "No pets? How come?"

"I moved around a lot." Folding the worm in half, Logan hooked it.

"Was your dad in the service?"

Logan frowned. "No, why?"

"Well, my dad moves around a lot, because he's in the service. That's why I never see him."

Logan didn't quite know what to say to that, so he busied himself securing the fish. Flinging the line out into the water, he glanced over at Jason. The little boy was intent on getting his worm fastened, and finally, he flung his out, as well. "I have three cats," he announced when he got the line where he wanted it. "And two goldfish, and a dog that kind of runs away whenever he wants, but comes back when he gets hungry. They all stay outside, except for the turtle."

"Your mom must like animals."

"Yeah," he said. "She moved around a lot when she was a kid, too. She never got to have pets. So whenever I bring one home, she usually lets me keep it, unless it's wild or something. She doesn't like the idea of locking up something wild."

He wondered if that had anything to do with her own free spirit. Did she ever feel locked up, confined to this tiny town? If she did, he hadn't yet seen any evidence of it.

"Your mom is a very special lady, Jason."

"I know," Jason said, matter-of-factly. "She's fun. She's not exactly like other moms."

"How do you mean?"

Jason shrugged. "Well, a lot of the guys are jealous because their moms don't ride motorcycles. They think she's cool."

"Has she taught you to fly?"

"We're working on the ground school," he said. "But I need to learn math a little better before I'll get good enough to fly. Maybe when I get in third grade." When Logan laughed, Jason said, "Really! It could happen. I saw a kid on TV who flew across the country when he was ten. If he can do it, I can! At least, if I get better at math, I could."

"I'm pretty good at math. If you ever need any help . . ." Logan felt something tugging at his line, and he got to his feet quickly and began trying to pull it in. A big, floppy fish hung from his hook, and he laughed aloud as he grabbed the line and pulled it in. "I'll be damned."

"All *right*! That's big, Logan! We can eat that for supper. I'll get Mom to cook it, and you can eat with us!"

Logan was too distracted by the flopping fish to respond, but when he'd wrestled it off the hook, Jason took it and hooked it on the stringer that hung in the water.

Some overwhelming feeling—pride, or maybe childish pleasure—came over him, and Logan sat back down. He couldn't remember ever feeling such a burst of pure excitement. Jason, however, took it all in stride and handed him the bucket. "Here, get another worm. We're gonna catch a million of those today."

The thought of repeating that pleasure suddenly became Logan's foremost goal, and he found another worm and baited his hook again. "You do this all the time?"

"Every Saturday, almost," Jason said. "Sometimes Mom comes with me, but I don't bring her to this place because it's a secret. It wouldn't be a secret anymore if I brought my mom."

Logan threw his line back out and watched an egret as it flew across the water. In the tree above him, birds chirped and sang, and the breeze whispered smoothly through the leaves, relaxing him more than a stiff drink ever had.

He regarded the child, who sat quietly on his log, and realized that it had been years since he'd experienced a comfortable silence with another person. There was no sales pitch on the tip of his tongue, no scheme concocting in his mind, no new angle that he was trying out. There was no need for pretense, and the pretenses he'd started out with today—his Gucci loafers, Hilfiger shirt, and custom-tailored slacks—seemed awfully silly now.

"You sure we've got enough bait?" Logan asked finally.

"If we don't, we'll dig for some more," Jason

said. "But it should be enough. Mom told me to be home at three."

"Yeah," Logan said. "That's probably because I have a class with her at 3:30."

"You will come back and eat with us, won't you?"

Logan squinted into the sunlight and gave it a moment's thought. "Uh . . . no, I don't think so, Jason. Matter of fact, if you tell your mom that I came with you here, she'll probably go ballistic. She really doesn't want me around you."

"I know," the boy admitted. "Why do you think that is? I mean, you're a nice guy. I wouldn't just take any old jerk fishing with me. Not to my secret place."

Logan smiled. "Well, maybe your mom has a different standard of judging people. She's just looking out for your best interests."

"I know, but she goes overboard sometimes. Everybody in town knows you're a good guy. The park is gonna be so great. . . . Oops, I'm not supposed to talk about that with you, am I?"

"I guess not." He studied the surface of the water, watching for a ripple. "So does your mom see anyone special?"

"What do you mean?"

"Does she have a boyfriend?"

"Oh, she has lots of them. She's real pretty, you know. That's another reason so many of my friends are jealous. Their moms don't look like mine."

"You can say that again."

"But I don't think she wants just one boyfriend.

She doesn't go out on dates too much. Sometimes, when I spend the night at Nathan's, she might go to a movie with one of them. Mostly Nathan spends the night at my house, and we make popcorn and watch movies and stuff. Have you seen *Homeward Bound*?"

Logan's mind wandered as the boy rambled on about the movie he'd just seen, but Logan couldn't help dwelling on the fact that Carny had lots of suitors, but that she preferred to stay home most of the time. And there wasn't a doubt in his mind that was her choice. She wasn't looking for a relationship. She was happy with her life as it was.

That he envied that life of hers surprised him, and he couldn't put his finger on why. In a few days, he would be moving on, richer and wiser, and the town of Serenity would be nothing more than a distant memory that he could never return to. But for the first time in his life, he almost wished he could stay.

That was foolish, and Montague would be the first one to tell him: You're getting too involved, my boy. You're letting the people con you, instead of the other way around. And worst of all, you're thinking too much.

But as the day went on and the fish kept biting, Logan realized that it wasn't going to be as easy as he thought to leave. Serenity lived up to its name. He wondered if it still would after he'd finished with it.

\* \* \*

Carny was looking out the window of her office next to the hangar when Logan drove up in that rented Mercedes. The fact that she'd seen it parked at the Trents all day riled her. Apparently, David and Janice were buying into the scam. She had stewed all day, trying to find a way to make the people of Serenity listen to her. But those who were stupid enough to give him their money sure didn't want to hear anything negative on the matter. Everyone's patience with her seemed to wear thin as soon as she got on her soapbox.

She turned around to the plane parked in the hangar behind her and saw Jason sitting in the cockpit, making flying noises and talking into the radio like a top gun who'd just sighted the enemy. As long as she and Jason were safe from Logan's clutches, she supposed, she should let it go. Let the town learn its lesson. As for her in-laws, well, she had put the money Logan paid her for her class in a safe place, to return to them when he skipped town. She only hoped they hadn't paid him more than that.

Glancing out the window again, she watched Logan get out of the car and wave at her with that devilish grin on his face. It almost wiped out her reservations and made her feel that there was nothing worse than a little mischievousness in his soul. For a moment, she tried to consider the possibility that she *was* wrong, and he wasn't a con artist, just a big businessman about to change the face and heart of Serenity.

She still didn't like it, but it was a little easier to stomach. Somehow, she couldn't buy it, though.

Opening the door, Logan stuck his head into her office. "Are we still friends?"

She feigned distraction and headed for the classroom at the other end of the building. "We've never been friends, Brisco."

"Well, okay. Then are we still just mild enemies, or is it worse since last night?"

She frowned. "What are you talking about?"

He looked a little too smug as he came in and dropped his notebook and car keys on his desk. His nose was the slightest bit sunburned, and vaguely, she wondered when he'd had time to get any sunshine since last night.

"You seemed a little disgusted at my attentions to the pretty Miss Miller. Isn't that why you left?"

She laughed then. "You thought I left because of you? Get real, Brisco."

He leaned on her desk as she straightened her papers, and he crossed his arms with cocky insouciance. "I don't know. I noticed a definite chill when you looked at me on the dance floor."

She knew he was baiting her, so she came around the desk and faced him squarely. "All right, Brisco. It did disgust me. There's not a woman in this town who deserves to be strung along by you, used, and then dumped when you disappear without a trace."

"And what if I stayed, Carny?" he asked, annoyed. "What if I actually did what I say I'm going to do, and built the park, and made Serenity my home?"

"And what if the sky turned green, and grass was pink, and the Loch Ness Monster turned up in our lake?"

For a moment he stared at her. "You think you've got everything all figured out, don't you? You never have to think about where you came from and who you really are. The possibility that you're wrong never even occurs to you, does it?"

"Where I came from is no excuse for anything I do now, Brisco. I'm an adult, and I have choices. When I'm wrong I can admit it."

"Are you sure?"

She looked him dead in the eye. "Tell you what, Brisco. When you prove me wrong, I'll prove I can admit it. Until then, we have nothing really to talk about. Now do you want to take your lesson or not?"

Logan sat down. Pulling his pen out of his pocket, he said, "Teach me. I'm listening."

Her heart hammered with anger as she launched into her next lesson about federal air-traffic regulations. She wondered how much longer she'd have to endure this.

Logan didn't know what had provoked him more: Carny's dead-right attitude about him, or the questions the citizens had been asking about the park. But in his motel room only days later, he found himself poring over research books he'd ordered in an attempt to get a better working knowledge of theme parks. He read about the inner workings of such an enterprise, the people who had done it in the past, the impact on the towns around them, the potential revenue of an endeavor like this one. As always when he researched a part he was playing, he found himself absorbed in the subject matter, meticulously planning out details and adding up figures. By the end of the next week, he had the facts as clearly as he would have if he'd been legitimate.

The problem was, he'd been there too long already. In another week or two, the first of his hot checks, which had been routed all over the country due to the computer-confusing code he'd laser-printed at the bottom, would start being hand-sorted and make their way back to the bank in Serenity, and everyone would know that he'd fleeced them. The printer, the hotel, the diner, the department store, the rental agency . . . They'd all know that he was a fraud.

But there was still a week or so of safety, in which he had to finish the job and skip town. The checks he'd collected from the citizens so far had already cleared, and all he had to do was push those undecided investors over the hump, take their money, and disappear. It was so simple.

So why hadn't he done it already? To console himself, he decided that he wasn't getting soft, that Carny Sullivan hadn't gotten under his skin, that Jason's fishing hole had made no difference. He was here to score, and score big.

*And then what?* came that annoying voice in the back of his mind, that voice that reminded him of the three-year-old child who still believed in mother and bedtime stories. What then? Would he buy that ranch that had been Montague's dream and live there alone, isolated and hidden, so he wouldn't get caught? Or would he just keep moving, keep scoring, keep deceiving everyone he ever met for the rest of his life?

A knock on the door to his room startled him, as though he'd been caught with his incriminating thoughts. He glanced at the appointment calendar on his computer to see if he'd forgotten someone. He hadn't.

Tucking his shirt in and finger-combing his hair, he went to the door. Slade Hampton, the barber, waited there with his dog Jack at his side. "Slade, come on in," Logan said, shaking the man's hand.

"I hope I'm not interrupting anything," Slade said. "I didn't have an appointment, but I just made my mind up this minute."

It was exactly the kind of thing Logan liked to hear. Bending down to pet Jack, he said, "What's on your mind?"

"My retirement," Slade said. "I think I told you that I've been planning for it for years. Saving a good portion of what I made, so that one day, I could retire in style and do some traveling, some gardening, some loafing . . . just the kinds of things I've never had the chance to do."

"Sounds like heaven," Logan said. "Are you planning to do it soon?"

Slade hesitated for a moment, then looked Logan squarely in the eye. "No. Actually, I've decided to keep working a little while longer. I want to invest my retirement money into the park. When it starts paying me back, then I'll retire."

Logan stared at him for a moment, wondering at the conflicting sides of his conscience that seemed to be at war in his mind. Slade was offering him his life savings, the money he'd earned and grown, the money that would allow him finally to do the things he deserved after a lifetime of working on his feet.

But on the other hand . . . Slade was someone who loved his work. He loved cutting hair, always having someone to talk to, always having a line of friends and neighbors waiting for his services. Retirement would probably not suit him. He was the type who needed to work until he simply couldn't anymore.

"So do you think that's realistic? That I'll earn it back, and then some, in time to retire?"

Something inside Logan—something that had never been there before, something quite unwelcome—prohibited him from lying and making a quick killing. "I can't promise that you'll earn every penny back in the next ten years, Slade. In fact, I can almost promise you won't."

"But you said—"

"I know what I said, but I could be wrong." Logan went to his logbook, opened it up to a clean page, and wrote Slade's name in at the top. "Everyone who invests stands to make a fortune. Just not overnight." He looked up at Slade, and noted the disappointment on his face. "Look, don't give me the whole thing, Slade. Keep some back, just in case. I can promise you dividends enough to supplement your retirement. They'll grow every year, I know that."

Wearily, Slade sat down on the edge of the bed,

and Logan noticed that his face looked pale. "I came here prepared to give you all I had."

"I know, but I can't take it. Not all of it."

Slade rubbed his face, slumping slightly. "You see, I'd like to have enough to live well on in retirement, but still leave something behind to my daughter and her husband. They don't expect anything, 'cause I've never been a rich man. But wouldn't it be nice if I could take care of their kids' educations, maybe a down payment on a house? I don't quite have enough for that as it is, Logan. But I might if I invest with you. I could leave them my share of the park, and that would be just as good."

Logan took a deep breath and leaned forward, planting his elbows on his knees. He tried to block out Montague's voice blaring through his ears: *Take it, my boy. Stop that thinking. Stop it right now.* But Logan couldn't stop thinking.

Finally, faced with choosing between his conscience and his practicality, Logan put those condemning thoughts aside, slammed the door on his conscience, and gave in. "All right, Slade. I'll take whatever you're offering. And I'll do my best to see that it helps you reach your goals."

Slade smiled like a lottery winner as he fished the checkbook out of his back pocket and picked up a pen from Logan's table. "Thank you, Logan. You're practically saving this town, you know. You couldn't have come along at a better time."

Logan watched him tear the check out and hand it to him, and his heart jolted when he saw the amount of a hundred thousand dollars. It was enough, he thought. Enough to call the mission accomplished and get out of town. There was no point in being greedy. No point in waiting for more.

Excitement welled inside him as he made the careful log entry, trying to keep up the appearances of legitimacy. When he'd finished, he laid the check carefully on the log entry's page, and closed the book. "Thank you, Slade. You won't regret it."

Slade took his hand, but it was unusually limp and clammy as he shook. Perspiration glistened over his lip and at his temples, and his face became even more pasty than it had been when he came in. "Slade," he asked softly, "are you feeling all right?"

Slade tried to chuckle, but the effort fell flat. "Just a little angina, I think," he said. "Chest feels a little tight."

Alarmed, Logan got to his feet. "Do you . . . do you want me to call an ambulance?"

"No, no," Slade said. "I'll go up the street to see Dr. Peneke."

"Right now? Do you want me to drive you?"

He waved him off. "I'm fine, Logan. I can make it."

Logan hesitated at the door as Slade went through it, walking with a pained slump, but trying to hide it. When he stumbled and fell against the wall, Logan ran out and caught him.

"That's it," he said under his breath, easing Slade to the floor as Jack began to whimper. "Doc!" he called in his loudest voice. "Help, Doc! We've got an emergency! Please! Somebody call an ambulance!"

In seconds, the motel manager, Doc, who had

never been a real doctor, came running out of the office downstairs, looked up at Logan holding Slade, then dashed back to the phone. And as Slade clutched at his heart and winced in pain, Logan could only remember Montague.

"You're gonna be okay, buddy. Just hold on."

The memory of the teenaged kid he used to be, and the death of the only person in his life who had cared for him, flashed repeatedly through Logan's frantic mind.

Jack began to whimper and lick Slade's face.

In moments that seemed to stretch into eternity, the area outside Logan's room was crowded with paramedics and machinery. But before they could get him on the gurney, Slade Hampton was dead.

# 9

*The funeral home was* crowded with people from the first moment of visitation. Flowers lined all four walls of the viewing room, where a few mourners clustered beside the coffin, paying their last respects to the barber who'd been such a vital part of the community. Logan felt a tinge of apprehension as he signed the guest book, and a great sadness fell over him as he noted how vastly different this was than it had been when Montague died.

They hadn't bothered with visitation for Montague, since they'd been in the town solely to score, and the only "friends" they'd made were marks who had believed them to be government employees selling "surplus" real-estate holdings at a dirt-cheap rate. Since Montague had never spoken of family back home in England, Logan had arranged a small, private funeral at which the only guests were Logan and the preacher he'd hired. He had taken the money they had made thus far on that score—several thousand dollars—and bought the best coffin he could afford and a headstone with Montague's final con, an epithet that claimed he was "a pious man, beloved of all who knew him."

But it wasn't a con in Slade's case, for everyone who came by to pay their respects to Slade's daughter had tears in their eyes and stories to tell of special ways Slade had touched them. It was so sudden, they all said, so unexpected. He'd had so much living yet to do.

But no one felt that as vividly as Logan, as he waited for the small group at the coffin to break up. As they did, he saw Jack, curled up on the floor at the foot of the coffin, looking as forlorn and confused as an abandoned child.

Logan didn't know where the tears came from, but he blinked them back as he looked down at Slade's slumbering body. "You weren't supposed to die, you old fool," he whispered under his breath. He drew in a long, deep breath, and turned away.

Carny stood behind him, looking up at him with uncertain eyes.

"Carny."

"I heard he was with you when he died," she said, and though he expected it, he found no accusation in her voice.

"That's right."

She didn't say anything for a long moment, and he wondered when she would ask him how much he'd gotten from the man before he collapsed. If she knew he held a check for one-hundred thousand dollars in his pocket right now, she'd probably break her neck getting to a phone to call the police.

He looked back at Slade's body. "He was talking about retiring. Traveling. Doing all the things he'd never had time to do." His voice broke, and he cleared his throat.

Carny looked down at Slade, her eyes filling with tears. "Serenity's not gonna be the same without him." Then she looked up at Logan. "Are you all right?"

The question threw him, and for a moment, he searched the words for hidden meaning. Why wasn't she condemning him, blaming him? "I . . . I'm fine." He looked down at the dog, still lying there. "Look at Jack. He won't leave Slade's side."

"It's gonna be awfully hard for him," Carny said. "I wonder if dogs grieve."

Logan stooped down next to the dog and scratched his ear. "Of course they do."

As he stroked the animal, Slade's daughter Betsy left the cluster of people surrounding her and approached them. "We don't know what we're going to do with Jack," she said, wiping her eyes. "He wouldn't leave Daddy's side all night. Mr. Nelson, the undertaker, said he had to lock him out of the building last night, but he slept right beside the door until he let him in this morning."

The image of Jack refusing to leave Slade's side touched Logan in a place that had been numb for as long as he could remember. "How do you explain death to a dog?" His eyes filled again, and he blinked the sting of tears back. "He'll just keep expecting him to come back."

Carny touched Betsy's shoulder. "Are you all right? Have you slept any?"

"Some," Betsy said. "It's been a shock, but . . . we'll make it. Mr. Brisco, I know he was with you when he died . . . I know you did everything you could. . . ."

Logan looked at her and wondered at the emotions assaulting him from so many directions today. Coming to this town had been a mistake, he told himself. A serious tactical error. Montague would have been long gone, and he'd have already cashed that one-hundred-thousand-dollar check.

But Logan wasn't Montague. For the first time in his life, he embraced that fact, rejecting the thought that it meant he was weak. Perhaps he had strengths that Montague had never known.

"He . . . he came to me to talk about an investment, Betsy," he said, and Carny's head snapped up. "He had a dream of retiring and traveling and doing whatever he wanted, but still being able to leave an inheritance to you to put your kids through college, help you financially . . . he wanted to invest his retirement into the park, so he could make it grow enough to do both of those things."

"He gave you money?" Carny asked, keeping her voice as calm as she could manage.

"Yes," Logan said. "He gave me everything he had. A hundred thousand dollars."

Betsy gasped. Carny's mouth dropped open, but it was Betsy who got out the words.

"I had no idea . . . that he had . . ."

"He's been saving for years," Logan said. "Your father might not have made a lot of money, but he saved it well."

He could see the recriminations in Carny's eyes, the murderous accusations, the I-told-you-so's. But for now, she had too much decorum to vent those feelings in front of Slade's body, his grieving daughter, and a room full of mourners.

Logan looked into the young woman's eyes, and realized he had two choices. He could lecture Betsy about how much money this investment was going to make for her and her family, or he could do the right thing. The thing Carny least expected. The thing he would never have expected of himself.

Reaching into his wallet, he pulled out the check, unfolded it, and handed it to Betsy. "I haven't cashed the check yet, Betsy. And in light of what happened to Slade, I can't do it in good conscience. This money should go to you."

Bursting into tears, Betsy took the check in trembling hands. Reaching up to hug him, she whispered, "Thank you, Logan. You're a good man." Then she disappeared back into the other room, leaving him alone there with Slade's body, Jack, and Carny.

Carny was speechless, he realized, when he finally met her gaze. She'd been all pumped up for chewing him out, and now she didn't know what to say.

"What did you think I was gonna do?" he asked. "Skip town with his life savings?"

She drew in a deep breath. "I thought I had you all figured out," she whispered. "But I never would have expected you to do what you just did."

"Yeah, well, life's full of surprises."

Then, unable to take another moment of her scrutiny, and unable to hold back his emotions and his self-recriminations and Montague's ravings as he rolled over in his grave, Logan made his way back through the crowd and left the funeral home.

The motel room was too cold when he got back to it, and Logan shut off the air conditioner, wondering why there was no way to regulate the temperature in it. It was always too cold or too hot, musky and humid or filled with the acrid stench of cigarette smoke from the person who'd occupied it before him.

Quickly, he went to the closet, pulled out the bag he'd carried into town, and began rolling up his clothes. He'd bought some since he'd come here, but there was no room for them, so he left them hanging in his closet and went into the bathroom to pack his shaving kit.

It was past time to leave, he told himself. Too much had gone wrong here. First he'd run slam-bang into Carny, who was intent on exposing him for the fraud that he was, and then he'd become his own worst enemy by growing too close to the people in the town.

Disgusted with himself, he gathered up all the paperwork and books that he had lying around the room, stuffed them into his briefcase, and took one last look around the room. It was best just to leave and start over somewhere else, where there were no Carnys and no Jasons. Where no one came to his room and died. Where he didn't get tears in his eyes thinking about a dog.

He locked the door behind him, pocketed the key, and went out to his rented car. Throwing his stuff into the backseat, he got behind the wheel and pulled out of the space.

What was happening to him? he asked himself as he drove down the main street of town, mentally identifying every store by its owner and his family, the employees who worked there, and the stories he'd been able to gather about each of them. Some of them had given him money, and others had been considering it.

But he was getting too soft to wait around. Giving back that check had been the last straw. Montague would have washed his hands of Logan right then and there.

He reached the outskirts of town, where the land lay empty and abandoned—the area he claimed would be developed into the park. And as he wound around it, without seeing the vision he had planted in the minds of the people of Serenity, he asked himself why he had given that check back. Was it for his own conscience, a conscience that had never spoken up before, no matter how much money he took? Or was it for Carny? Was it really nothing more than part of the scam? Just another hustle, until he could make the biggest score of all?

He drove for over an hour before he realized he had no direction. No place to go. He wasn't ready to set up another scam in some other town. He needed some time to cleanse his mind of Serenity. He needed a little time to forget.

But something told him that he wouldn't forget. Serenity wasn't like any other town he'd ever encountered, and Carny Sullivan wasn't like any other woman. He thought of what she would say when she learned that he was gone. Would the fact that he'd given back Slade's money diminish the fact that he'd taken off with everybody else's? Somehow, he doubted it. She would realize, then, that she'd been right about him all along. That he was nothing more than a fraud and a thief.

He didn't like the fact that it disturbed him so deeply. Finally, Logan pulled his car to the side of the road, kept it idling there a moment, and tried to think. Never before had he allowed himself regrets about the people he left behind. Never before had he given a thought to what they would think of him. Never before had he cared if they figured him out or not, as long as they couldn't find him.

But this time, he cared deeply.

Jerking the car into gear, he turned it around, and headed back to Serenity. It wasn't time to leave yet, he told himself. Not like this. Not when there was a funeral to attend.

People would expect him to be there, and for the life of him, he didn't want to let them down.

\* \* \*

"Why do people have to die?"

Carny finished tying the knot in her son's tie and looked into his freckled face. Usually, she had a ready-made, carefully thought out answer to these profound questions, but today she was at a loss. "I don't know, Jason. Maybe he had finished doing whatever God meant for him to do."

"Will he go to heaven?"

"I'm sure," she said, swallowing the lump in her throat.

"Do you think Logan will be at the funeral?"

The question seemed to come from left field, and Carny stood up and got her purse. "I don't know. Why?"

"Just wondered." He looked quietly at her for a moment, then said, "Mom, you look real pretty."

"Thanks, honey," she said, bending to kiss his forehead. "But I don't think black is my color."

"You look pretty in any color," he said. "Logan thinks so, too."

Frowning, she turned back to him. "Logan? When did he tell you that?"

Jason hesitated for a moment, then shrugged. "Maybe at church. No, it was at the dance. That must have been when."

Something about the way he answered alerted her that something wasn't quite right, but they were going to be late, so she let it go. She was just about to ask him what else Logan had said, when Jason popped another question out of thin air.

"Can we have Jack?"

Starting the car, she shot him a look. "I don't

think so, honey. We have enough animals, and he's used to living inside. Besides, I think Betsy's family will probably take Jack in."

"Poor Jack," Jason said, gazing out the window.

She blinked back the tears misting in her eyes and tried to concentrate on getting to the church.

Carny had almost given up on Logan's attending the funeral, when she saw him walk into the church after the service had started, his head down and his shoulders slumped. She saw him slip into the back pew, and look toward the coffin at the front of the church. Jack lay curled next to it, still unwilling to leave his master's side. The other mourners had related to her how Betsy had tried to get him out of the church for the funeral, but he'd growled at her, so she'd left him alone.

Carny couldn't help playing the facts over in her mind. Had she been wrong about Logan? Would he really have given back a check for a hundred thousand dollars if he were, indeed, a con artist? No matter how attached her father ever got to someone, she couldn't imagine a scenario in which he'd give back a hundred grand.

Logan had seemed truly shaken by Slade's death, and the tears she'd seen in his eyes when he'd stood at the coffin had been real. She knew she wasn't wrong about that. But she'd been sure she wasn't wrong about his being a fraud, either. Now she was just confused.

Jason snuggled closer, leaning his head against her

as the service progressed, and dear old friends stood and told stories about Slade. *He would have enjoyed it,* she thought. It was a shame that people waited until you were gone to say good things about you.

When the service ended, Brother Tommy instructed them all to convene around the grave site outside, where the coffin would be taken by the pallbearers. Slowly, the crowd spilled from the church and headed across to the small cemetery next door, where all the members of the congregation were buried when they died.

Carny saw Logan slip out of the crowd and hang on the outskirts, waiting for everyone to go by. Something about his forlorn posture moved her, and quietly, she went toward him. "You okay, Brisco?"

He nodded. "Yeah. Fine."

"Are you coming?"

Logan saw the side door open, and the pallbearers brought out the coffin. Jack followed behind them.

"Yeah, I'm coming."

Jason reached up for his hand, and Logan hesitated for a moment. Finally, he took it, as if it provided the rescue he needed from the edge of his emotions. And holding Jason's hand for dear life, he walked with them to the grave site.

Jack whimpered as the pallbearers lowered the coffin into the grave. He lay there with his chin on the dirt, his eyes trained on the coffin, until the closing prayer came to an end and the crowd broke up. Logan couldn't have said why that sight touched him so, but an unspeakable despair, rooted deep in his heart, came over him. Struggling with the tears that were so foreign to him, Logan let go of Jason's hand, and went to the dog.

"It's gonna be all right, boy." He scratched behind the dog's floppy ear, and Jack looked up at him in confusion. He sat down next to the dog, stroking him and talking softly to him, until the last of the guests had offered condolences to Betsy and her family, and only a few stragglers remained behind. Among them were Carny and Jason, offering to take Betsy's children for the night, so that she could rest.

"No, I think it would be better if they were home," Betsy was saying. "But I appreciate it, Carny. I really do." Wiping her eyes, she turned to Logan, sitting beside the dog.

"I don't know how I'm going to get him away from here," she said. "He almost bit me earlier. And we can't keep him. John's allergic to dogs."

Logan didn't stop his reassuring stroking as he asked, "What are your options?"

"Honestly," Betsy said, "we're considering having him put to sleep. He's old, and he was so attached to Daddy. . . ."

Logan stood up. "He's not that old. He's just confused right now, Betsy. He doesn't understand."

"I realize that," she said, "but we can't just let him hang around in the graveyard. I honestly don't know what else to do."

Logan looked down at the dog, who still gazed down at the coffin with no intention of leaving. "I'll take him," he said suddenly.

"What?" Betsy's eyes lit up. "You would do that?"

He looked from Betsy to Carny, who looked even more confused than she had when he'd given back the money. "Yes," he said. "I feel a special affinity with Jack for some reason. Besides, I've always wanted a dog."

Carny's eyes narrowed. "Logan, are you sure? You're not exactly set up for a dog."

*And what are you gonna do with Jack when you have to skip town?* Logan asked himself. But that didn't seem to matter right now. There were times in a person's life when logic had to be overruled. This was one of them.

"Jack's easy to take care of," he said. "He's housebroken, polite, and he'll just go with me everywhere I go. Just like he did with Slade."

*But you can't blend in with a dog, young man!* he could almost hear Montague shouting. *You can't run and clear the slate and change identities. The authorities will catch up with you, simply by identifying the dog!*

None of that mattered as he reached down and scooped Jack up in his arms. Jack whimpered and looked back at the grave, but he didn't struggle as Logan carried him to his car.

Carny didn't like being confused. It disturbed her, and it blurred the lines and grayed all the colors. It made her feel unbearably vulnerable, a trait she'd always shaken off before.

But these new developments with Logan had

thrown her. How could a con artist give back a hundred thousand dollars that no one even knew he had? How could he take up the care of a grieving dog, when he had to stay on the run?

The remote possibility that she could have been wrong about him tiptoed, once again, through her mind, until she had to come face-to-face with the thought. No matter what he was, Logan Brisco was a man with a heart, as well as a conscience.

Carny pulled her motorcycle into Logan's motel parking lot, reached for the bag she'd strapped to the seat behind her, and tried to straighten her windblown hair.

He didn't answer immediately after she knocked, and just when she was about to give up, the door opened.

The room was dark, lit only by a small lamp in one corner, and she immediately felt like an intruder. "Carny," he said, surprised to see her.

"Did I wake you up?" she asked.

He ran his fingers through his hair. "No. I was just reading. Jack was asleep in my lap, and it took me a minute to move him."

She came into the room and saw Jack, curled up on the bed, looking up at her with sad, sleepy eyes. "Is he all right?"

"He will be. We've kind of been bonding."

She smiled and turned back to him. With his face half in shadow, half in light, he looked almost compassionate, and almost as vulnerable as she felt. "You know, you're blowing all my theories about you. I hate it when that happens."

He breathed a laugh. "Well, I guess something good came out of all this." He went to clear the books off a chair so she could sit down. "Where's Jason?"

"He's at Nathan's. I had to go over to Betsy's, to take her some casseroles I cooked. She's going to have a lot of company for the next few days."

"That was a sweet thing to do."

"Yeah, well, that's what you do in Serenity when there's a death in the family. You don't know what to say, so you bring them food. Anyway, she asked me to send all this stuff over to you."

She handed him the bag, and he reached into it.

"It's just Jack's food, and the blanket he likes to sleep on and his bowl. Familiar things . . . to make the transition a little easier."

Logan took the bag and set it down on the table. "I fed him a hamburger for supper. He ate some of it, but he didn't have much appetite." Dropping into his chair, he rubbed his face.

"A lot of responsibility, isn't it? I mean, after being alone for so long, suddenly having to worry about someone else," she said softly.

She could see that he was in a reflective mood, and his guard was down. Why that fascinated and attracted her, she wasn't sure.

"A few years ago, I knew a fourteen-year-old kid who had no home, no place to go, and no money except what he could make hustling pool," he said softly. "And someone came along, at just the right moment, someone who had every reason to keep going and not look back. But he stopped and took that fourteen-year-old kid in, made him his partner, and taught him to believe he was somebody. You know who that kid was?"

"You," she said without a doubt.

"Yeah. And if Montague Shelton could encumber himself with a fourteen-year-old runaway, then I can take care of an orphaned dog."

For a moment, Carny couldn't think of a reply, and she only looked at him. His eyes were weary and defeated.

"Tell me about your parents," he said softly.

She couldn't tell if he was changing the subject, or if it had everything to do with what they'd been talking about. "What do you want to know?"

"Are they still living? Do you see them? Talk to them?"

"Yes, on all three," she said. "I may have wanted to escape their lifestyle, but they're still my parents."

"Didn't it ever bother you that they might not approve of your going straight?"

"I'm not sure they believe I have," she said with a rueful smile. "They haven't had many breaks in their lives. I think they're a little doubtful that things will work out for me."

"Do they love you?"

Her smile faded. "Of course they do. I'm their daughter."

"That doesn't matter. Lots of parents don't love their children."

"Well, mine do. I'm the only child they ever had. There was never any question that they loved me."

"Then why did you leave?"

Sighing, she got up and walked across the room, then turned back to him. "I wanted peace," she said. "And stability, and a home. I wanted to stay in one place, and belong there, and raise my child to belong."

"I envy you," he said.

"Why? You can do the same things."

"Not really. I think I'll always be an outsider."

"It doesn't take a lot to be an insider in Serenity," she said. "They're very accepting people. You've already seen that."

Sliding down in his seat, he leaned his head back. "Do you ever miss it, Carny? Traveling, I mean? Do you ever miss the gypsy life?"

"Never. I spent too many years wishing for a backyard where I could plant a tree and watch it grow. The first year I had my house, I planted three trees in the yard. In a few years, they'll be big enough to climb."

Again, that contemplative silence filled the room, and she wondered what he was thinking. Her eyes roved around the room and landed on the books he had stacked on the table. She scanned the various titles and realized they all had to do with amusement parks.

"Why all the reading?" she asked.

"Just trying to anticipate any problems that might come up," he said. "It's kind of like comparing notes with others. I was particularly interested in seeing how other parks have affected the communities around them."

Again, she was at a loss. His interest indicated that he was sincere, that he wasn't a fraud, that he had every intention of building a park.

But she just wasn't sure.

He saw the conflicting thoughts in her expression, and asked, "What are you thinking?"

She sat back down. "Oh . . . I was just thinking that my parents have good hearts. My father used to have a miniature horse he exhibited in a freak show, and he sometimes let it in our trailer when it was cold out. And I've seen him give a kid a free teddy bear for his girlfriend, just to help him earn points with her."

"What's your point?" he asked, knowing that it somehow related to him.

"My point, Brisco, is that compassion doesn't necessarily preclude fraudulent behavior. A con artist can rob someone blind in one minute without one stirring of conscience, then turn around in the next one and save a cat from a burning building. That you may have a good heart doesn't mean that you're a good person."

"It doesn't mean I'm a bad one, either."

"No, it doesn't," she said. "And there's the problem. I'm having trouble deciding which you are."

"Maybe you just need more data," he suggested quietly.

"Maybe so," she said with a smile. Then, getting to her feet, she said, "Well, I have to go now, Brisco. I have to get Jason to bed."

He got up and walked her to the door, and paused a moment before opening it for her. "I like you like this," he said.

"Like what?"

"Sweet, soft, gentle . . . even if you are still suspicious."

She didn't like the warmth that spread through her at his words. "I've got to go now, Brisco. You are coming to the lesson tomorrow, aren't you? It'll be the first one in the cockpit."

"Jack and I will be there," he said.

"Jack's already taken the course," she said. "I taught Slade two years ago. Jack has enough hours in the cockpit to get his own license." Then winking, she said, "See you later."

As she walked out to her bike, she felt him watching her, and her face warmed. She didn't look back until she was on the motorcycle, pulling out of her space.

Logan was leaning on the rail above her, watching as she drove out of sight.

# 10

*The dilemma that* grew inside Logan was getting harder and harder to resolve. It was time to go, and he knew it. The problem was, he didn't want to leave.

This had never happened to him before, and he hadn't believed it was possible. Oh, there had been times over the years when he'd grown fond of a woman, enjoyed her company, and regretted leaving her. But this was different.

Telling himself he didn't want to leave because he hadn't made enough of a score, he decided that he'd just have to get himself refocused. He needed to step up the promotion of the park. Try to go in for one last sweep of the town, and get the money out of anybody else who was likely to give it to him. He needed something new to tell them. Some new morsel of hope to seal the deals brewing in the minds of the citizens. He needed a gimmick.

As he thought, his fingers absently flicked the remote control of the television, changing channel after channel, until finally he came to the country-music video station. Dolly Parton sat in a bar with some of her music cronies, singing "Romeo." Logan had been to her park in Pigeon Forge, Tennessee two years ago, and he'd thought then that someone with more imagination could have done a better job of planning it. But it didn't matter, for it was her name that drew crowds.

And suddenly it came to him. That was what Serenity needed for its park. They needed a star to link his name with it. A star who could be a partial investor, whose name would draw millions, not just from Texas, but from all over the country.

He watched Billy Ray Cyrus as he walked through the bar in Dolly's video, and thought of what a response he might get from the town if he attached Billy Ray's name to it. People would be lining up outside Logan's door to give him more money, and those who already had would be digging deeper.

Logan tried to think of possible names for the park. Cyrus Land came to mind, along with Billy-World . . . or better yet . . . the Achy Breaky Park! Laughing aloud, he wondered if the town would buy it. Something told him they would.

But as Jack got off the bed and came to lie at his feet, Logan reached down to stroke his coat and realized that there was not much joy in figuring new ways to fleece the town. It had become a job, instead of a challenge. A lonely job. A job he'd rather not have, but one he was stuck in, because he'd already dug himself so deep.

In a job like his, there was no turning back. He'd made his own prison, and no one else could set him free.

News spread like a forest fire the next day, starting in the diner where Logan and Jack ate breakfast, and making its way through the barbershop and the beauty salon, down through the drugstore and printer, across to the hardware store, and up to the post office and florist. Billy Ray Cyrus was investing in the park, and it was going to be named after him.

Carny heard it first from Lahoma at the Curl Up & Dye, when she brought her the delivery she'd picked up for her in Dallas that morning. "Who told you this?" she asked.

"Well, Logan. He's been telling everybody. Billy Ray's gonna come for the opening, and give a special concert for all the investors, and folks are sayin' he might even build a house here and live here part of the year! Can you imagine it, Carny? Billy Ray in Serenity?"

"No, actually," Carny said. "I can't imagine it."

"Well, it's gonna happen. And I'm gonna be a part of it. I've got an appointment with Logan this afternoon. I'm gonna get a piece of this action. Have you invested yet?"

"Of course not," she said. "I'm still not sure it's legitimate."

"Oh, Carny," Tea Ann Campbell said from under the dryer. "When are you gonna stop suspectin' him? He's the nicest man I've ever met. How can you watch him traipsing around town with that dog and not just know he's pure as the driven snow?"

Carny didn't argue, for she knew that no one in town would buy her objections anymore. Logan had convinced them. And the truth was, she was starting to wonder herself.

But Billy Ray Cyrus? Something about that didn't ring true. Where would Logan have gotten a connection like that?

She left the beauty shop and started up the street to the hardware store to make another delivery, while she turned the new information over in her mind. As she passed the barbershop, she saw Logan and Jack shooting the breeze with Cecil, to whom Slade had left the shop.

Slowing her step, she looked at the dog, sitting where he had always sat, though his head was tipped and his ears were cocked, as if he waited for Slade to come in at any moment and take him home. Slowly, she went through the door. The men in the shop looked up when she came in, and she said, "Hey, guys."

"Hey, Carny," Cecil said.

Logan grinned that big, irreverent grin. "Well, look who's here, Jack."

She bent to pet the dog. "How's he doing?"

"About as well as you could expect. He's a little confused. A little sad."

"Do you think it was a good idea to bring him here?"

Logan shrugged. "I don't know, but I figure a little familiarity never hurt anybody."

"Maybe." She straightened up, and sliding her hands into the pockets of her khaki shorts, said, "So what's this I hear about Billy Ray Cyrus?"

Logan looked at the others, allowing them to take the rumor and run with it.

"We're namin' the park after him, Carny," Cecil said. "The Achy Breaky Park."

She couldn't help the amusement passing over her face. "The Achy Breaky Park? Don't you think that's a little silly?"

Logan laughed. "Hey, if he's willing to invest millions of dollars, we'll name it anything he wants."

"And he really suggested Achy Breaky Park?"

"Well . . . no," Logan said. "Actually, that was sort of my idea. I haven't run it by him yet. But he's 90 percent committed, and I'm giving Serenity a few more days to invest. It's not too late to throw some in, Carny."

"I don't think so, Brisco. How do you know Billy Ray?"

"I don't know him," he said, prepared for the question. "One of my investors, a bank down near Houston, does business with him, and he was looking for some new ventures. It was actually his idea. He got the idea from Dolly Parton when they were shooting that 'Romeo' video. My investor decided to hook him up with us."

"So, do you have a contract?"

Undaunted, he shook his head. "Nope. None of this is a done deal. It all depends on my getting enough enthusiasm here to convince my bigger investors that Serenity's the place to build it. Billy Ray can't sign anything until he knows for sure there's going to be a park."

It all sounded so pat, so logical, and yet there wasn't one shred of authenticity to the story, Carny thought. She couldn't forget that Logan had just appeared here out of nowhere, that they still didn't know who the major investors were, or that he was taking money from her friends like there was no tomorrow, or like tomorrow was about as long as he'd be around.

"What if it all falls through? Do the investors get their money back?"

"Of course."

"With interest?"

He laughed. "No, not with interest. It's a risk, and I've told everybody that. They won't lose their money, but if the park falls through, they won't make any, either."

He wasn't the same man she had seen, ruffled and alone, in his motel room last night. He was on stage now, all charm and salesmanship, the man with all the answers.

"You sure you don't want to come in with us, Carny?" Cecil asked. "You stand to gain more than any of us in Serenity. They'll have to expand the airport, and you could make a killing."

"Not interested," she said, going to the door. "I didn't come to Serenity to get rich."

"Well no, but wouldn't it be nice if you did?"

"It's kind of a moot point, isn't it, Brisco?" she asked over her shoulder as she left the barbershop.

She knew, even as she walked away, that he watched her, realizing that she wasn't entirely convinced just yet.

As she drove home, she couldn't shake the feeling that he had almost counted her among his marks. He had almost persuaded her that he was legitimate. He had almost made her think he was a man with pure motives.

But something about his persona today reminded her of that con artist facade, that charismatic smile with the poison to kill . . . or at least injure. She really didn't know that much about him, other than what he'd told her. And she'd hit dead ends about the holes in his life. All she knew was that he'd met a man when he was fourteen. . . .

Montague! That was the man's name. Montague Shelton. He'd told her about him last night when his guard was down, when he hadn't been covering up or putting on, when he'd only been himself. Quickly, she turned her truck around and revved it, heading for the sheriff's office to dig a little deeper into Logan Brisco's past.

Joey Malone was Carny's primary connection at the sheriff's office, though she knew everyone there. Two of the six deputies had been past suitors, whom she had finally shaken off, politely but firmly. Joey was the only survivor among them, and he counted himself honored that she had decided to pay him a visit.

"I need a favor," she said, when he'd bought her a soda from the machine and offered her a seat at his desk. "I know you can help me."

He smiled. "I'll do anything you ask, Carny, you know that. Unless, of course, it's illegal."

"No," she said. "It's not. I want you to run a name through your computers. See if he has a record, any arrests, anything you could tell me."

"Yeah, I can do that," he said. "Who is it?"

"Montague Shelton," she said. "I don't know if that's his real name. Would his aliases be registered?"

"Maybe, if the FBI or somebody ever had reason to investigate him. What's the deal, Carny? Is he one of your father's carnies?"

"No, no," she said quickly. "This doesn't have anything to do with my father. Actually, it's a long story."

Satisfied that she didn't want to divulge why she needed the information, Joey punched a few keys on his computer. "Let's see," he said, waiting for it to come up. "Montague Shelton."

In a moment, the screen filled with data, and Joey stared at it, fascinated. "Wow. Look at that. Went under three other aliases. Maurice Hinton, Shelton Ainsworth, and Montague Black. Died twelve years ago."

She got up and came to stand behind Joey and scanned the screen. "Are those arrests?"

"Yeah," Joey said, moving the cursor down. "Had one conviction in 1968 for mail fraud.

Served six months. Another conviction in 1970, for passing counterfeit checks. Only served three months that time."

Mentally, she calculated when Logan had told her he took him in and realized that both convictions were before he'd met him. "Does it say anything about a partner?" she asked. "Any accessories to his crimes?"

He scanned the rest of the report and shook his head. "No, nothing. There is something else here, though. Apparently, between the time he got out of prison the last time and the time he died—which would be about ten years—there were twenty-four warrants out for his arrest."

"Twenty-four?" she asked. "Where?"

"All over," he said. "There's even one in Paris and another in Copenhagen. The charges range from theft by swindle to counterfeiting. Looks like he managed to evade the authorities until he died."

For some reason she couldn't name, Carny felt as if a fist had just gone through her stomach. Those were the years when he would have been with Logan. And if he was involved in swindling, then Logan was a part of it, too.

And that meant she wasn't wrong about him.

"Are you sure there's no mention of anyone else in these arrest warrants?" she asked. "Maybe even a child? A teenaged boy?"

"Nothing," he said. "The FBI file might have something a little more detailed."

"Joey, could you get that?" she asked. "It's real important."

He frowned. "Why? Who is this guy?"

She sighed and glanced around, making sure no one overheard them. "I think he was someone real close to Logan. In fact, he might have been his mentor. If I'm right, that gives us a big clue to Logan's credibility. Please, Joey. Can you do this for me?"

He sat back in his chair, and stared at Carny. "I'll do my best, Carny, but I should tell you. I ran a check on Logan myself, just because you were so upset about him at the meeting. Turns out, he has no priors. None at all."

"That only means he's never been caught," she said, getting to her feet. "And that may not be his real name. Call me when you get the file, Joey. And try to hurry. Serenity might be running out of time. If he leaves and takes all that money with him, we might never be able to find him again."

"You're assuming an awful lot, Carny."

She looked at him sharply. "Are you going to help me, Joey, or not?"

"Yeah, I'll help you, Carny," he said. "Just don't get your hopes up. And I gotta tell you, I hope to God you're wrong. My dad just cashed in his IRA and his life-insurance policy and invested it with Brisco. And my uncle's taking out a second mortgage on his house."

Closing her eyes, she whispered, "Why is everyone so stupid?"

"Because he's bringing us hope, Carny. It would be so nice if he could do what he said he could."

\* \* \*

Logan wished that it wasn't a scam, that he could do what he'd promised, as he stood in the assembly hall of the local elementary school and looked out at the faces of those bright, clean, hopeful children who expected him to change their world into something magical. They didn't know, he thought, that Serenity already had magic. He was only going to taint it. But a guy had to make a living.

"So what I'm proposing," he went on, standing and pacing across the stage, with Jack close on his heels, "is that you children help me by drawing pictures, writing down ideas, brainstorming, if you will, until you come up with wonderful, outrageous ideas of the kinds of rides you'd like to see in the park. We're going for originality and the more fantastic the better."

He saw a hand go up in the middle of the auditorium and recognized Jason. "Yes, Jason," he said.

Jason smiled, puffed up with pride that Logan knew him by name. "Do you want the rides to have something to do with Billy Ray Cyrus?"

"They can," he said, "but they don't have to. Just anything that we can say is ours. I'm looking for ideas that we can develop, things that no one else has, that will draw people from all over to our park."

Another hand went up. "Yes?"

"What if a kid wanted to invest?"

Logan hesitated. "Well, now, every little bit helps, sure, but I think ideas are more what I'm trying to get from you."

"But if we did have some money, and we gave it to you, would we be partners, too?"

"Of course," he said. "Everybody who invests is a partner."

"And would we get free passes?"

"Every one of you who comes up with an idea that we use will get free passes," he said. "I guarantee it. You don't have to give me your allowance."

"But we could if we wanted?" someone else asked. "And then, when the park started making lots of money, we'd make money, too, wouldn't we?"

"Theoretically, yes," Logan said, "but like I told you, I'd rather have your ideas."

The bell rang, saving him from any more questions about investments, and he breathed a sigh of relief as the children were dismissed. He shook the principal's hand and thanked him for allowing him to come again, when he felt someone tap his side.

Jason Sullivan stood behind him, his big eyes wide and admiring, and when Logan stooped down to the child's eye level, Jason said, "That was good, Logan. And I have lots of ideas."

"That's great, Jason," he said, "but you know, it's too bad we can't reproduce your fishing hole and offer it as a part of the park. That was the most fun I've had in years."

"We can go again! How about today?"

"Isn't your mom expecting you home?"

"No," he said. "I'm going home with Nathan today, because she had a couple of flights she had to make. You could come over, and we could all three go!"

He looked out at the children dispersing from

the auditorium, and realized that he really had no reason not to. His work was finished until the children went home and worked on their parents. Tomorrow was the day he expected to sweep up. Between the enthusiasm of the kids and adding Billy Ray Cyrus's name to the park, very few citizens would be able to turn away from this.

"Besides, you told me you could help me with my math. Well, I'm having a little trouble with my fractions. I could bring my book, and we could work on it while we fish."

The boy was too persuasive to turn down, and Logan realized that he had very distinct con artist genes. All he needed to do was hone them into the same kind of charisma that Logan had developed, and there was no telling what Jason could do with his life. Even in legitimate business, he'd go far.

"All right," he said finally. "Let me go change, and Jack and I'll meet you at Nathan's in half an hour. How does that sound?"

"Great!" Jason said, jumping down from the stage and heading out of the auditorium. "See you in a little while. We're gonna catch a zillion fish today!"

Logan only laughed, and hoped that Carny wouldn't find out.

Nathan and Jason were armed with bait, poles, and math books when Logan got to the Trents' house. Taking his share of the load, he went with the two boys and Jack through the woods, around the lake, and to the special, private little area where he and Jason had fished the other day.

While Nathan held their poles, patiently waiting for one of the lines to get a bite, Logan looked over Jason's fractions. "Ah, here's what you've done wrong," he said, pulling the pencil out of his pocket. "You haven't found the common denominator."

"I don't understand about common denominators," the boy said.

Patiently, Logan explained how each of the fractions could be broken down. Rapt, Jason listened. When he thought he understood, he attempted a problem himself, and his eyes lit up with pride when he got it right.

"So what does Mom mean when she says that the park will reduce us all to the least common denominator?"

Logan chuckled. "She means that the bad people will bring the good people down, instead of the good ones bringing the bad ones up. But she shouldn't worry, because there won't be any bad people here. We'll keep them all out."

"Anyway, if they did come, I think bad people can turn good, don't you?" Jason asked.

Logan knew he couldn't have put it better himself. "That's exactly what I think, Jason. And if there's ever a place where a person could turn his life around, it's got to be Serenity."

They fished for a while then, until they'd caught more fish than they wanted to carry home, and then they pitched Jason's baseball until it was time for Logan to make his way back.

"I have a lesson with your mother at 4:30," he said.

Jason wasn't ready to leave. "You go on, and we'll stay here for a while longer. And don't tell Mom we did this, okay?"

"All right, kiddo," Logan said, picking up a stick for Jack to fetch as they made their way back through the woods. "See you later."

"Tomorrow?" Jason asked hopefully.

Logan laughed. "Yeah, okay. Tomorrow. And I want to see that math paper again. See if you can have all those problems corrected by then."

"Piece o' cake," Jason said. "And don't rile Mom, okay? I don't want her coming home in a bad mood."

Logan couldn't help laughing as he walked back through the trees.

# 11

*Carny was leaning* against Logan's car fender when he and Jack made it back to the Trents' house, and instantly she saw the look of guilt pass across his face. "Where's my son?" she asked.

"Down at the lake fishing."

"Have you been with him?"

She already knew he had, for she had canceled her flight and had come home early. When she'd confronted Janice about where the kids were and why Logan's car was here, she discovered the truth.

"Yeah, we did a little fishing."

"You've got a lot of nerve," she said through her teeth.

He hadn't expected to defend himself after such

a pleasant afternoon, so he sighed and slumped against the car. "What exactly is wrong with my going fishing with your son?"

"You didn't ask my permission, and I warned you to stay away from him."

"Look, Jason came to me," he said. "He's a hard kid to reject. He looks up to me, God knows why, and I can't help responding to that, because I don't think anyone else ever has."

"Give me a break," she said, her face reddening. "Every kid in town looks up to you. I heard about your little assembly at school today. You're the Pied Piper, for heaven's sake."

Her words stung him, and he turned away. "That's different. That's business. Jason looks up to me for different reasons." He brought his gaze back to hers, and for a moment, she almost believed she saw sincerity there. "He needs a man around, Carny."

Something about those words enraged her, and she blinked back the tears that only seemed to come into her eyes when she was angry. "He has me, and he has this town. There are men all around him who love him. His grandparents, our neighbors, our friends, coaches . . . that's a whole lot more than a lot of little boys have."

"Tell me about it."

"Don't feed me that, Brisco. You had a man in your life. A very dominant influence."

He frowned. "And who would that be?"

"Montague Shelton," she said. "I know all about him, and the things he taught you."

For the first time since she'd met him, she saw fury in his eyes. "What are you talking about?"

"I'm talking about your friend the grifter, Brisco. I'm talking about the two convictions for fraud and counterfeiting, and the twenty-four warrants out for his arrest when he died."

Compressing his lips, he said, "And what conclusion has that brought you to, Carny?"

"That I've been right all along," she said. "That you're nothing but a low-life swindler."

"Let me tell you something about Montague Shelton," Logan said, his eyes blazing as he stepped closer to her. "He was the only person in my entire life who gave a damn what happened to me. And he may not have been the most honest man in the world, but his crimes were pretty much victimless. He never hurt anyone. It wasn't in his nature."

"You think taking someone's life savings is a victimless crime?" she asked. "You think because he didn't pull a gun on them and tie them up, that he was somehow above the scum who do?"

"People can recover from temporary financial setbacks."

"Yeah," she said with a bitter laugh. "If they're willing to work two jobs, and never retire, and sell everything they own to buy food! You don't get it, do you, Brisco?"

"All right, so he was a con artist. So are your parents. You can't assume that I'm one any more than I can assume you are."

"Hey, I live here. I work here. I'm raising my

son here. You're the one who blew in on a train with nothing but a smile and an idea."

"It's a damn good idea, Carny, and you know it. And I may have a questionable past, but that doesn't mean I don't get the chance to settle down myself, build anything, or have a family of my own! I'm no different from you, Carny. You should just be glad that when you came to Serenity, no one here judged and accused you the way you've judged and accused me!"

Something about the fervor in his words struck her, and she suddenly realized that none of this was an act. She hadn't found anything on him, and the fact that he'd known a con artist didn't mean he'd become one. She had departed from the ways of her family, even though dishonesty had been drilled into her all her life. It wasn't so farfetched to think that he, too, could have chosen a cleaner path.

She let out a heavy sigh. "If I'm wrong about you, Brisco, I'm sorry."

"Wow, that's some apology."

"Yeah, well, I'm not prepared to go any further than that."

"That's fair."

They stood quietly for a long moment, and finally, he asked, "Does all this mean that you're canceling my lesson for today? I was really looking forward to getting into the cockpit."

She shrugged. "Meet me at the hangar," she said. "You've already paid, after all."

Carny left him standing there and went to her pick-up truck, got in, and slammed the door. And as she pulled out of her driveway, she told herself that she was losing her mind. There was no reason on God's green earth that she should trust him.

And yet, somehow, she almost did.

The lesson in the plane was fraught with tension, and Carny's words were clipped and to the point. She had already tested Logan's knowledge of the plane's controls, navigational equipment, and check sheets, all of which they'd covered in the ground school, and it was past time for him to take the plane up and apply what she had taught him.

But it wasn't the first time Logan had flown. Several times before, when he'd deadheaded on a commercial airline, pretending to be a pilot en route to his hub, between flights he'd sat in the jump seat in the cockpit. Occasionally, the captain would ask him to take the control while he went into the cabin. Knowing the first officer could handle the plane, Logan had always stepped confidently into the captain's seat, as if he knew what he was doing. He wondered if many of them realized yet that he had been a fraud without an hour of pilot's training under his belt.

That seemed like such a long time ago. The pilot's uniform Montague had finagled for him was in a storage building in Atlanta. Now, he almost didn't care if he never saw it again. Yet he knew that it would always be there, in case he ever needed to step back into his pilot role again.

"Not bad," Carny said, watching him turn the plane and circle back over her hangar. "You have a good feel for this."

"I told you I'm a quick study."

She refrained from saying that all con artists were quick studies, for something about his pensive, quiet attitude confused her. There was real sincerity in his eyes. Authentic vulnerability. And he'd seemed genuinely hurt by the fact that she kept accusing him, or that she'd said anything derogatory about his friend.

But Carny knew that the pride of a great con lay in the fact that the mark saw some degree of authenticity and hung all their trust on it. She wondered if she was just getting soft. "Tell me something," she said, taking back control of the plane and preparing to land. "When you and Jason were fishing, what did you talk about? The park?"

"No," he said. "In fact, I don't even think the park came up. We talked about fishing, and I helped him with his fractions, and we had an interesting talk about 'least common denominators.'"

When she glanced at him, she noted the slight grin on his face, and she knew instantly that Jason had repeated something she'd said. "You helped him with his math? Why didn't he ask me?"

"I don't know," he said. "But I'm good at math, and I think I explained it so he can understand. He was gonna take it home and work on it, and bring it back for me to look at tomorrow. We had planned to go fishing again."

"I'll check his work," she said.

She started to land, and both of them were quiet until the plane was on the ground.

"Look," he said finally, as she taxied to the tarmac, "this thing with Jason. I honestly wasn't trying to go behind your back. It's just that I'd never been fishing before, believe it or not, and the first time I went with him I enjoyed it so much that I couldn't wait to do it again."

Her head snapped back to him. "The first time? This wasn't the first time?"

He sighed, kicking himself for letting that slip. It wasn't like him to set himself up that way. "No. There was one other time. You thought he was with Nathan, but I went instead. Carny, for the most part, we sit and fish and don't say anything. He taught me something valuable that I hadn't experienced before. He's a great kid, and I liked being around him. But I won't do it anymore."

She cut off the engine, and for a moment they sat still, neither speaking. "You have to understand, Brisco. I want to protect my son. That's why I never went back to the carnival. That's why I kept him here in Serenity."

"I don't blame you," he said, staring off into space. "He's the most precious possession God gave you."

Another eternal moment passed, and she whispered, "That sounds funny coming from you. I didn't have you pegged for someone who believes in God."

He didn't answer right away, and she saw the turmoil in his eyes as he stared out the cockpit window, wrestling with the question. "I used to. My mother used to say prayers with me, take me to Sunday school. But that was a long time ago. As you grow older, you kind of start questioning the logic in believing."

"Whether you believe or not doesn't change God's existence at all."

"I know," he whispered. "The hell of it is, I think I really do believe, whether I consciously want to or not. I'm just not so sure God believes in me."

"You might be surprised," she said. "I was picking pockets when I was seven years old. Helping to fix games when I was ten. I used to feel like I had too much baggage to ever turn around. But then I found that He's a shepherd over even the black sheep."

He smiled softly, and brought his eyes to her. "I don't think I've ever heard it put quite like that. Still trying to convert me, Carny?"

"Heavens, no," she said. "I'd never believe it if you did convert."

"That's right," he said on a chuckle. "You'd just be sure it was a part of a con."

For a moment, they sat quietly, until finally, she sighed and looked over at him. "Look, Brisco. I guess it wouldn't hurt for you to go fishing with Jason now and then. As hard as it is for me to admit, I guess he needs that."

He was both surprised and touched at the tiny step she'd taken toward accepting him. "Thank you, Carny," he whispered. "I promise I won't do anything to hurt him."

She opened the cockpit door and got out, the

stiffness of her posture indicating that the conversation was over. Only then did Logan realize how much the concession had cost her. But it had cost him, as well.

As she walked back into the office, he stood still in the middle of the hangar, and realized that there wasn't much he liked about himself right now. For he had almost succeeded in earning her trust, knowing all the while that he intended to betray it.

When Logan drove up the next afternoon, Jason was waiting for him, armed with two fishing poles and a bucket of bait that he'd dug out of his backyard. Out of his pocket stuck a fat envelope, and his shirttail was half out of his pants. His face had grown more freckled since he'd spent more time in the sun, and Logan couldn't help smiling at the sight of him.

"Logan, I've got something for you!" he said, running to the car and dragging one of the poles in the dirt. "Something really great."

Logan got out and took the poles from Jason to lighten his load, as Jack hopped down from the front seat. "What? Tell me."

"Our investment." The boy was out of breath, and he stopped and tried to catch it. "At school, everybody brought their investment, and they gave it all to me. . . . "

"Whoa," Logan said, bending down and getting eye level with the boy. "Start over. What do you mean everybody brought their investment?"

"I mean, the kids. We each brought what we had. And I've got three hundred dollars here. Is that enough, Logan? Can you go back to those bankers now, and get them to start building the park?"

Logan straightened slowly and took the envelope from Jason. "Three hundred dollars? Where did everybody get it?"

"Allowances, birthday money, piggy banks. I had sixty dollars that was last year's birthday money and the money in my stocking last Christmas, and another sixteen dollars and fourteen cents in my piggy bank. And don't worry. I made a list of all the investors and how much they gave, so when we get rich, you'll know who gets what. That's how you do it, isn't it?"

"Yeah," Logan said quietly. "That's how, all right. But I thought I told you all that I wasn't trying to get money from the children. I just wanted ideas."

"Oh, they've got those, too, only I couldn't bring them. The teachers are collecting them, 'cause there's so many. But isn't this great, Logan, about the money? Aren't you happy?"

"Yeah, sure," Logan said, trying to sound enthusiastic. "It's great. Really."

"Is it enough? 'Cause we could probably raise some more, if we had more time. We were thinking we could have a bake sale or wash cars. . . ."

"No," Logan said. "This'll be fine. It's real close."

"Are we gonna be rich, Logan?"

Logan ran his fingers through his hair and looked off into the breeze. "Probably, kiddo. If it's at all in my power."

"Wow!" the boy said, punching the air with his fist. "You know what's the first thing I'm gonna buy? One of those pretty red dresses like they have in the window of Miss Mabel's Boutique, for my mom, so she can get a husband."

Logan laughed in spite of himself. "I don't think your mom is too worried about finding a husband."

"Then he has to find her," he said, "and I think that red dress is just the thing that'll lure 'em. Come on. The fish are really biting today. I just know it!"

Logan watched as Jason ran off ahead of him and disappeared beyond the trees.

It didn't pay to have a conscience, Montague had always told him. And all afternoon, as Logan talked and played and fished with the little boy who trusted him, he discovered how true that statement was.

His conscience, which he'd always managed carefully to ignore, since he'd rarely gotten close enough to anyone to consider the pain his scams might be causing, had begun to rear its ugly head with amazing frequency lately. Even Jack seemed to look at him with shameful eyes, as if to say that he knew what he was up to and didn't want any part of it.

Stupid. That was what he was. He was stupid to get involved with Carny Sullivan's son. He was stupid to take on the care of a dog who depended on him. He was stupid to have stayed this long.

He threw back all the fish he caught that day, despite Jason's protests, and walked pensively back to his car before the boy was ready to leave. Something had to be done, he thought. He was sinking so deep that, if he didn't act now, he might never get out. There was a lot in his life that he could tolerate—running from the law, changing his name every couple of months, having self-recriminations that kept him awake at night. But it was hard to tolerate his own fatal weakness.

Even as he drove back to the motel, he made the decision that it was time to cut his losses, take what he'd already gotten, and get out of town. But the thought gave him little comfort. Reaching over to the dog that lay curled on the seat next to him, he said, "So Jack. How would you like to see the world?"

The dog gave him a blank look, and he stroked his soft coat and realized how difficult it would be to travel now. No more posing as a pilot and deadheading across country. No more vague descriptions from people who'd figured him out. Now there was Jack, and he would complicate Logan's life drastically.

But something about the way the dog looked at him made it impossible for him to leave him behind. Logan knew what it was to be alone, and he knew what it was to be confused. He understood abandonment and grief. No one, until Montague, had been there to care what happened to him. Nurturing Jack meant, in some small way, nurturing the child in him who had had no one. It was silly, he thought, and some shrink would probably have a field day with it, but it was there, nonetheless.

He pulled into the motel parking lot, and Jack followed him up to their room. It still smelled of musk and stale cigarette smoke from the previous occupants. He had fantasized more than once of buying a little house in Serenity, putting a few pieces of furniture in it, and actually unpacking his bag for a while, but his practical side had told him how ridiculous that would be.

Locking the door, he pulled out his bag, rolled up the clothes he'd brought here with him, gathered all of his toiletries, and left the clothes he'd bought since being here in the closet. Then he gathered up all the paperwork and log sheets that he'd kept for appearances, and all the notes he'd taken on building a real park, and all the books he'd studied about it. He was definitely leaving here with more than he'd come with, breaking another of Montague's rules.

But there was probably time for him to get out of the country for a while, before the people of Serenity realized they'd been had. Even with extra baggage and a dog, he'd probably be all right.

After boxing up his computer and printer, he made one last check of everything in the room, and satisfied that he'd gotten everything, he sat down at the table to count the cash he'd gotten from the citizens of Serenity. While it wasn't as much as he'd hoped for, it was still enough to live off for a couple of years, while he kept a low profile in Brazil or Sweden or Greece . . . just long enough for the Feds to stop looking for him.

Reaching into his pocket, he pulled out the fat envelope Jason had given him. Opening it, he pulled out the three hundred dollars, mostly in dollar bills. At the front of the stack of money, he unfolded a list in Jason's crude handwriting, listing the investors by their first names only, and the amounts they had contributed.

*Are we gonna be rich, Logan?* The boy's words echoed through his mind, and he tried to imagine what Jason's innocent little face would look like when he learned that he'd lost all his friends' money, and that Logan had been nothing more than a crook.

He searched his mind for the rationalizations that usually came so easily. Jason needed to learn this lesson. It might save him a wad of money later in life. He needed to realize that he shouldn't trust someone so readily. He needed to understand that crooks came in all shapes and sizes, and that they needn't look scruffy or questionable to stab you in the back.

But none of those rationalizations worked, for Logan knew that Jason would be worse for the lessons, not better. That was why Carny had chosen to raise him in Serenity, after all. She was trying to protect her son as she had not been protected.

And what would she think? That she'd been right? That he was nothing more than a two-bit thief with an expensive smile? That the tiny trust he'd begun to cultivate in her was worthless? Would she ever go that far again?

He didn't like the sudden black hole that seemed to form in his heart, and he couldn't stop the disturbing questions that kept racing through his mind. Finally, he sat down, made out a new envelope, addressed it to Jason, stuffed the money into it, along with the list, and sealed it.

Then he set about to harden himself enough to leave the town behind forever.

# 12

*The evidence was indisputable.*

Carny gaped at the broken piggy bank on Jason's desk, its pieces left scattered over the wooden top as if he'd been distracted by something else. It had been almost full, after she made him return the money to it, yet there was no sign of the money now.

She told herself to stay calm, that there was probably an innocent explanation. He'd probably forsaken the go-cart he'd been saving for, and decided to buy a pair of skates or a new fishing pole, instead. The fact that he'd done it without consulting her, thus breaking a major rule in their household, didn't mean anything. He was a child, after all, and had probably forgotten.

Still, she went looking for him, and found him in the woods on his way back from the lake, carrying the string of fish he'd caught, and talking to himself as he went. He was alone, a fact that relieved her somewhat, though she was sure she'd seen Logan's car parked nearby earlier.

"Jason!" she called.

He spotted her and, smiling, picked up his step until he was running toward her. "Mom, we caught fifteen, but Logan threw all his back. I kept six of mine."

"I need to talk to you," she said. "In the house."

He noted her tone immediately, and looked up at her with saucer-shaped eyes. "What's wrong?"

"Come on, Jason. In the house."

"Is it about Logan?" he asked, walking as fast as he could to keep up with her as she headed back to the house. "You said we could fish together. Don't you remember?"

"I remember," she said, almost feeling sorry for him. She opened the screen door and held it for him as he went in. "Put the fish in the sink. You can clean them later."

He did as she said, then washed his hands, and turned back to her. "What is it, Mom?"

"Jason," she said, pulling out a chair and sitting down, so she could face him eye to eye. "I want to ask you something, and I want you to tell me the truth. Where's the money that was in your piggy bank?"

He immediately glanced away. "I'm sorry I broke it, Mom, but it was taking so long to shake it out, that I finally just whacked it. I know I was supposed to ask you."

"Jason, where is it?"

"Well, I decided I didn't need a go-cart. There are more important things."

Some overwhelming feeling of injustice washed over her, and she felt her heart tightening. "What things?"

"Well, you know how you're always teaching me to save. Some things are just like saving . . . only they make you more money later."

She knew then where the money was, and why he was trying so hard to evade her. Closing her eyes, she whispered, "Jason, did you give that money to Logan?"

He was silent for too long, and when she finally opened her eyes, she saw him staring stubbornly at her.

"Jason, I asked you a question. Did you give that money to Logan?"

"Yes," he said through tight lips. "And the money I had under my mattress, too. Last year's birthday money and my Christmas money, too. But so did all the other kids at school. We raised three hundred dollars. We're gonna be rich, Mom!"

Instantly, she shot to her feet, almost knocking over the chair. "And he took it? He actually took the money from little children?"

"Well, why wouldn't he? We want to be partners, too. We're gonna be VIPs, Mom."

"No, you're not!" she shouted, her face reddening. "You're not going to be anything, because I'm getting your money back tonight! And if he won't give it to me, I'll press charges and have him thrown in jail!"

"No, Mom! You can't do that! I want him to have it! All the kids want him to!"

"How much of it was yours, Jason? Exactly how much?"

"Seventy-six dollars," he said. "But I don't want it back. If you get it, I'll find a way to give it back to him. It's not your money. It's mine!"

Carny was livid. "Go to your room! Now!"

"I hate you!" Jason screamed. "If you go to Logan, I'll never forgive you! I'll hate you for the rest of my life!"

Taking his arm, she dragged him to his bedroom, forced him through the door, then set him down on the bed. "Now you stay here until I tell you to come out," she shouted, "and while you're in here, you can clean up that broken bank!"

"It's *my* money!" he screamed as she slammed the door behind her.

Carny collapsed against the closed door, and before she could control it, tears assaulted her, and she covered her mouth as the sobs rose to her throat. Damn him! Logan Brisco was not only destroying her child's innocence, but he was causing a huge rift in her relationship with Jason. A rift that hadn't been there before.

Logan had to be stopped.

Pulling herself together, she ran to the phone, and called her in-laws. They answered on the third ring.

"Hello?"

"Bev, I need you. Can you come over for a little while and watch Jason while I go out?"

Betsy hesitated. "Carny, are you crying, honey?"

"Can you come or not? It's urgent, Bev."

"Yes, of course. We'll be right over. Are you all right?"

"I will be," she said, her voice quavering. "Please . . . just hurry."

She hung up the phone, then sat down at the kitchen table, and covered her face with her hands. Jason had never in his life told her he hated her. Their conflicts had been few and far between, and the ones they'd had were minor. The words cut her more deeply than she would have ever predicted, and that she'd been made into the bad guy made her furious. But it wouldn't stop her from going to Logan and getting Jason's money back.

How could he take money from the kids? The idea made her sob even harder, for she had just begun to trust him enough to let him alone with her son. That was her own stupidity, and she supposed that she deserved as many lessons as the rest of the town was going to get from Logan. But Jason didn't.

She heard the car drive up in the driveway, and she got up and met her in-laws at the door. "Jason's in his room," she said. "He's grounded, so don't let him out."

"Carny, what's happened?" J. R. asked, taking her by the shoulders. "I've never seen you like this."

Carny realized that, even when Abe had abandoned her, she had never let her in-laws see her cry. "Jason gave Logan all his money, J. R. Seventy-six dollars, and Logan took it. I know you think he's legit, but a man with any integrity would not take money from babies! I'm going to get it back, and Jason doesn't like it."

Bev looked at J. R., and finally, he nodded. "Whatever you need to do, Carny. Logan shouldn't have taken it without your permission."

"And he knew how I felt about it," she said. "He knew!"

Wiping her eyes, she grabbed her keys. "Let me just tell him you're here, and then I'll go."

She went back to Jason's door and flung it open. "Jason, your grandparents . . . "

Her voice dropped as she realized her son was gone. The window was open, and the curtains flapped in the breeze.

"Jason!" By then, her in-laws were right behind her and, in a mad panic, she pushed past them and rushed back through the house for the door. "Jason!" she screamed. "Jason, you get back in here right now!"

When there was no answer, she ran across the lot separating her from the Trents and banged on the door.

Janice answered it right away. "Carny, what's wrong?"

"Where's Jason?" she asked breathlessly. "Is he over here?"

"Well, no," she said. "Nathan had a lot of homework, so he hasn't been playing today. We haven't seen Jason since they got off the bus."

"Are you sure?" Carny asked. "You wouldn't hide him from me, would you?"

Janice gaped at her. "Carny, you know I wouldn't!"

"I've got to find him. He can't have gone very far." Helplessly, she started running blindly into the woods behind the house, and Janice followed her a few feet. "Carny, don't go back in there. It's dark! He wouldn't go there after dark!"

Still, Carny ran as fast as she could through the brush, between trees, calling as she ran, until she reached the lake. "Jason! Jason, please come home. It's not safe for you to be out here when it's dark. We can talk about this!"

The silence of the water threatened her, and she listened for the sound of a crackling leaf, a breaking limb. All she heard was an occasional cricket, or the rumble of a bullfrog. "Jason, please!" Two flashlights came from out of the woods from the house, and she saw they were being carried by David Trent and J. R.

"We looked in our storage room and in the tent in the backyard, Carny," David said. "He's not there."

"And we searched the house," J. R. told her, coming up behind David. "Carny, where do you think he is? He's just a baby!"

"I don't know," she said, "but keep looking around the lake. I'm calling the police! And then I'm going to see Logan Brisco."

Logan checked his watch and decided it was too late for UPS, but he still had time to get his boxed equipment to Federal Express before they closed.

Setting his bag on the middle of the bed, he dialed the closest airport, which was an hour away in Odessa, to get departure times. There was a flight around midnight, and he booked it.

The knock sounding on his door was unexpected, and for a moment, he sat still, unwilling to answer it.

But the knock continued, incessantly, and finally, he cracked the door open just enough to see Carny, without allowing her to see into the room.

Her face was alive with fury, and her eyes were red. "Where's Jason?" she demanded.

"Jason?" he repeated, puzzled. "Didn't he come home?"

"Of course he came home!" she said through clenched teeth. "And then he left again. Where is he, Brisco?"

"Carny, I don't know!"

With more force than he would have expected from her, she shoved him back from the door and pushed her way inside. "Jason?"

"He's not here!" he said, trying to block her way so she wouldn't see the bags on the bed.

But it was too late. She stopped, stunned, and looked from the bed, to Logan, and back again. "Going somewhere?" she asked as fresh tears filled her eyes.

"Yes . . . no! Carny, why are you looking for Jason? What's wrong?"

"You!" Grabbing his bag with both hands, she flung it off the bed. "You're what's wrong! You took money from my baby, turned him against me, and now he's gone . . . and you . . . you're getting ready to leave, aren't you? Just like I said! Only I didn't want it to be true!"

Logan took her by the shoulders and turned her around. "What do you mean, he's gone? Where did he go?"

"He ran away, you scumbag!" She shook his hands off. "Who knows where he'll go, because he doesn't have any money! He gave it all to you! And it's dark, and he's so little!" Her voice broke, and she lost herself to uncontrollable sobs, a sight that Logan was quite sure few people had ever witnessed.

"I wasn't going to keep the money, Carny," he said softly. "You've got to believe me." He went to his coat lying over the bag, and fished out the fat envelope with Jason's name on it. "It's all there, Carny. Every cent the kids gave me."

Wiping away her angry tears, she looked up at him. "And what about the adults, Brisco? Are you giving theirs back, too?"

He turned away, and knew that she saw right through him, to all the dark, ugly places that had never seemed dark or ugly before.

"No, I didn't think so," she said. "God, I hoped I was wrong about you. You had so much potential." Catching another sob, she headed back to the door.

"Carny, wait!"

"I can't. I have to find my son!" she cried.

The door slammed in her wake, and Logan stood there for a moment, reeling from the impact of her words, from the feeling that had come over him when she'd told him he'd had potential. She had wanted to trust him, that woman who'd seen so many reasons not to trust. And he had just given her one more.

He turned to Jack, who sat up on a chair, whimpering slightly, as if asking if he was really as bad as she'd depicted him. And as he looked at the bed, where his whole life was packed neatly away in one bag, a briefcase, and a couple of boxes, he realized that he couldn't leave town.

Not yet.

Grabbing the keys to his rental car, he said, "Stay here, Jack. There's something I have to do."

Logan found Jason in the first place he looked. He was in his secret spot at the lake, a place Logan knew the boy had never been to at night, a place that seemed more ominous than peaceful with the moonlight playing through the trees and the shadows dancing beneath him.

At first, he saw only the soft mound on the fallen log, but when he got closer, he realized it was a sleeping bag, opened up and draped over the boy, not to keep the warmth in, for it was May and not very cold, but to keep out those things he feared the most. The things he hadn't counted on hurting him when he'd resolved to run away. But little boys never thought anything would hurt them, least of all the grown men they counted as their friends.

Logan stepped closer, and in a quiet voice said, "Jason?"

Startled, the boy looked out from under the

sleeping bag. "Oh, Logan," he said, catching his breath. "You scared me half to death."

"I'm sorry," he said, sitting down on the log next to him. "But you shouldn't be out here at night by yourself."

"I'm not going back."

Logan looked at the boy, staring off into the lake, his features stubborn and angry, but they still seemed so young. "Why not?"

"Because my mother treats me like a kid."

"Your mother happens to be worried sick about you. She came to me crying, Jason. Do you want to make your mother cry?"

Jason didn't answer for a moment, and finally, he asked, "What did she say?"

"She was looking for you. Everybody's looking for you. Jason, running away is no answer. Why don't we go back, and—"

"No!" he said. "If you came out here to talk me into that, then you can leave. I'm not scared to stay here by myself."

Logan sighed. "I know you're not. Look, what do you plan to do? Spend the night on this log? What about tomorrow? What will you eat?"

"I'll fish," he said. "I'll start a campfire and cook it myself, and live like Huck Finn, without anybody telling me what I can do with my money."

"Jason, your mother was right about the money. I never should have taken it from you. I gave it back. Your mother has it."

"See?" the boy said, shaking off the sleeping bag

and standing up to face him. "I knew she would do that! She's ruining everything!"

"She's trying to protect you, Jason."

"Well, I don't need protecting. I can make my own decisions."

For a moment, Logan stared quietly at the boy, knowing that nothing he said right now was really going to make any difference. "All right," he said finally. "I won't try to talk you into going back. But I hope that sleeping bag will fit two, because I'm staying here with you."

Jason gaped at him. "What?"

"You heard me. I'm not making you go back, but I won't leave you here, either."

"What about Jack? You gonna leave him alone all night?"

"He'll be all right."

Jason didn't quite know what to say. "Yeah, well, you can stay tonight, but tomorrow, I'm taking off, and you can't come. I don't need anybody slowing me down."

Logan would have found his words amusing, but he remembered making the same decision himself over and over when he'd been trapped in foster families he hated. He hadn't really ventured out until he was fourteen, but in many ways he'd been as unprepared as this eight-year-old. "It's lonely out there, Jason."

"I don't care."

He patted the log, urging the boy to sit down, and finally, Jason did. Logan put his arm around him and pulled him against him. Weary from the battle, Jason laid his head against Logan's chest. "Jason, I know how you feel. I really do."

"No, you don't."

"Listen to me, Jase. Listen real close, because I'm gonna tell you a story, and I'm only gonna tell it once. It's not easy to tell, and I've never told it before. Are you man enough to keep it to yourself?"

"Sure I am," Jason said, looking up at him.

Logan hoped the boy couldn't see the mist in his eyes as he cleared his throat. "Once there was a little boy who lived with his mother, and she was the most wonderful person alive. He didn't know his father, but it didn't really matter, because his mother gave him so much love that nothing seemed to be missing."

Jason pulled back slightly and looked down, and Logan knew that he thought he was talking about him. "Did she keep him from making really important investments?"

Logan set a finger on the boy's lips, shushing him. "This little boy was only three, and money was the farthest thing from his mind. He liked to be read to, and he liked singing songs with her, and he loved bedtime, because that was when she tucked him in, and they cuddled while they said their prayers."

He hadn't expected the memories to be so painful, and he found his mouth going dry as he got the words out. Jason was quiet now, listening.

"The little boy stayed with a baby-sitter while his mother went to work, and every day she came just before suppertime and picked him up. But one day, she didn't come."

"Why not?" Jason whispered.

"The little boy didn't know. He waited and waited, and finally the baby-sitter fed him, and then she told him that he would be staying with her that night, that his mother wasn't going to make it."

Logan's voice wavered, and he stopped and waited for a moment, trying to rein in the emotions he had never voiced before. But the words had to come out. "He kept thinking that she'd be there soon, but the next day, she hadn't come. He waited and waited, sitting by the door most of the day, watching out the window, but his mother never came.

"Finally, a social worker came to the baby-sitter's house, and she took the little boy. She told him that his mother wouldn't be coming back for him, and that they were going to find him a new home."

"Why?" Jason asked.

"He didn't know. All he knew was that, when his mother came back for him, she wouldn't be able to find him. They put him in a home with people he didn't know, people who didn't have much patience with him, and he sat by the window most of the time, staring out, waiting for his mother to come. But do you know why she never came, Jason?"

Jason's eyes were moist as he considered that for a moment. "Because she didn't know where he was?"

"That's what the little boy thought," Logan said, taking a deep breath. "That little boy got real angry, and he threw a lot of fits, so the family he was with didn't want him anymore. They wound up moving him from one foster home to another. And year after year he waited for his mother to come get him. When he was eight years old, he was sitting in the social worker's office one day, waiting for her to assign him to a new home, when he saw his records and learned that his mother was dead, that she'd been in a car wreck when he was three. That was the worst day of his life."

Jason stared up at him, horrified. "Did anybody ever adopt him?"

"No one ever did," Logan said. "And all his life, all he wanted was to have a real family, where someone loved him, where he could count on people, where he was important. He didn't care if he got to make his own decisions, or if he got to spend his own money, and he didn't even care if it was a poor family. He just wanted to belong somewhere. But that never happened, so one day, when he was about fourteen, he decided he was old enough to be on his own, and he ran away."

"Just like me."

"Not exactly like you," Logan said. "He was running to something. He was looking for a place to belong. You already have a place to belong."

Jason considered that for a moment. "What happened to him? He was all right, wasn't he? On his own, I mean?"

"No, Jason, he wasn't. He was very lonely, and he had to do dishonest things to make a living. He lost whatever childhood he had left, and he never really found what he was looking for."

Enraptured with the story, Jason gazed up at Logan with sad eyes.

"Jason, do you know what that little boy's name was?"

He shook his head.

"It was Logan Brisco. That little boy was me."

Jason caught his breath, and stared at Logan with a new reverence. "Really?"

Logan swallowed the emotion in his voice. "Yeah, really. And you know what? If I'd had one person who loved me like your mom loves you, my whole life would have turned out differently."

As he held the little boy's gaze, he saw the tears forming in Jason's eyes. When they dropped over his lashes, Logan pulled him against him and held him while he cried, without saying a word.

After a moment, Jason looked up at him. "Logan, I want to go home."

# 13

*Carny's face, when she ran* to embrace Jason, brought back a fantasy that Logan had had all his life. It was of someone—anyone—running to him with that look of pure love and unconditional belonging. It was to see the tears that spoke of terrible fear and concern over him.

Trying to restrain his emotion, he watched as she clung frantically to the boy, tears streaming down her face. Then, pulling back, she made a lame attempt to look angry. "Jason, I could kill you for pulling such a stunt. Don't you ever do that again!"

"I'm sorry, Mom."

She crushed him back against her and held him tighter. "Where were you?"

Jason couldn't seem to answer, so Logan stepped in. "He was at his secret place at the lake."

"I looked at the lake, Jason! And Grandpa and David—didn't you hear us calling?"

"Yeah, I heard," Jason said. "But I didn't want you to find me."

She wiped her eyes and stood up, looking down at him. "Jason, I love you. Don't you know that?"

"Yeah, I know, Mom," he said weakly. "I love you, too."

"And you won't ever run away again, will you?"

"No, I promise."

She looked around at Nathan's parents and her in-laws. "You hear that, everybody? He promised."

Laughing with relief, the Trents said good night, and the Sullivans herded the weary child to his room to get ready for bed.

Carny watched until he was out of sight, then turned back to Logan. "Thank you," she whispered.

He swallowed. "Don't mention it."

Their eyes locked for a long moment, and finally, he said, "I'm sorry I caused all this trouble."

She gave a mirthless laugh. "I honestly thought you'd be halfway to Mexico by now."

He didn't know what to say, for there was nothing he could hide from her. "I'm not going anywhere, Carny."

"I saw the suitcase, Brisco."

"That doesn't mean anything." He was quiet for a moment, thinking of all the things he wanted to say. But chances were, she wouldn't believe any of them. Finally, he said, "You'd better get to bed,

Carny. We have an early lesson tomorrow. I think I'll be able to take off with no problem, but I need some special care in learning how to land."

Understanding flickered in her eyes, and she whispered, "I'm not sure you're ready, Brisco."

"You know, Carny, sometimes it's just easier to glide. But sooner or later, a man has to come down. I just need help learning how."

Carny didn't say another word as she watched Logan walk back to his rented car, which was parked down the street near the trees beside Nathan's house. As he drove away, he wondered if she even believed that he'd still be in town tomorrow morning.

When he reached the motel Jack greeted him at the door, glad to see him, and Logan realized that the dog had finally stopped waiting for Slade. He depended on Logan now. In some small way, that was a victory to him. There *was* someone who cared whether he ever saw him again. There was someone who needed him. Even if it was a dog.

Squatting, Logan petted the animal, and Jack licked his face. "Did you miss me, boy? I don't think anybody has ever missed me before." Standing up, he opened the door again. "You need to go out? Come on, I'll take you."

Together, they walked down the stairs and across the parking lot, to the cluster of trees where Jack had been doing his business. As the dog sniffed around for the perfect place, Logan talked quietly.

"Jack, if a guy was going to make good on a promise, and do something he'd never really intended to do, where would he start?"

The dog gave him a sidelong glance, then kept sniffing the trees. "I mean, where would you start?"

No answer came to him, and he felt the weight of Serenity on his chest, blocking his breathing. Maybe it was stupid. Maybe it was too farfetched, to think that he could actually build the park and stay here in Serenity.

When Jack had finished, they went back in, and the dog sat on the bed and watched him as he unpacked his bags. "I have to approach it like a con," he said. "Look at all the possibilities, as farfetched as they may be. I've done impossible things before, and I've persuaded people to do outrageous things. Why couldn't I convince the bankers?"

As he talked, the ideas began to whirl through his head. He *could* do it, if he just planned it out carefully enough. It didn't matter that he had lied about other investors, or that he'd never even tried to communicate with Billy Ray Cyrus, or that he didn't even know who owned the land he was proposing to build it on. He could find a way to make good on those claims after the fact. He could do it now.

Ideas teemed through his mind as the night grew older, but Logan stayed up, making his plans, checking his facts. And as dawn brought the first rays of sunshine through his window, he felt better than he remembered feeling in a long time.

The challenge breathed new life into him, and he was ready to pull the biggest con of his life. The one that wasn't a con at all.

Carny was almost surprised to see Logan when he pulled up at the hangar the next morning, for even though he had helped her find Jason, and they'd had that quiet, vulnerable moment last night, she had convinced herself that he had disappeared in the dead of night.

Yet here he was, with Jack at his heels, ready to take a lesson as if it were any other day in Serenity.

"How's Jason this morning?" Logan asked her when he entered the office.

She smiled. "Fine. I was going to keep him home from school, since he didn't get a lot of sleep last night, but he wanted to go."

"Good," he said. "I'm glad he's okay."

It was only then that she noticed he was holding something behind his back. "What's that? What are you hiding?"

With a rueful grin, he brought the wrapped box around and handed it to her. "It's for you. I hope I got the right size."

"For me?" She looked almost distressed as she took it. "Logan, you shouldn't have gotten me . . . "

"No, it's really from Jason," he cut in. "Sort of. Open it, and I'll explain."

Slowly, she opened the gift, and pulled out the red dress that had been on the mannequin in the window of Miss Mabel's Boutique for the past two weeks. She had noticed it, but she would never have bought it for herself. It was too expensive, for one thing, and too revealing, and would call too much attention to her—something that made her uncomfortable. Still, she tried to smile. "It's . . . beautiful. But . . . how could it be from Jason?"

Logan leaned against her desk, smiling. "Yesterday when Jason gave me the money, he started talking about what he would do with his earnings. He said the first thing he'd buy was that dress in Miss Mabel's window, so that you could wear it and find a husband."

Carny caught her breath. "What?"

Logan couldn't help laughing. "Yep. That's what he said. He wanted you to look nice so you could find a husband."

Dropping the dress back into the box, she tried to fight her smile. "I hope you told him that I'm not in the market for a husband."

"I told him I had that feeling," Logan assured her. "But he said it didn't matter, that the dress would make husband-candidates find you."

She moaned and dropped into her chair. "That child."

"It was sweet," Logan said, leaning one hip on her desk. "And this morning I thought it was kind of sad that Jason wasn't going to earn that money now. I hated to think of you going through the rest of your life without finding a husband, so I thought I'd go ahead and get it as soon as they opened."

Twisting her lips to keep from laughing, Carny threw the dress at him and hit him in the face.

"Hey, now!" Laughing, Logan caught the dress and shook it out. "It really is gorgeous, Carny. I think you should wear it."

"It's not me," she said. "But thanks anyway. You can take it back, now."

"Oh, no," he said. "I insist that you keep it. Your son has excellent taste, even if his motives are a little questionable."

She took the dress back and sighed. "Where on earth would I wear this?"

His smile faded, and his voice was more serious as he said, "I guess someone will just have to take you out someplace fancy."

"I'm not the fancy type."

"Oh, but I think you are," he said. "There's a beautiful French restaurant in Houston, and it would do that dress justice."

"Well, Houston's a long way from here."

"Not by plane."

She laughed. "Right. We're supposed to hop in the plane and jaunt down to Houston for one dinner? I don't think so."

"The woman who drives a Harley can't be spontaneous enough to do that?"

She regarded him soberly. "The truth, Brisco, is that I used to do things like that all the time. But I've settled down. I have Jason to think of and a business to run. . . . "

"What if it coincided with business?" he asked.

She smiled at his persistence. "How could it?"

"Easy. I hire you to fly me to Houston, and then Dallas, and later to Austin, where I have to meet with some of the bankers who will be my bigger investors in the park. While we're there, I take you to dinner . . . in that red dress."

Something about the easy way he mentioned his investors took the amusement out of the moment. Quietly she folded the dress and laid it back in the box. "Come on, Logan. We both know there aren't any investors. And I'm not interested in flying your getaway plane."

"Getaway plane?" he asked, throwing his hand over his heart. "I'm hurt. Carny, you'll know my every move. We'll get adjoining hotel rooms if you want. And I'll have to leave Jack with somebody. He can stay with you, sort of as collateral."

She hesitated, wanting to believe him. "Logan, are you forgetting that I saw the packed suitcases last night?"

"Carny, you never gave me the chance to explain."

"Explain what? You were on your way out of town."

"Yes, but why? Carny, it was this trip I was going to take, but I was planning to go by car. Your reaction made me realize what people might think if I just disappeared like that. So I'll keep my room here, leave all my stuff, and one of Serenity's most upstanding citizens will fly me wherever I need to go and keep an eye on me while I'm there."

For a moment, she only stared at him, wondering if he could, indeed, be trusted.

"Come on, Carny. I have to meet with these people. It's very important. I'm offering you the chance to make sure I don't run out with the money."

"All right," she said, finally. "I'll do it. But it's going to cost you."

"I never doubted that for a moment."

"When do we leave?"

"I was thinking about Monday. That should give us time to get all our ducks in a row. And we won't have to miss the church picnic Saturday."

"Okay," she said. "I'll make sure that time is free."

"And don't forget the dress," he said.

She held his gaze for a second longer than she should have. "Thanks, Brisco. For the dress, and for Jason . . ."

Logan shrugged. Their eyes locked for an eternal moment, eloquent with words that couldn't be spoken.

"I guess we should go out to the plane now. You wanted me to teach you how to land, didn't you?"

Logan only smiled and followed her out.

The sheriff's office was a slow-moving, quiet place where a handful of men in uniform sat with their feet up on their desks, reading the paper, talking on the phone, and waiting for a call to come in so they'd have something to do. Carny saw Joey sitting at his desk in the corner, intent on a *Newsweek* article he was reading.

"Hey, Joey," she said, startling him.

Instantly, he got to his feet. "Carny. I thought you weren't coming until later."

"You got me so curious on the phone," she said. "I had to come on over."

"Yeah, well, we got the FBI file back on that fellow." He set the magazine down and reached for the folder at the corner of his desk.

"Montague Shelton," she said. "Was there any mention of Logan?"

"None." He sat back down and flipped through the file. "But there was something interesting. Several accounts say that Shelton always traveled with a companion. Some said it was a teenaged boy, but others claimed he was a man in his late twenties, who went by the name of Mark Sanders, Larry Bird, or Skip Parker. And listen to this."

Carny leaned forward, reading over his shoulder. "One of their victims, a wealthy lady who gave them ten thousand dollars to invest in a real-estate venture, described the younger man as having 'a charming, friendly grin, rather nice looking, brown hair, blue eyes, and a demeanor that made you trust him instantly.'" Joey looked up at her. "Sounds like she still liked him, even after he suckered her. Does that sound like anyone we know?"

Carny studied the report, frowning. "It could describe any number of people."

Joey looked surprised. "Carny, it sounds just like Logan. The smile, the eyes, the hair . . . the fast-talking. And his age . . ."

"Teenaged to late twenties? Come on, Joey. It could be two different people." She flipped through the pages in the file, and stopped at a page full of pictures. Most had been taken by video cameras at banks and automated teller machines, but there was no way to identify either of the men, for they were obviously wearing disguises. "How long ago was all this?"

"At least fifteen years," Joey said. "When Shelton died, they must have closed the file."

"And they never looked for the other guy?"

"They didn't have any leads on him. He was slippery." He pulled out another file and opened it. "I got them to send me everything they had on all three aliases, and there honestly isn't much here. After Shelton died, they seem to have lost his trail. Either he's operating under a different name everywhere he goes, or wearing disguises, or he's given up that life altogether."

"Or he's just real good at what he does and never gets caught," she whispered.

But that wasn't what she wanted to believe anymore. She thought about the things Logan had told her the other night, when she had confronted him about Montague. What if he had been telling the truth, and his con-artist history had died with Montague Shelton? What if he'd been on the level ever since?

"Carny, I'm thinking about sending a picture of Logan to the FBI, so they can check with other scam victims to see if they can identify him."

"No," Carny said quickly. "I don't think that would be right."

He looked at her as if she were crazy. "Why?

You're not defending him, are you? You're the one who was suspicious."

"No, Joey. It's just that . . . I'm having my doubts now. And I'd hate to start some big FBI investigation about an innocent man. It might blow the whole deal with the park."

"I thought you didn't believe the deal was really going to happen. What's changed, Carny?"

She sighed. "Last night, it was Logan who brought Jason home. I was scared to death, Joey. And Logan didn't have to look for him, but he did. The dog confuses me a little, too. Why would a con man take on the responsibility of a dog? It doesn't make sense. And then there's the trip he's scheduled for next week. He has meetings with his big investors in Houston. . . . "

"You're falling for him, aren't you?"

Carny gasped. "No! Of course not! How could you even suggest that?"

"If he's a swindler, Carny, then he's a good one. And if he can make you believe in him, then he can fool anyone."

"Maybe he's not fooling, Joey. Maybe this is all for real."

"Do you really think so?"

She paused for a long moment, trying to decide. Finally, she gave in. "No, not really. Go ahead and send the picture in, Joey. I guess it couldn't hurt too much to find out."

"All right," Joey said, pleased. "Now all I have to do is get one. That shouldn't be too hard. Is he going to the church picnic Saturday?"

"Yes," she said. "He mentioned it this morning."

"Then I'll take a camera."

As Carny left the station, a sense of dread washed over her. It suddenly occurred to her that she was beginning not to want to know who Logan Brisco really was. For she liked the illusion he was beginning to paint for her. The one where he was just a nice guy, with a big idea, and a talent for persuasion. The one where he was someone she could allow herself to care for.

Jason seemed pensive that night at supper. Worried that he was still angry at her, Carny took his hand and made him look at her. "What's wrong, Jase? Let's talk."

He shrugged. "Nothing. I was just thinking about Logan. It's sad about his mom."

"What about her?"

"Well, he told me all about her. He said he loved her. And she died when he was three. Mom, no one told him, and for all those years, he just waited and waited for her to come get him. He didn't know what had happened to her." Carny didn't like the uncomfortably sympathetic feeling grabbing hold of her. "That is sad."

"He only found out she was dead when he saw it in his file. Did you know he grew up in foster homes?"

"Yeah," she said. "I heard something about that."

"Mom? I think Logan's lonely, don't you? Oh,

he's real friendly and all, and makes friends real easy, but I think deep down he's real lonely."

"That's why he took Jack."

"Huh? What do you mean?"

She looked at her son. "Well, I just wouldn't have predicted that he'd do that. He travels a lot, you know, and a dog will make it harder. But he had some kind of bond with him. Maybe it was abandonment."

"I don't get it."

She smiled softly and patted her son's hand. "It doesn't matter. You're sweet to worry about Logan. I'm sure he appreciates it."

"Mom, he wouldn't have given me back mine and the other kids' money if he was a crook. He would have kept it."

"Maybe so," she said softly.

That night, Carny E-mailed Ruth again on her computer, knowing she always checked her messages when she came back to her trailer after working, and told her she needed to talk to her. Ruth called her just after midnight, when the carnival had closed.

"You okay, baby?"

"I'm fine," Carny said. "Just a few weird things have been happening around here."

"Weird things? Like what?"

"Like Jason running away."

"Jason ran away?"

She heard a fumbling and her mother got on the

line. "Honey, have you called the police? Have you called all his friends?"

Her father snatched the phone then, and said, "Was there a ransom note, Carny? If there was—"

"No, no!" she shouted, cutting him off. "Pop, we found him. He came home."

"Oh. Just like that, huh?"

"Well, he was kind of talked into it. As a matter of fact, the guy who did it is the same guy I was asking you about."

"The scam artist?"

"Yeah. Only I'm not sure he is one. Anyway, how are things with you?"

"They're great. We have some good news for you."

Fumbling again, and then Carny's mother was on the line. "Honey, wait 'til we tell you. You won't believe it!"

"What?"

"We made a huge score last week. Your father's a genius. Course we had to leave Arizona real fast."

"Where are you now?"

"Durango," Lila said. "Anyway, it looks like your father and I might be able to retire by the end of the year. And guess where we want to settle down!"

Her heart plummeted. "Where?"

"Serenity! Won't that be a hoot? All of us together again? Cooking up God knows what! And I'll get to see that little grandbaby of ours whenever I want! And we can set up some of our flat stores in that amusement park there."

Carny tried to tell herself that this could be just another of her parents' whims. Her father took the phone again, and closing her eyes, she wished Ruth had never surrendered it.

"Honey, what's the progress on the park? I think we need to be in on the planning stages, if we're going to get involved."

"Mama, Pop, it could be years before the park is built, if ever. Besides, you'd hate it in Serenity. It's boring and dull and nothing ever happens. All we do is work and go to church. I'm telling you, you wouldn't last a month."

"Well, if it's so boring, why do you live there? Our Carny wouldn't settle for a life of humdrum. Nosirree. If it can satisfy you, it can satisfy us."

"Besides, I don't think they're planning the kind of rides and booths you have. They're sort of creating all new, original ideas. And there won't be any games or freak shows. And they're doing complete background checks before they'll hire anyone." She was lying, making it up as she went along, but she was desperate. "Mama, if you and Pop apply, they'll find out your history. Besides, they all know my background. They'd know yours the minute you introduced yourselves."

"Details," her mother said. "Your father will work that all out."

Her head was beginning to throb, and finally, she said, "Mama, I hear Jason coughing. I need to check on him. Can I talk to Ruth real quick first?"

"Sure honey. The days are going fast. Before you know it, we'll be right there in Serenity! Bye."

Carny let out a heavy sigh as Ruth came back to the line. "Carny?"

"You've got to talk them out of this, Ruth. They can't come here."

"I know."

"Really. They'd never fit in. I mean, I know the people here are innocent, and that Mama and Pop can just about convince anybody of anything, but they can't do it!"

Ruth hesitated for a moment. "Well, frankly, Carny, I was thinking about coming, too. At least for a while."

Carny sighed again. "Don't get me wrong, Ruth. I love you, and I'd love to have you here. I love Mama and Pop, too. If they weren't always looking for an easy mark . . . do you think they could ever change?"

"It would be about as easy as me dropping three hundred pounds."

"Do I need to worry? I mean, do you think it'll ever really happen, or is it just a whim?"

"Maybe, maybe not."

Carny wasn't satisfied. "Well, I'll just have to talk them out of it. Jeez, they should put a badge on me here. I feel like I'm single-handedly keeping Serenity clean."

That night, as she tried to sleep, she kept dreaming about Logan picking pockets at a huge amusement park with rides that looked like crude children's drawings, her parents selling chemotonic, guaranteed to fend off all types of cancer, as well as gout, gallstones, and toothaches, and Ruth sitting in all her glory while people paid to look at her.

One thing was certain. If all this came to pass, Serenity could never be accused of living up to its name again.

# 14

*Like the town dance,* the church picnic was another excuse for the people of Serenity to get together. Over the music of High Five, the sound of laughter and talking rippled across the air, along with varying scents of apple pie, grilled hamburgers, fried catfish, and a pig roasting in a barrel grill. Across the lawn, a group of people prepared for the three-legged race, while pony rides went on in the south side. On the east side of the church, someone had brought a crane, and a short bungee cord bounced from it, waiting for its first victim.

As Logan got out of his Mercedes and started across the lawn, with Jack beside him, he was confronted, again, with the odd feeling of familiarity and belonging. These were people who made him smile, people he enjoyed, people who welcomed him. "Hey, Logan!"

He saw Jason running toward him. "Will you run the three-legged race with me, please? Mom was going to, but they talked her into bungee jumping. They're about to start! Hurry!"

"Well . . ." Before he could protest, Jason grabbed his hand and dragged him toward the race, yelling for them to wait for him. And as they tied Jason's little leg against his, he looked over toward the crane, preferring to be there, instead. He might have known Carny would be the first one to jump, he thought with a chuckle. You could take the woman out of the wild, but you could never take the wild out of the woman. Something about that pleased him.

The whistle blew, and before he was ready, Jason took off running, pulling him with him.

"Whoa, hold on!" Logan shouted. "We have to do this together."

"Hurry, Logan! Nathan and his dad are getting ahead of us."

Logan eyed David and Nathan just ahead of them. "Okay. Left, right, left, right . . . good. Come on, we can do it." When they had their legs moving together, he shouted to David, "What's the matter, old man? Can't you go any faster than that?"

"Come on, Nathan!" David shouted. "Let's make 'em eat our dust!"

The competition went into new gear as they left all the others behind. Neck and neck with Logan and Jason, the Trents battled to get ahead.

Logan and Jason put everything they had into the final stretch of the race and made it over the finish line a nose ahead of the Trents. Whooping like a kid, Logan hopped around with Jason. But they had stopped too soon, and suddenly the rest of the racers were stampeding them.

Logan tried to run left, and Jason tried to run right, and within seconds they were on the ground, laughing and trying to break free as the others fell on top of them.

Everyone around them seemed to be drowning in laughter as Logan finally untied them and got to his feet.

"Way to go, Logan!"

"That was great, Logan! You've found your calling!"

Logan ruffled Jason's hair, glad he'd had a part in putting that pride on his face.

Carny hadn't jumped yet when Logan made his way over to the crane and pushed through the crowd forming at the bottom. It was a long way up to the platform where they tied her to the cord, and his stomach flipped at the thought of her falling that far.

"She's crazy," Lahoma muttered.

"I hope they hook her up right."

"Can't we stop this before someone gets killed?"

"She'll be all right," Logan said. "Carny's tough."

The crowd grew deathly quiet, except for the music and laughter on the other side of the church, as Carny stepped to the edge of the platform. "Are you guys ready?" she shouted down, without a hint of the fear in her voice.

A chorus of discouragement was the crowd's reply, but Carny only laughed. Then, counting to three in a loud voice, she hurled herself headfirst off the side of the platform and fell seventy-five feet, bounced back fifty, and yo-yoed back and forth, hanging from her feet, for what seemed forever.

When she finally stopped bouncing, Logan reached her before anybody else could. Bending over, so he'd be upside down with her, he asked, "How was it?"

"Fantastic!" she said, breathless. "Now get me down so I can do it again."

He hesitated. "I don't know, Carny. Something about being tied up by your feet and hung upside down becomes you. It makes you seem more . . . vulnerable. Puts color in your face, too. I think I like it."

"Brisco, let me down!"

"Not until you agree to let me go with you on the next jump."

"You mean, you and me together?" she asked, her face turning even more crimson.

"Yep. Right now."

She flashed him a wicked grin. "Okay, Brisco. You're on."

Grabbing her around the hips with one arm, he unhooked her feet with the other and flipped her down to the ground.

Like an acrobat at the end of a glorious stunt, Carny raised her arms, inviting applause. "You should all try it. It was such a rush! Come on, Lahoma! Brother Tommy, you can do it!"

Lahoma backed away, and Brother Tommy only laughed. "I'll wait until God intends for me to fly."

"Oh, you coward," she teased. "It's a piece of cake. Like stepping off a curb."

Jason ran forward and shouted, "I will, Mommy! I'll go!"

The crowd laughed. "Sorry, Jason. Not until you're a little older. You have to be eighteen."

"Aw, I never get to have any fun."

"I know," she said. "You're such a deprived child. But you're still staying here." Turning to Logan, she smiled her biggest smile. "So are you ready, Brisco?"

"You bet I am." He bowed and swept a hand to the ladder. "After you, m'lady."

Flushed with the excitement, Carny started climbing the ladder.

"Have you done this before?" he asked her as he came up behind her.

She looked down at him. "No, but I've ridden plenty of roller coasters. I loved them. I loved the feeling of being completely out of control, staring danger right in the face, unable to do anything but ride it out."

"I would have guessed that about you."

She laughed. "It's not hard, Brisco. It doesn't take a psychoanalyst."

"But you live such a quiet, risk-free life. I mean, except for the planes and the motorcycle."

"Balance, Brisco. That's the key. I have balance. Now let's go look death in the face and spit at it! Whoa!"

Logan laughed, but as he got to the top of the ladder and peered down, he realized this wasn't really that funny. "Uh . . . maybe it would be better if we went separately, instead of together. You can go first."

"Not a chance, Brisco!" she said. "A deal's a deal."

"Yeah, but it was supposed to scare *you,* not *me!*"

Carny laughed. "Don't let it scare you. Just completely get rid of the thoughts that it's eighty-five feet to the ground, and that if something goes wrong and the cord snaps or comes unhooked, you'll die at the moment of impact. Unless, of course, you land in just the right way, and then you might live long enough to have a few minutes of the worst suffering of your life. Just think about how much fun it is!"

"Gee, Carny, you're just full of comforting thoughts, aren't you?"

"Actually, it's real safe, Brisco. I checked out everything carefully before I jumped."

"Right," he said, feeling a little sick. "And you're an expert. You'd know if something was going to snap."

"I'd feel it in my gut," she said. "And I don't feel it about me. You, on the other hand . . . Nah, it's probably safe."

He shot her a somber look, and laughing with delight, she said, "I'm kidding. Are you coming or not?"

"Yeah," he said. "Let's do it."

They put on a harness that strapped them together, back to back, then the crew hooked them to the bungee cord. As they stood at the edge of the platform, preparing to jump, Logan tried not to look down.

"How did you talk me into this?"

"You talked *me* into it," she said. "Now, at the count of five . . ."

"Five, hell," he said, taking her hand. "We're going now!"

And before Carny could prepare herself, Logan had jumped, pulling her with him.

She screamed all the way down, and when they reached the bottom, he began to laugh hysterically as they bounced back up. For several moments they bounced and bobbed, laughing like children.

When they finally stopped bobbing, Carny said over her shoulder, "That was better than sex, wasn't it?"

He grinned. "Actually, no. But it was darn close."

A crew member came to let them down, and from the crowd, he heard someone shout, "Hey, Logan!"

He glanced up and saw Joey standing with a camera, about to aim it.

Quickly, he spun around, putting his back to the camera.

"Hey," Joey said. "You messed up my picture. Turn around."

The crew member let Logan out, and he hit the ground running. "Wait. Jason's calling me. Catch me later."

Carny's laughter died a sudden death as she watched him disappear. Shooting Joey a look, she said, "I think I heard Jason, too. Try him again in a minute."

"I will," Joey said, lowering his voice. "Try to hem him in when you eat. I'll get him then."

But Logan kept close watch on Joey and his camera for the rest of the day and managed to avoid him. When the pressure seemed to get too intense, and he worried that he couldn't avoid the camera any longer, he decided to slip away from the picnic, unnoticed.

The hell of it was, he wasn't ready to go, and as he and Jack went back to the musky-smelling room at the motel, he realized how soul-tired he was of running. But he'd come this far, and he planned to do one of the first legitimate things in his life. He'd already deposited enough money into his account to cover the bad checks he'd written when they finally managed to route their way to the Serenity bank. He'd been on the phone all week making appointments in Houston for next week. If he didn't have big investors now, he'd certainly have them by the time he came back. That is, if someone like Joey Malone didn't get the Feds on his trail before he had the chance to try.

\* \* \*

Clyde Keppler's hot-air balloon floated over their heads as they ate, but instead of looking up, Carny kept scanning the crowd looking for Logan. Where had he gone? One minute, he'd been standing in a cluster of people, campaigning about the park, like a politician who reveled in the chance to get so many constituents together in one place, and the next minute he was gone.

"Mom, did you see Logan leave?" Jason asked her.

She looked down at her son and with her thumb dabbed the barbecue sauce smeared across his face. "No. Did he leave?"

"I guess so. I haven't seen him in a while."

"Why would he?" she asked, frowning. "He was having a good time."

"I think he didn't want his picture took," Jason said. "Mr. Joey kinda made him mad."

"So he just left?"

"I guess," he said with a shrug. "I don't know why. He's a good-lookin' man. I'd like to have a picture of him."

"Then I'll get you one," she said with greater resolve than she'd had before. "Next week when I fly him to Houston, I'll get a picture of him then."

"Are you gonna wear the red dress?" Jason asked, lifting his brows.

"I might," she said. "If I go someplace nice enough to wear it."

"Oh, you will," Jason said. "Logan's gonna take you someplace real nice. He said he hoped you had some dancing shoes."

Carny tried not to smile. "Yes, well, Logan says lots of things."

"He means them all," Jason said, biting into his pork again. "You'll see."

The air was thick with tension as Carny and Logan took off Monday morning for Houston. Logan seemed preoccupied and pensive, and Carny couldn't help wondering if this trip was proof of his legitimacy or just another con to get him out of town quickly.

While he loaded his bag into the back of the plane, Carny had peeked into the appointment book he'd brought with him and laid on the seat, and she saw that he did have appointments with bankers penciled in. Either he was really going to talk to them about the park, or he was going to rob several banks. Gloomily, she realized that the former would have surprised her more than the latter.

"So what's this trip all about?" she asked him when they'd reached their desired altitude and were cruising south.

"Just an update meeting for the investors and potential investors," he said. He pulled a calculator out of his pocket, and began recomputing numbers that were listed on a computer printout.

"Are you going to be seeing Billy Ray Cyrus?"

"Don't know, yet," he said. "We'll see."

Carny grew quiet as he worked, and she told herself she didn't believe for a minute that Billy

Ray Cyrus had anything to do with this "Achy Breaky Park." It was ludicrous. Yet . . .

Logan seemed so serious, so intent on his work, preparing for his meetings. He wouldn't get this uptight about a con, would he?

Trying to break the tension and still get some information out of him, she decided to make her own confession. "I talked to my folks the other day. They want to retire from the carnival and settle here in Serenity."

Logan looked up. "Is that good or bad?"

She sighed. "I'm ashamed to say it, but I think it's bad. Don't get me wrong. I love my parents. I really do. But I don't think they belong in Serenity."

"Because of their pasts?"

"No," she said, "because of their present. Their lifestyle isn't exactly conducive to small-town life. Besides, they want a piece of the park. They want to set up some booths and rides and run them."

"And you think that would be a bad idea?"

She hesitated. "Brisco, the only way this could work is if we can preserve the integrity and hometown sweetness of Serenity. As much as I love my parents, I don't think we can do that if they come here with their entourage of carnies and try to run the show."

"You're right," he said. "We'll have to be strict about who's involved in the park. In fact, we should probably have a park commissioner who regulates the activities there."

"Good idea."

He looked at her then, grinning. "Do I detect a

hint of faith in you? Are you starting to believe I'm not a liar?"

She sighed. "I don't know what I believe." She glanced over at him. "So what am I supposed to do while you're meeting with the bankers?"

"Stay in the cockpit and keep the plane running," he said with a wry grin.

She shot him a look. "I knew this was the getaway plane."

He laughed. "That was a joke, Carny. Actually, you can do whatever you want. Stay in your room with Jack, or go shopping, or go sightseeing, or you could even come with me."

The last line wasn't one she'd expected, and she looked at him again. "Really? Come with you?"

"Sure," he said. "Of course, you couldn't actually come into the meetings with me, since these are mostly old boys, and I'll have better luck with them if I'm alone. But you could wait in the waiting area, if you want. I did tell you you could keep an eye on me, after all."

Carny thought for a moment, then decided to call his bluff. "All right. I'll do it."

"Good," he said, and went back to studying his notes.

The fact that he didn't object, or try to find some way out of it, surprised her again. This was getting too confusing. How was she supposed to figure him out, if he kept acting normal? She'd based her whole perception of him on his being a swindler. If he wasn't one, then she didn't quite know how to feel about him.

She'd get her mind back on track with the camera, she thought. She'd try to take his picture, and he wouldn't let her. That would remind her that he was a crook. It would reinforce, yet again, what she already knew.

Somehow, she needed to hang on to that belief, for trusting him meant that she'd eventually have to deal with the feelings she'd been trying to deny—the feelings that had the potential to hurt her even more than his duplicity might have.

Logan got them adjoining suites at the Adams Mark Hotel in Houston, a luxury hotel that made Carny wonder who was paying for it—the big investors from the banks, or the small ones in Serenity. He told her to take an hour or so to relax while he made some phone calls. He would come to get her for lunch, and then they'd proceed to his first appointment.

The first call Logan made was to a limousine service, from which he ordered a chauffeured Rolls-Royce to pick up Carny and him at 2:00 P.M. to transport them to the first bank. It had worked for him before, when he'd opened accounts with bad checks, taken out loans under the guise of a wealthy New York businessman, and perpetrated more than a few cons of bankers. The first impression was the most important, and when the bankers saw him drive up in a chauffeured limo, and come in dressed like a Wall Street winner, they immediately got the idea that he was someone whose business they wanted. The rest was just a matter of persuasion.

He then set about to call all the bankers he'd made appointments with, confirming that they would see him, and reaffirming the fact that he was shopping for investors, but that he was choosy about who he went into partnership with. That, he hoped, would set the tone of urgency and of competition. Nothing made a banker want a client more than the possibility that he may not be able to have him.

After the phone calls, he sat still for a moment, staring at Jack, who looked a little queasy and tired after the flight. "That was nothing, boy," he said softly. "The real ride's about to start."

Could he really pull this off? Getting real investors would take all the talent he had as a con artist. That it was for a legitimate venture wouldn't matter. He'd have to con them, as much as he'd ever conned anyone, if he was, indeed, going to make them give him the amount of money he needed. He'd have to pit one bank against another, drop lots of names, and look uncommitted to whatever bank he was visiting at the time. And it would all be done in the name of the town of Serenity.

He'd done his homework, and he hoped it would pay off. He knew the age of every one of the bankers he had targeted, how long they'd been running that bank, what other banks they'd worked for, where they'd gone to school, whether they were married, their spouses' names, how many children they had, what big ventures they had funded. . . .

But he didn't plan to use any of that information today. The background was just so that he could read them more accurately, judge them, gauge them. It was only so he could determine what kind of pitch they would respond to.

He hoped Carny wouldn't throw a wrench in his plans. Even though he would make her wait in the lobby, one wrong move on her part could blow his whole cover. One wrong word and he wouldn't be able to make them give him the time of day.

When he stopped by her room to get her, he was pleasantly surprised at the way she had transformed herself. As if she realized the importance of the meetings, she had twisted her hair up and donned a little yellow suit that looked expensive enough to suit the bankers, though he suspected it had come from the sale rack at Miss Mabel's. The high heels she wore defined her shape and her height, and made her look not only sophisticated and sexy, but sassy, as well. She was the perfect match for a man who was supposed to be able to afford a chauffeured Rolls. And suddenly he felt completely at ease. It was all going to work out as fantastically as the scam would have, if he'd gone through with it.

"You look perfect," he said, closing her door behind him.

"You don't look so bad yourself." She reached into her bag for the camera she'd brought, and waited for him to blanch. "Smile and let me get a picture."

Surprising her, Logan grinned his sexiest grin and allowed her to flash three pictures right in a row. "Now, are you finished?" he asked. "We've got a lunch reservation."

She set the camera down, confused that he had allowed her to take the pictures. "Sure, I'm ready."

Bemused, she followed him out, locking the door behind her.

She hadn't expected to eat a five-course meal in the hotel's fanciest restaurant, but Logan's tastes were evidently more opulent than her own. Not certain whether it was his employers, or the citizens of Serenity, who financed this trip, Carny ordered only a salad and glass of iced tea.

"Aren't you hungrier than that?" he asked as she eyed the steak the waiter had brought him.

"Not hungry enough to pay what that costs."

He laughed. "What do you care? I'm paying for it."

"With what?" she asked. "My in-laws' money, or the Trents', or Brother Tommy's . . . ?"

He sighed. "You'll never give up, will you? For your information, one of the investors I'm talking to today happens to own this hotel. He's putting us up, and all the meals are on him, too. He'd be insulted if we didn't enjoy it."

Carny didn't waver. "I don't like taking handouts."

"Handouts?" Logan asked. "Carny, I'm going to make this man a fortune. This is peanuts."

"Still . . ."

He smiled at her for a moment, that charming, persuasive grin almost convincing her she was being silly. "You want me to order you something else?"

She smiled. "I'll wait until you finish, and then maybe order some dessert."

He let out a frustrated breath, then slid back his chair. "Well, then, if you'll excuse me for a minute, I'm going to find the men's room. Don't eat my lunch while I'm gone."

Smiling, she watched him walk out of the restaurant and wondered if the rest room had windows. Any minute now he was going to make an escape and leave her holding the bag.

Then she told herself she was being silly again. Logan wasn't going anywhere, except to the bank to talk to his investors. Maybe it was time she started ignoring her suspicious instincts and started believing him. After all, he *had* let her take his picture. He wouldn't have stood there and let her take it so easily, if he'd had something to hide. It would be too easy for the FBI to match it to descriptions by recent crime victims, if, indeed, there were any.

Sighing, she finished her salad, content that things might be on the level, after all.


Logan never went to the men's room. Instead, he rushed to the elevator, rode to the floor their rooms were on, and trotted up the hall. When he'd checked in, he had gotten the desk clerk to give him two keys for each room, just in case he needed to get into hers for something like this. Fishing it out of his pocket, he opened her door and slipped inside her room.

The camera was still sitting on the table, right where she'd left it. Quickly, deftly, he opened the back, exposing the film. Popping it out, he took it to the window, unrolled it, and allowed the sun to expose whatever prints she had there. Then, carefully, he rolled it back up, popped it back into the camera, and put it back exactly where he had found it.

Chances were that she wouldn't know she had a "bad" roll of film until they were back in Serenity.

Smiling, he slipped back out of her room, hopped the elevator, and cut back across the lobby to the restaurant, where Carny was waiting.

# 15

*They had just finished* the last of their desserts when the maitre d' approached their table. "Excuse me, Mr. Brisco? Your limousine is here."

"Thank you," Logan said, laying down a couple of bills that Carny couldn't see. "This should cover the check and the tip."

"Thank you, sir."

Carny waited until the maitre d' disappeared. "Did he say your *limousine?*"

"Yes," Logan said, getting up. "Haven't you ever ridden in one before?"

"Well . . . yes," she said, though she honestly couldn't remember if she ever had or not. Baffled, she followed him across the lobby and out the front door.

A chauffeur waited beside a gold Rolls-Royce, and upon seeing Logan, he opened the back door for them. "Good afternoon, Mr. Brisco."

"Hello." Logan shook the chauffeur's hand. "We're going to see Mr. Gastineau at the MidSouth Bank on Congress Street."

Carny hesitated before getting in. "Logan, are you sure . . . ?"

"Get in, Carny," he whispered. "The man's waiting."

Clumsily, she slid onto the seat and made room for Logan. "Who is this person who sent this?"

"The banker I'm talking to," he said. "And please, if you meet him, don't say anything about it. He's funny about gratitude. He likes to know you feel it, but if you say too much it makes him feel uncomfortable. Besides, he sees me as a successful young consultant. We don't want him to think we're not used to this kind of treatment."

The lies weren't meant to fleece her, he thought, looking out the window as the chauffeur got in. They were only thrown out to appease her, so she'd stop questioning everything he did. It probably hadn't been smart to bring her along, but he realized as the car began moving that he wanted to prove to her he was legitimate more than he wanted to persuade the bankers to buy into the scheme that would help make him legitimate.

Why was that? Why did he care more what Carny thought of him than anybody else?

Deciding to examine that later, he looked at her and grinned. "So what do you think?"

She feigned nonchalance and shrugged. "It's nice, for a Rolls."

He laughed aloud, and the chauffeur glanced into the rearview mirror.

"So who's your first victim?"

Logan shot her a disgusted look. "Carny, you're too negative. They hired me, remember? I found them a location for their park, and now all I have to do is convince them it's the right one."

"And why are you so sure it is?"

"Because the town needs it, Carny. And because wherever we build it, I'm going to have to live there. And Serenity is where I want to live. And because I think it'll make my investors a killing."

She let her gaze drift out the window and ran his words through her mind, analyzing and processing them. "Will you know from this trip whether they'll approve the Serenity site or not?"

"Maybe," he said. "I hope so."

"And what if they don't?" She brought her gaze back to him. "What if they tell you that isn't what they had in mind? Will you give back all the money you've collected from Serenity?"

"They won't say that," he said. "I can be very persuasive. Besides, the amount of money I've already raised speaks volumes about Serenity's level of commitment to the project. That's the kind of community they're looking for."

"You didn't answer my question. If they don't, will you give the money back?"

He faced her directly. "All right, Carny. If they decide not to build the park there, yes, I'll give the money back, just like I've told you before. I'll have to, won't I?"

She didn't answer, but again looked out to the street.

The limousine turned onto Congress Street, and ahead, Logan saw the MidSouth sign on a black marble-and-glass building. Just as he remembered, the first floor was showcased in glass. Perfect, he thought. The officers of the bank would see him driving up in the limo, and if his hunch was right, he'd be greeted at the door by someone who mattered and noticed by everyone who could see the street.

He got his briefcase, checked the contents, then snapped it shut as the chauffeur pulled to the curb. Carny reached for her door handle, but Logan stopped her. "Let him," he said, as the chauffeur got out and came around to open the door.

Carny stepped outside and noticed at once that people along the sidewalk were watching them, waiting to see what celebrity or billionaire would be making an appearance today. From inside the bank, she saw that the secretaries looked at them curiously, as well, and she instantly wanted to slink back into the car.

Logan asked the driver to wait for them, then set his hand on the small of Carny's back and escorted her in.

They had scarcely reached the door when a man in a suit opened it for them.

"Good afternoon, sir," he said, shaking Logan's hand. "I'm Andrew Seal."

"Good afternoon," Logan said. "Logan Brisco, and this is Miss Sullivan. I have an appointment to see Mr. Gastineau."

"Yes, of course, Mr. Brisco," the man said. "Miss Sullivan. I'll take you up myself."

Carny wondered whether she should decline to go all the way up, and wait in the lobby here, or follow all the way until she was no longer welcome. She chose the latter, just to fulfill her curiosity.

All the way up, Mr. Seal talked about the weather in Houston, about the fact that rain was expected, and he questioned Logan about the length of his stay. That he didn't seem familiar with him didn't bother Carny much. It was a big bank, after all, and one man couldn't be expected to know all of their consultants.

They stepped off the elevator into a plush lobby with secretaries working quietly along the perimeter. Mr. Seal escorted them to the bank president's office and asked them to have a seat while he alerted Mr. Gastineau that they were here.

Logan seemed infinitely more relaxed than Carny as they took the elegant sofa against the wall. "So what do you think so far?" he asked with a grin.

Carny smiled. "It's okay, if you like having your feet kissed. And you do like it, don't you, Brisco?"

He chuckled. "Doesn't everybody?"

"No, actually," she said. "It makes me very uncomfortable. Makes me feel like I'm lying about something."

"Well, don't worry. Mr. Gastineau isn't a foot-kisser. When I go in, you just wait here. And be patient. It could be a long meeting. If you decide to leave, you can take the limo. I'll call the chauffeur when I'm ready to be picked up."

She smiled. "I'll stay here, Brisco."

"Still afraid I'll break and run?"

She laughed softly. "Well, I don't think you can easily escape from a twentieth-floor window, so I feel pretty safe here."

"As long as you're in the same building?"

"Something like that," she said.

Mr. Gastineau came out with Mr. Seal, and Logan mused that he'd probably been told that Logan was someone important, and should not be kept waiting.

"Mr. Brisco, it's nice to see you," he said, reaching for his hand.

Logan stood and shook the president's hand, but instead of introducing Carny, he rather hurriedly slipped into the man's office. Carny bristled slightly, then consoled herself with the fact that he knew the temperament of the bank president better than she.

Logan made himself comfortable in the chair across from the bank president, an overweight, balding man who carried his extra pounds with a polished dignity. As unassuming as he seemed, though, Logan had done enough homework to know that he was as shrewd as they came. His name carried a lot of weight in Texas financial circles, and if Logan could nail him, the other bankers would be more likely to hear him out.

"I have two reasons for wanting to meet with you today, Mr. Gastineau," Logan said. "One is to open an account in your bank. I'd like to start with two hundred thousand dollars, and within the month, I'll deposit a million more." That, he thought, was how long it should take for him to get his hands on all the money he'd stashed in safe deposit boxes all over the South in the last ten years.

Gastineau cleared his throat and immediately pulled out the necessary paperwork. "Certainly, Mr. Brisco. Will this be a transfer from another bank?"

"I have a cashier's check," Logan said.

"Wonderful," the man said. He took the check Logan proffered, made the necessary notations, then took off his glasses and sat back. "And do you want this account in your name?"

"I'll be the only signatory on the account for now," he said, "but I want the account to be in the name of the town of Serenity, Texas."

"You want it in the name of a town?"

"Yes," Logan said. "I've been hired by Serenity to raise money for a huge amusement park we're planning to build in that area. Billy Ray Cyrus has tentatively agreed to allow his name to be used in the promotion of the park, as well as possibly making it a theme park for him, much like Dollywood in Pigeon Forge, Tennessee. And I have several other banks that have committed to investing in the venture. The money I'm depositing is just a portion of the cash the citizens of Serenity have invested already.

We're planning to build it on a scale even bigger than AstroWorld."

Gastineau took off his glasses and sat back, listening carefully with the mathematical mind that had gotten him to the position he held today. "An amusement park."

"Yes," Logan said, plowing right past the doubt in his voice. Digging into his briefcase, he said, "I've brought you my business plan, my projected costs for the venture, projected profits over the next ten years, comparisons of other parks across the United States. . . ." He paused, and chuckled slightly. "Actually, Mr. Gastineau, I should probably go over one thing at a time with you. We'll start with the projected profits, so you can see what an opportunity this is for you."

He handed him the booklet he'd printed on his own laser printer, then taken to Julia Peabody to bind. Sitting back, he opened his own copy.

"You say other banks in the Houston area have agreed to invest?"

"Some I've nailed down, others are more tentative. I'm meeting with Alex Green at First Trust Bank this afternoon, and tomorrow with John Van Landingham at South Federal. I also have several bankers in Dallas and Austin who have committed. One—and it wouldn't be prudent for me to tell you which one—has even offered a sizable investment from his personal funds, in addition to what his bank has put up. It's an opportunity you don't want to miss, Mr. Gastineau. The profit margin is very high."

Frowning, Gastineau opened the booklet and zeroed in on the numbers. "Interesting," he muttered, and Logan grinned.

One down, a dozen to go, he told himself. If he could just keep the con going long enough, he'd be legit before he knew it. And then all of his lies would turn to truth.

Carny had almost begun to regret waiting when an hour and a half had passed, and Logan still hadn't come out. For a moment, she considered sending the secretary in to make sure he hadn't slipped out some back door, but then she told herself that was ludicrous.

When the door finally opened and Logan came out, laughing with the bank president as if they were old friends, she breathed a sigh of relief.

"I'll call you at the hotel and let you know what time my board of directors plans to meet, Logan. I'd very much like you to be there yourself."

"I'll make it a point," Logan said. "And if you think of any questions in the meantime . . . "

"I'll certainly call."

Carny got to her feet, and the older man smiled. "Why Logan, you didn't tell me your lovely wife was waiting."

"Mr. Gastineau, this isn't my wife. This is Ms. Sullivan. She's my pilot."

"Pilot!" Gastineau said. "Well, I never would have guessed!"

Carny smiled. "It's nice to meet you, Mr. Gastineau."

He took her hand in both his own. "Forgive me for keeping Logan so long."

"That's all right," she said.

Gastineau saw them to the elevator, and when the doors closed, Logan didn't look at all drained from the meeting.

"Well, how did it go?"

"It looks good," Logan said. "I'm meeting with his board of directors tomorrow."

"Will they make the final decision about where to put the park?"

"They might. But I'm expecting to have to fly everyone to Serenity and show them the site before they make a final decision. How many people can your plane accommodate?"

She thought for a moment. "Six, comfortably."

"That'll be fine," he said.

The chauffeur was still waiting when they reached the car, and as Carny got in, she couldn't help the confusion taking hold of her. She was almost getting excited about the prospect of getting the park under way. She was almost relieved that he'd been successful with Gastineau.

But that wasn't how she was supposed to feel, she told herself. She was getting too soft. Too easy.

As Logan took the seat next to her, she couldn't help telling herself that it wasn't her fault. Logan could convince a tiger that it was a zebra. And she was beginning to wonder if that was exactly what he was doing to her.

\* \* \*

Logan was secretly relieved that Carny opted to go back to the hotel while he met with the second banker that afternoon. It didn't pay to have her around too much when he was wheeling and dealing. One inconsistency could blow everything, and he had no doubt that she was mentally recording every word that was spoken. Maybe she was starting to trust him, he thought. Maybe the scene with Gastineau had been just what she needed to convince her.

If it had, the scene with Alex Green, the president of First Trust Bank, would have sent that faith tumbling down.

Logan looked out the window as the sun began to set, and told himself he could relax now. There was no harm done.

But he hadn't been so sure of that when he'd driven up in the limo, gotten out, and made a big deal of telling the bank officer who greeted him that he had an appointment with Mr. Green.

Mr. Green had turned out to be a woman, a fact that Carny Sullivan would not have missed. Since he'd told her that he'd already been dealing with all of these bankers, he probably would not have been able to talk his way out of that one. Fortunately, Ms. Green never had to know about the mistake and neither did Carny.

But Alex Green had been as difficult to deal with as he'd expected Mr. Gastineau to be. Logan had turned his charm on full tilt, but if it affected her, he couldn't tell. He had also turned his intelligence up several notches, citing figures and statistics and comparative analyses of other parks. Her continued reluctance became an even bigger challenge to him, and he found himself nursing the same kind of adrenaline burst that he'd nursed when he pulled off a particularly challenging scam.

By the end of his interview, he had persuaded her to come to Serenity to tour the area so that she could decide for herself whether her bank's money would be well spent there. She had finally agreed, and as he'd left, instead of feeling energized by the success, he felt exhausted.

He paid the driver for the day's use of the limo, plus a substantial tip, then went up to his room and collapsed on his bed. He couldn't believe how much harder it was to pull off the truth—albeit with a few variations—than to pull off pure fiction. He wondered how that could be. Hadn't enough been at stake before, when he feared getting caught and sent to prison?

The difference, he told himself, was that there was more than prison at stake now. If he succeeded, he'd be a hero in the little town he'd come to care so much for. Carny would trust him entirely. Jason would continue to look up to him. And he would still be treated as though he belonged.

All he had to do was accomplish the impossible, make no mistakes, and pray for a couple of miracles.

After shedding his coat and tie he went to Carny's room.

"Tough day, huh?" she said with a smile.

"Yeah, but it was worth it." Jack inched around

Carny as Logan came in, and Logan stooped down to pet him. "Hey, boy. You've probably been wondering where I was, haven't you? You didn't think I left you, did you?"

The dog licked his face and neck, and Logan laughed. "I think he's getting used to me, Carny, don't you?"

"Yeah. Slade would feel real good knowing that he's happy." Closing the door, she turned back to the enigma crouched on the floor with his dog. "I walked him a few minutes ago."

Logan got to his feet and handed her the bottle of wine he'd been carrying. "I stopped on the way back and bought us a bottle of wine. Sort of a pre-celebration celebration."

"What does that mean?"

"It means that we're getting real close to having something to celebrate."

She went to the wet bar in the corner of her room, and found a corkscrew there. Deftly, she peeled the foil off the cork, dug the corkscrew in, and pulled the cork out. "So when do we know for sure?"

"Could be weeks," he said. "I have lots more meetings. But you and I need to put our heads together tonight and decide exactly when we can come back to pick up Gastineau and some of the others on his board and take them to Serenity. Then we need to plan another day to take Ms. Green and her people. Are you up to this?"

She poured his wine into a glass and handed it to him. "Depends. Are you paying me?"

"Of course. Although I was hoping to combine some of these trips with my flight lessons, so I can log some hours. Can that be done?"

"Sure," she said. "As long as they're not solo hours, we can work it out."

Smiling, he took his wineglass and waited for her to pour herself one, but instead she stuffed the cork back into the bottle. "Aren't you drinking with me?"

Carny laughed and went to the couch that sat in front of the huge picture window overlooking the city. "I don't drink."

"Well, you sure opened the bottle like a pro."

"I have lots of experience at things I don't do anymore," she said.

He sat down next to her. "A little glass of wine isn't going to hurt."

She smiled and raked back her hair. "Maybe not, but I don't need it. I have lots of fun without it."

He sipped his wine and gazed at her with those sexy eyes that, she suspected, were his biggest source of success. It was the eyes that could nail her, she thought. The eyes that could persuade her. The eyes that would make her forget her suspicions of him.

"Don't you ever just want to relax? Sip a glass of wine, put your feet up?"

She laughed. "With my background, Brisco, there's a fine line between relaxing and running amok."

"What does that mean?"

"It means that with a little juice, I could either

sleep for ten hours or do a trapeze act on the power lines. It could go either way."

"So you have a problem with alcohol?"

She shook her head. "I'm a woman of extremes. Of course, if I don't drink, I don't have a problem."

Disappointed, he swirled the wine in his glass and watched it slosh against the sides. "Well, I was just hoping we could have a toast together. I was also kind of looking forward to seeing you tipsy."

Her laughter almost surprised him. "I know what you're up to. You were hoping to get me drunk so I'd pass out, and you could steal my plane."

"Actually, I was hoping to get you drunk so I could have my way with you. We still have that bet, you know."

Again, her laughter shot through to a place in his heart that wasn't frequently visited. "Let's see, what was it again? Something about my begging you for sex before the month was up? Don't look now, Brisco, but the month is almost up."

"*Almost* being the key word," he said with that maddening grin. "I've lived a lot of my life on almosts."

"I'll just bet you have."

Something about the conversation, the laughter, and the flirtatious way he looked at her was intoxicating in itself, and for a moment she only gazed at him, considering the way he made her feel when she had forbidden herself to feel anything at all.

"So, let me ask you something," he said, moving in until his face was dangerously close to hers, "if you had never nursed this tremendous doubt about me, if you believed who I said I was, if you thought that I might have a shred of decency . . . would there be any chance for us?"

Instead of backing away, she looked unabashedly into his eyes. "To do what?"

"To get involved. To have a relationship. To get to know each other better."

"With our clothes on or off?" she asked with the barest hint of a smile in her eyes.

"Off would be nice," he said, his grin growing even more maddening.

"Mm . . . hmm." She smiled. "Well, let me think. When surfboards become a big-selling item at the North Pole, and Saddam Hussein applies for U.S. citizenship, then maybe . . ."

"I knew it," he said. "I knew we had a shot."

Her eyes twinkled as he moved even closer, and she whispered, "Is this how you sweet-talk all the notches on your briefcase?"

"Every one," he said, his gaze dropping to her lips.

She wet them just then, allowing her tongue to slide along her bottom lip, knowing the effect she had on him.

"But you know," he whispered, "there haven't been any in Serenity. Not that there haven't been opportunities. I just haven't taken them."

"And why not, pray tell?" she asked softly.

"Maybe I had my eye on first prize," he whispered. "Maybe I didn't have the heart to settle for less."

"And what does heart have to do with it?" she asked.

"Everything," he said.

"Isn't sex just sex?"

"No, it isn't. Believe it or not, Carny, with me there's a lot of heart involved. There has to be, or I don't do it."

When she laughed, he looked hurt.

"You don't believe I have a heart?"

Her grin faded then as she considered that for a moment, and her eyes softened infinitesimally. "Yeah, Brisco. I know you have a heart. I'm just not sure you know what to do with it."

As Logan's serious eyes locked with hers, he realized that, perhaps, she was right. Maybe he didn't know what to do with it. Maybe he'd never had the chance to learn. "I told you, I'm a quick study," he whispered.

She swallowed and let her gaze fall to his lips, wet and inviting, and smelling faintly of wine.

"Yes, you are," she said. "I just wish I knew how much you needed to learn."

"A lot," he assured her, looking as serious as she'd ever seen him. "I need to learn a lot . . . about love . . . and commitment . . . and friendship . . . But I've learned harder things, and I don't give up easily."

Somehow, she knew that. She gazed at him, suddenly stricken with the strength of her desire for him, the strength of her need for him, the strength of her faith in him. . . .

Of its own accord, her hand came up to touch the triangle of hair at his open collar. Gently, her fingertips stroked the curls there.

Something about the simple touch beckoned

him in a stronger way than he'd ever been beckoned before, and before he had the good sense to stop himself, his lips were hovering over hers, offering her the chance to break and run, offering her the chance to pull away, or knock him to his knees. But she didn't move.

He wasn't sure if it was he or she who breached the final millimeters between their lips, but when they came together, it was a dual effort. Her hand came around to the nape of his neck, up through his hair, and he pulled her closer, his mouth probing gently, sweetly, though urgently.

Carny felt weak as she melted further into the kiss, weak as though her heart would collapse, as though her breathing would stop, as though all sense and logic would abandon her. She had felt something close to this on her father's roller coaster once . . . the one that had later jumped the track in a trial run and crashed into the dunking booth. And that was just what she feared would happen to her now.

Slowly, she broke the kiss, and pulled back. "Well, Brisco," she whispered, her forehead still pressed against his, "I can see that's one area that you don't need to learn about."

He smiled. "And as far as experience goes, well, you're not lacking either."

His lips touched hers again, and for a moment, she let herself fall into the warmth of his kiss, the security and commitment of his embrace. But the security was shaky, and the commitment was false. And she liked to think she was no fool.

Again, she broke the kiss, and pressed her hand

on his chest. "I have experience in other areas, Brisco. Areas of getting involved with the wrong men. Areas of letting passion sweep me away."

"There's nothing wrong with passion," he said, "and what makes you so sure I'm the wrong man?"

"Because I still don't entirely trust you. Because I still question every move you make. Because I don't really know who you are."

"I'm whomever you want me to be," he whispered. "I'm whomever you need."

"That's what I'm afraid of," she said softly. Slipping out of his embrace, she stood up. "I don't want a custom-tailored man, Brisco. How can I trust a chameleon?"

"A chameleon?" he repeated. "You think I'm a chameleon?"

"You change according to your environment, Brisco. One minute you're the good ole boy shooting the breeze in the barbershop, the next you're riding in a chauffeured Rolls and going to meetings with bank executives."

"So I can relate to all types of people. Is that a crime?"

"No, of course not."

"Then what's the problem?"

"The problem," she said, thinking hard, since she wasn't entirely sure what the problem was, "well, the problem is . . . the problem is that I was dead sure you were a con artist. Dead sure. And then the dog, and Jason . . . and today I saw you with those people, only . . . I'm still not sure it all rings true, Brisco. I'm still not sure I trust you."

He looked genuinely hurt as he got up and poured another glass of wine. "So you're saying that you still don't believe I'm legitimately trying to help Serenity?"

For a moment, she turned over the things in her mind that she did believe. "I think I believe that you're trying to build the park," she said, "although I'm not absolutely sure that you're as far along as you say. I think I believe that you genuinely like the people in my town, and that you'd like to help them."

"You think you believe?" he asked. "Thanks, Carny. Thanks a lot. And what about you? What do you *think* you believe about the way I feel about you?"

"I think I believe that you're attracted to me," she said. "No, I take that back. You're obviously attracted to me. But that may partially be because of the challenge I represent. I don't think you've been turned down many times in your life."

"You missed your calling, Carny. You should have stayed in the carnival as a fortune-teller." Angry, he tossed the wine down his throat, and set his glass down hard.

"You know as well as I do that the biggest talent a good con artist has is the talent to read people. I was raised learning to read people, Brisco, and I think you were, too. After a while, you start noticing details about people, expressions, words they use, and slowly, your mind starts working out the puzzle, until you've got all the blanks filled in, and you know how that person feels, how they think, how they'd react. . . . "

"And what about the margin for error, Carny?"

"You're right," she said. "There is that possibility. But I haven't often been wrong. And neither have you."

"You were wrong once," Logan said. "You sure didn't know the kind of man Abe Sullivan was."

"That's because I let passion blind me," she said. "I made that mistake once, but I won't make it again."

For a moment, Logan only stared at her, then finally, he nodded. "Good for you," he whispered. "I wouldn't want you to make that mistake again. Not even with me." His eyes were soft, sweet, as he looked at her. "I don't want to hurt you, Carny. I really, really do like you."

A gentle smile crept across her lips, spilling into her eyes. "Believe it or not, Brisco, I really, really like you, too."

He couldn't remember when he'd had a better endorsement, or a more touching affirmation, and for a moment, he couldn't answer her. The lump in his throat obstructed his voice, but finally, he managed to smile.

For a moment, Carny only smiled back. Then, finally, she said, "So are you gonna feed me or what?"

"Sure," he said. "I'm taking you to Great Caruso's, like I promised. You did bring the red dress, didn't you?"

"You bet I did. Jason insisted."

"Yeah, Jason and me . . . we've got a strategy."

"A strategy for what?" she asked on a laugh.

"For finding you a husband," he said, going to the door. "Whether you want one or not."

Carny threw a towel at the door as Logan and Jack ducked out.

# 16

*"This reminds me of* that restaurant in *Scent of a Woman,"* Carny said when they'd been seated at their table, in what looked like an old-world opera house. "Remember that scene when Al Pacino dances with that girl?"

"I don't go to many movies," Logan said, admiring the woman across from him rather than their surroundings.

"Don't you like them?"

"I used to. When I was a kid, it was a terrific escape. Now I don't have much time for it. By the way, have I told you how gorgeous you look in that dress?"

She smiled. "At least half a dozen times."

"Is that all? Because you really do look beautiful. Jason knew what he was doing."

Feigning disgust, she looked at her watch. "Well, I've had it on for almost an hour now, and I haven't had any proposals yet. This husband-hunting isn't all it's cracked up to be."

He laughed. "I'd ask you, but I don't think you'd say yes."

"No," she said with a sigh as she propped her chin on her hand. "Marriage is not for me. There are some women who need that in their lives. I'm not one of them."

"Oh, really?" he asked, not convinced. "You don't need security, commitment, romance? You don't need sex?"

She laughed. "Your question implies that I could get those things in marriage. It's hard to be secure when your spouse chases everything in panties, and commitment is nothing more than a crude joke. And as for romance . . . well, that's why I read and go to movies."

"And sex?" he asked with a half grin.

She returned his smile. "Some of the most platonic relationships I know are within the bonds of marriage."

"Don't your parents have a good marriage?"

She sighed and looked off across the restaurant, considering that for a moment. "I think they do. They were certainly more wrapped up in each other than they were in me. But nothing about my family is conventional, and I wouldn't want to emulate any of it. Which reminds me . . . remember that I told you my parents are thinking of retiring and settling in Serenity? What if I can't talk them out of it? What if they come anyway, dead set on getting you to include them in your plans?" Her eyes were piercing as she fixed them on him. "How would you feel about that?"

He thought for a moment. "Well, no offense, Carny, but I don't think they fit the profile of the kind of employees I had in mind."

Relief flooded through her, but she didn't show it yet. "And what if they were to invest a big hunk of money?"

He stared at her for another moment, realizing that a week ago he might have taken it. But that was before the park was legitimate . . . before he had plans to make his lies into truth. "I'm sorry, Carny, but no. I wouldn't take it."

A slow smile dawned across her face. "Thank goodness."

He frowned. "What do you mean?"

"I was testing you," she said. "And miraculously, you passed."

"Why? Your parents aren't really coming?"

"Oh, they're definitely talking about it." She shifted in her seat. "You see, Brisco, I'm still not absolutely sure that I believe there's going to be a park. But if I were to believe you, my next concern would be the integrity of my town. I'm still against it. But if it is what the rest of the town wants, all I can do is try to make sure the town isn't violated by it."

"I realize that," he said. "Which is why I've been thinking about a specific role for you in the park."

"Oh, no. I don't want anything to do with it."

"You might want this," he said. "I was thinking of making you the park commissioner. You could actually be in charge of maintaining the park's integrity. Making sure you only have honest people working there, with only honest attractions, and that the park represents the best and cleanest of Serenity."

Her expression didn't change noticeably. "That would make me a direct adversary of yours. As you built the park, I'd be second-guessing every step of it."

"Aren't we already adversaries, to a large extent? Frankly, I kind of like it."

"You've got to be kidding. It would be like shooting yourself in the foot."

"No, it would be like making sure I didn't overlook anything. I'll be real busy, Carny, and things could get past me. I can't think of anyone in the town who'd be better suited to sniffing out corruption."

She sat back and tried to think. "But what about my flying service, and my school?"

"That's up to you," he said. "You could keep running it, or turn it over to someone else to run it. I'm not kidding about our expanding the airport. It's got to be done. Now, you can have your present outfit expanded to accommodate all the traffic that'll be coming in, or someone else will build one in another place, and they'll be the ones to get rich. If I were you, I'd be the one to do it."

"I'm not interested in being rich, Brisco. My parents have chased money all their lives, and it hasn't gotten them anywhere."

"I think you have stronger values, Carny. You could handle money, if you had it. You wouldn't gamble it away on schemes and scams. And you'd have something to leave Jason."

"I'll leave Jason a childhood," she said. "And values. And security and peace of mind. Don't you realize how valuable those things are?"

For a moment, his eyes grew serious, and he looked down at his food. "Yeah, I do, Carny. What I wouldn't have given for those things when I was growing up."

"Me, too," she whispered.

The pianist started to play, lending an oddly romantic backdrop to the conversation that had little to do with romance. "We have a lot in common, Carny. A lot more than you like to think."

"I know."

Their eyes locked in a startling merge of emotions. Finally, Logan whispered, "Will you dance with me? You look too pretty not to be seen on the dance floor."

Her smile was more satisfying than all the scams he'd ever pulled off, and getting to his feet, he took her hand and pulled her with him.

He didn't know the name of the tune the pianist played, and it didn't matter. As if she'd always been his partner, as if he'd learned to dance with her, they moved across the dance floor with grace and finesse.

In the anonymity of the other dancers, they weren't adversaries at all, but two people who knew a lot about the locked chambers of each other's soul. Two people who were reaching an understanding. Two people who understood.

He looked down at her, his eyes stricken with how beautiful she was, how special, how delicate. But he knew better. She was also tough, like him . . . a survivor. A striver. A reacher. There wasn't much in Carny's life that would stand in her way of getting the kind of life she wanted. Not even Logan.

He didn't know if it was the romance or the music, or the way she felt in his arms, that compelled him to lower his lips to hers, but before he knew it, he had stopped dancing, and stood motionless in the center of the dance floor, holding her in his arms and kissing her with a deeper need than he'd kissed her before.

Carny allowed herself to get lost in that kiss, to revel in it, to respond to it. And as she felt her heart slipping away, some part of her pulled it back, clinging to it.

The song ended in sync with the kiss, and Logan led her back to their table. And as hard as she tried to get through the rest of the meal with her thoughts intact, she found that it was too late.

The spell had been cast, and she wasn't sure there was anything she could do about it.

Country music spilled out from the bar next door to the hotel when the cab brought them back. "Do you like country music?" he asked.

She shrugged. "Sometimes. Do you?"

"Sometimes," he chuckled. "I saw you two-stepping like a champ at the dance, but truthfully, I would have pegged you for the Led Zeppelin type."

She grinned. "And I would have figured you for the Milli Vanilli type."

Logan laughed. "You never give up." Taking her hand, he said, "Come on. Let's go in."

He pulled her toward the club, and they took a table at the back and looked across the crowd of people to the singer on the stage, doing his own rendition of a Clint Black song.

"He's pretty good," Logan said.

Nodding, Carny scanned the faces in the crowd, the way she'd always done as a child in the carnival. Her gaze landed on a man just coming in the door, a man with a cowboy hat and sunglasses. For a moment, the glasses snagged her attention, and she wondered why anyone would wear sun shades into a dark nightclub.

He slipped into the shadows near her table, and seemed to scan the place for an empty table. But she and Logan had gotten the last one.

Suddenly she recognized him.

"Eric Hart."

"No, that's a Clint Black song," Logan said.

"No, Brisco," she whispered. "Right there. That guy in the glasses. It's Eric Hart."

Logan looked up, squinting in disbelief. "It looks like him, but it can't be him. What would he be doing here all by himself? He's one of the biggest stars in country music."

"I don't know, but it's him. Look how he stands.

Look at that tattoo on his hand. That's Eric Hart! He's looking for a place to sit."

Before she knew it, Logan had shot out of his chair and was shaking hands with the star. She watched, astonished and a little embarrassed, as he pointed to their table, then started back with the star on his heels.

Carny stood up as they reached the table. "Eric, I'd like you to meet Carny Sullivan. Carny, Eric Hart."

"Nice to meet you, ma'am. I hope I'm not intruding. Logan invited me to sit with you."

"Of course," she said, shooting Logan an incredulous look. "Do you two know each other?"

Eric laughed. "No, but I've got a feeling that Logan doesn't meet too many strangers." He leaned forward at the table and, in a low voice, said, "I'm surprised y'all recognized me. I was hoping to be discreet."

"Oh, we won't call any attention to you," she assured him as he motioned to the waitress to bring him a beer. "What brings you to town?"

"Concert tomorrow night," he said. "I like to get to town early, just to relax before all the madness starts."

The band launched into a rendition of one of Eric's tunes, "Dream Scape," and chuckling, he glanced back at the band. "Hey, he's better than I am."

Carny and Logan laughed with him as the song played on.

\* \* \*

An hour later, Logan and Eric were deep in a conversation about the park, and Carny realized with some chagrin that he was making a sales pitch to Eric. Something about that riled her, for she didn't feel right taking advantage of the man's privacy by hitting on him for money.

But it wasn't so much money Logan was after, but Eric's name.

"We've been looking for a star to name the park after. You know, kind of like Dollywood. You're just the caliber we're looking for."

With a forced smile, Carny nudged Logan and said, "I thought you had Billy Ray Cyrus lined up."

Logan didn't seem daunted by her interjection. "No commitments have been made either way. And frankly, Cyrus is a relatively new star, who may or may not last. Eric has the kind of staying power we need. He's practically a legend." He set his eyes on the ceiling, and waved his hand as if creating a banner. "I can see it now. Hartland."

"Hartland?" Carny repeated, resisting the urge to stick her finger down her throat. But Eric didn't seem to find the idea silly.

"I like it," he said. "An amusement park. Hmmm. I never thought of that before. What kind of investment would I have to make?"

*That's it,* Carny thought. *Here's where he nails him for the money.*

"Well, that would be negotiable. The profit margin for you would be tremendous, because there would be licensing involved. The gift shops would be full of stuff related to Eric Hart and some of your specific songs, and the rides could go along with your themes. It may work out that we don't need any investment at all from you, if you could give us license to merchandise your name, in return for shares of the park."

"Merchandising, huh?" Eric asked. "This is sounding better all the time. How long will you be in Houston?"

"We'll be leaving day after tomorrow," Logan said.

"Perfect. Can you meet with my agent and me tomorrow? Say, ten o'clock?"

"Sure," Logan said.

"I'm in the penthouse here." Fishing through his hip pocket, he pulled out a card. "Here's the phone number so you can get through. Call before you come up, and I'll make sure you don't have any trouble getting in."

"All right," Logan said, shaking his hand. He stood up, looking at Carny. "You ready to go, Carny?"

"Yeah, it's getting late," she said. "It was great meeting you, Eric."

"You, too," he said. "We might be seeing a lot more of each other."

As they left the club and went inside and across the hotel, Carny gave Logan a curious look. "How about that?"

"Talk about being in the right place at the right time." The elevator doors opened, and they stepped in. "Do you realize what it could do for us if we could get a commitment from him? The investors would be calling *us!*"

"I thought the investors *were* calling you. And what about Billy Ray Cyrus, and all that Achy Breaky Park stuff? Brisco, was that all just a lie?"

"Optimism," Logan said. "I call it optimism. But I'd rather get Eric, and I think everybody in Serenity would, too. I just never dreamed we'd have a shot at him."

"Hartland," she said as the doors opened and she stepped off. "Sounds a little corny, don't you think?"

"Dollywood isn't corny? Opryland isn't corny?"

They came to her door, and as she stuck her key in the knob, he braced his hand above her head. "Hey, you're pretty good luck, you know that?"

"Don't count on it," she whispered. "You're not getting lucky with me tonight."

He smiled. "We had some nice moments at the restaurant, didn't we?"

She couldn't hold his gaze, so she looked up the hall. "Yeah, we did."

"The second half of the evening wasn't very romantic, but it could still end on a romantic note, if you let me come in."

"Jack's waiting for you," she whispered.

"Jack can wait," he said, leaning closer until his lips hovered millimeters from hers.

When his lips grazed hers, she closed her eyes, savoring the foreign feel of her heart pounding out its erratic rhythm. Finally, she touched his chest and broke the contact of their lips. "You're an interesting man, Logan Brisco."

"Does that mean you're interested?"

"It means I'm intrigued," she whispered.

"Then surely you could let your guard down a little."

"Oh, no," she whispered. "The fact that I'm intrigued only makes me want to raise it higher."

"You still don't trust me, do you?"

She smiled. "I think the problem is that I don't really trust myself. You were right when you said that before, Logan. I can't give myself enough rope to hang myself. There's too much at stake."

Then, pressing another kiss on his jaw, she went in and closed the door behind her.

# 17

*"I need a lawyer."*

Carny looked over at Logan who navigated the Texas skies on their way back to Serenity, and asked, "What?"

"A lawyer. Someone to represent the park. We're getting to the point to start drawing up contracts."

"Well, there are two lawyers in Serenity. Alan Robard is probably your best bet. He handled my divorce."

"I know Alan. He was one of our investors."

"So has Eric made a commitment?"

"He's that far from it," he said, holding up his thumb and forefinger. "He's coming to Serenity next week, but it's top secret, so don't tell anybody."

"And are the bankers top secret, too?"

"I'd rather they were, until everything is nailed down."

Something about the secrecy disturbed her. "You told us that Billy Ray Cyrus was almost committed, but he really wasn't, was he?"

"Well, not totally."

"So you were lying."

"Not lying. I never claimed it was a done deal. I was just playing all my cards."

"But your deck was stacked."

He shot her an annoyed look. "What's your point?"

"My point is that I think you used Cyrus's name to get others to invest. And then you used those investments to impress the bankers. Then you used the bankers to impress Eric Hart. And eventually, it has a snowball effect, but you aren't absolutely sure of any of the players, so you have to juggle it all very carefully."

"So I have faith in my juggling abilities," he said. "Carny, I've been in business a long time. I know how to make deals. I do it better than anyone I know."

"Then what other deals have you put together?"

He wasn't prepared for that question. "Lots of them, okay?"

"Name some."

"I put together several big real-estate deals along the east coast. Developed acres of property. And I helped with the buyout of a major hospital in Kentucky."

"What was the name of it?"

Aggravated, he glared at her. "What's your point? Do you think I made up Gastineau and his bank? Do you think Eric Hart was just some actor I planted in that bar to convince you I'm aboveboard?"

"I think that you're not above using dishonesty to reach a legitimate goal."

He shifted in his seat, and checked the controls. "It's not easy putting together an endeavor like this, Carny. Not just anyone could do it. It takes a lot of wheeling and dealing, and you can't go into a bank empty-handed and ask them to invest. You have to have other commitments. You have to have a plan. Haven't you read *The Art of the Deal?*"

"By Donald Trump?" She laughed. "Isn't he the guy with a mile-long line of creditors a few years ago who started selling off his assets one at a time?"

"He's back on his feet now, and doing very well, thank you."

"Right. According to his own press releases. And just because Donald Trump uses juggling techniques to make his deals doesn't mean it's right. It just sounds an awful lot like what my parents do."

"Don't be such a cynic," Logan said. "Everybody stands to get rich, Carny. I'm the man who just has to convince everybody. Thank God they're not all as hard to convince as you. The bottom line is that nobody's going to get hurt."

"Are you sure about that?"

He met her eyes, then, and felt almost glad they hadn't slept together, for the burden of her trust would be an awfully heavy one to bear. "Yeah, Carny, I am. I'm real sure. Do you believe me?"

For a moment, she only stared at him, then finally, she whispered, "I'm starting to."

Logan checked the controls again, then told himself that the day she trusted him completely would be the most significant day of his life. And he was determined not to let that trust be misplaced.

Over the next few days, Carny transported planeloads of bankers back and forth to Serenity, with Logan flying most of the time and logging his flight time. She listened to the conversations on the planes, real conversations about real logistics of the park, and was amazed at how prepared Logan was to answer all their questions.

And when Eric Hart made his discreet flight into their town, in his own Cessna, she realized that this might just turn into reality.

And Logan Brisco might just be here to stay.

Carny had been home for a week before Joey reminded her of the picture she was supposed to have gotten in Houston.

"I got it," she told him. "He stood right there like it was no big deal and let me take several pictures. I just haven't gotten the film developed yet."

"Bring me a copy when you get them," Joey said. "I need to get to work on this right away."

She hesitated. "Joey, I really think I've made a mistake about him. He really is working on the park. It just looks too real to be a scam."

"Hey, are you wimping out on me?"

"No," she said. "I just . . . I feel guilty going behind his back trying to dig up dirt . . . if he does happen to be legitimate."

"You're really hung up on him, aren't you? He's worked his magic on you, too."

"No," she said, though she knew her voice wasn't as adamant as she would have liked. "I'm just getting to know him better."

"And you trust him now?"

"I'm trusting him more," she said.

"Well, for that little flicker of doubt you still have in the back of your mind, and for mine, could you get the pictures developed and let me have a copy?"

Sighing, she started for the door. "Yeah. I'll do it right now."

"Hey, Carny? You don't really want to know if he is a crook, do you?"

"I want you to tell me," she said softly. "But I don't think there's a person in this town who wants to believe that's what Logan Brisco is. Besides, why would he have let me take his picture, if he has anything to hide?"

The moment Carny learned that none of the pictures had come out, that doubt in the back of her mind became more than a flicker. "Why wouldn't they have come out?" she asked Ben Walker, who developed most of the film in Serenity.

"Well, the film could have just been bad, or it

could have been exposed, or you might have some malfunction with your camera."

"My camera worked fine on the last roll," she muttered. "You didn't even get one picture out of this?"

"Nope. Sorry."

Her mind reeled through the possibilities as she walked back to the sheriff's office. It was just too coincidental. Yet it *was* a coincidence. It had to be, because the alternative was something she didn't want to consider.

"Was Logan ever near your camera?" Joey asked her when she reported back to him.

"No, never. It's just a coincidence. But don't worry," she said quickly. "I'll try again. Jason's birthday party is this weekend. I'll be taking pictures of the kids, and I'm going to see if Logan will come. I'll get him then."

Logan looked tired when he answered the knock on his door at the motel that evening, but his eyes lit up when he saw that it was Carny.

"I was just thinking about you," he said.

"Oh, yeah?" she asked, going in. "In what context?"

Chuckling, he closed the door behind her. "Well, you may not really want to hear this, but I was missing you. I've been caught in this whirlwind ever since we got back from Houston, and I haven't seen you except on the flights back and forth with the bankers. I think I like your company better than anyone else's in town."

"That's funny," she said softly, "since I'm the one probably giving you the hardest time."

"Not so much anymore."

The attraction between them had grown too powerful, and she tried to look away. "I came by to invite you to Jason's birthday party," she said. "He'll be eight on Saturday."

Something changed in Logan's eyes, and for a moment, she would have sworn that he was profoundly moved by her invitation.

"Really?" he asked. "You want me there?"

"I wouldn't invite you if I didn't," she said. "And Jason really wants you. It's at three o'clock."

"I'll be there."

Another profound moment passed between them, and a look so eloquent that it almost brought her to her knees. When he stepped closer to her, she didn't back away. He came close enough that she could feel his warmth through his clothes, could breathe his breath as it swept across her lips. "I think you should know something, Carny," he whispered, "only I don't really know how to say it."

"What?"

"Since I was a very little boy, my emotions have pretty much been on dim. But ever since I came into Serenity and met you, they've been as bright as anyone could stand. Sometimes, maybe it's better to stay on dim. But I don't think so."

Her own eyes misted over, and when he leaned over and kissed her, she felt her own emotions bypassing bright and heading for explosive. Her mind was beginning to trust, and her heart was beginning to need, and no matter how hard she tried, she couldn't repress her feelings any longer.

Slowly, he broke the kiss, and touched her face with tentative fingertips.

"I . . . I have to go," she whispered. "Jason's at Nathan's, and I said I wouldn't be gone long."

"Okay," he said, dropping his hand to his side. "I'll see you Saturday."

"Yeah." Her voice cracked, and she cleared her throat. "At three."

Then, taking her unruly emotions with her, she left his motel, suppressing the urge to run as fast as she could, either back to him, or far, far away.

Logan was the life of Jason's party, and as Carny videotaped his shenanigans with the children, she realized she wouldn't have expected otherwise.

"Do it again, Logan!"

"Throw me!"

"It's my turn, Logan!"

The children's happy voices rang out over the music playing at the picnic table, but the children were busy playing with Logan on the trampoline Carny had gotten him for his birthday. Without inhibition, Logan jumped on the trampoline, throwing each child and dribbling them like bouncing basketballs.

Not once had he seemed nervous about the fact that she was taping him—or embarrassed about looking foolish—but later when they assembled the children around the picnic table to cut the cake, when she got her camera and began flashing pictures, she noted a touch of apprehension. Logan managed to escape most of the pictures she took, and when she cornered him, he shoved a pair of big nose glasses she had given as party favors on his face and evaded the camera once again.

Annoyed, she finally got him alone. "Tell me something, Logan. Why don't you want me to take your picture?"

"Because I'm not very photogenic," he said. "The pupils of my eyes always come out with this demonic red glow. And I have that old Indian superstition about photography stealing your soul."

"That's ridiculous. You're not Indian."

"Besides, you got a picture of me in Houston."

"It didn't come out," she said. "Something was wrong with the film."

"Oh, that's too bad."

"Then let me get a picture of you and Jason together now. It would mean a lot to him. All I want to do is put it up in his room."

"No, you don't." His amusement faded, and he gave her a sober look that spoke volumes. "You want it so you can check me out. Do you want a fingerprint while you're at it? How about my dental records?"

"Do you have them?"

"No, Carny. Do you have yours?"

"Well . . . no."

"All right, then." Meeting her eyes, he said, "Go ahead. Take the picture. I don't have anything to hide. You've got me all over that videotape."

Backing away, she brought the camera to her eye. "Smile, Logan. Act like you're having fun."

Logan forced a smile, and she flashed a few pictures in a row. Finally, she lowered the camera. "Thank you."

His smile disappeared. "Tell me something, Carny. You do believe me about the park now, don't you? You don't think I'm going to skip town with all this money anymore."

"You still could," she said. "But no, I'm not expecting it anymore."

"Then why do you keep trying so hard to get my picture?"

"Maybe I'd just like a keepsake. Maybe I photograph all my friends."

"And maybe you send all their pictures into the FBI to see if they're on the top-ten-most-wanted list."

Feeling uncomfortable with how close he was to the truth, she said, "You sound worried, Brisco."

"Well, I'm not. So be my guest. Copy the picture and send it all over the country. Make billboards of it. Put it on milk cartons. That is, if you have nothing better to do with your time."

For a moment, she stood staring at him, trying to figure out if his nonchalance was genuine or affected. When a football rolled to her feet, she reached down and scooped it up. Tossing it to Logan, she said, "They're calling you, Brisco."

Logan only chuckled and headed back to the boys.

* * *

That night when Logan was alone, his mask fell, and the nonchalance he'd feigned about being photographed began to weigh heavily on his mind. He should have known he couldn't stop her attempts to photograph him forever. That was probably the only reason she'd invited him to Jason's party.

And he had believed it was because she wanted him there.

Jack rolled onto his side on the bed next to him, and Logan stroked his rich fur. "I always knew I'd have to pay for my sins," he whispered to the sleeping dog. "But I kind of thought it would just be jail."

But in many ways, this was worse. He was on the verge of doing something legitimate, something that he was pulling off with hard work, ingenuity, and the talent that he'd used to the wrong end so many times before. Carny was starting to trust him, and he couldn't help feeling that that was one of the biggest victories in his life. But it was a hollow victory.

If she sent that picture in to the FBI, and they showed it to some of those marks he had conned in the past, it was possible that they could identify him. Most of his scores had been to big corporations, like airlines, and where he wouldn't expect anyone to single him out in their memories. But the real estate scams were a little more personal, and those marks would remember him. . . .

So what was he to do? Sit here and wait for the FBI to knock on his door, ruining the one shot he had at redemption, at legitimacy? Or was he to break into her house and expose the film again?

Neither option was viable, and finally, he threw his wrist over his eyes, and tried to imagine how *she* would feel if the FBI came to her, and told her that she had been right to suspect him.

The kisses they had shared . . . so sweet . . . would seem like another con to her. The words they'd shared, the camaraderie, the laughter . . . it would all seem cruel. She deserved so much better.

Maybe he could give her better, he thought. Maybe, if he just went to her, he could persuade her not to do anything with the film. Maybe all it required was a little persuading. After all, he still was the master of persuasion. He had nothing to lose.

The house was lonely without Jason, and Carny lay awake in bed, listening for sounds of the boys in the woods behind their house, camping out with Nathan's father for a combination birthday and "school's out" celebration. But it wasn't the quiet that kept her awake. It was Logan.

He had been wonderful with the children today, and without him, Jason's party wouldn't have been nearly the success it was. The dichotomy in Logan Brisco was something she found hard to understand . . . and yet, part of her did.

Closing her eyes, she recalled the kiss in his motel room last week, when she'd gone to invite him to the party. He was at once gentle and hungry, sweet and savage. What would he be like in bed?

Their bet came back to her, and she realized that the month was over. She hadn't gone begging to Logan, though he had been partially right about winning her over. And bet or not, she supposed that the winner would take all. Body, heart, and soul.

The doorbell rang and she got out of bed quickly and pulled on her robe. It was probably Jason, she thought with a smile. He had probably heard a noise, or gotten cold, or had one too many mosquito bites.

She went into the living room and peered through the window. It wasn't Jason who stood there, but Logan.

Her heart jumped into triple time, and closing her robe and tying the belt around her waist, she opened the door. "Logan."

He looked as serious as she had ever seen him, but he made no attempt to come in. He merely leaned against the door's casing with his hands in his pockets. "I couldn't sleep," he whispered. "I was thinking about you."

Slowly, she stepped back from the door, allowing him entrance and closing it behind him. This was it, she thought. This was the moment when she came out from under the cover of her feelings. This was when she had to deal with the emotional havoc he had wreaked in her. "What were you thinking about me?"

"That I haven't been entirely honest," he whispered. "That you deserve so much more."

"I'm listening."

He took her hand, led her to the couch, and sat

down beside her. She pulled her knees up beneath her robe, hugged them, protecting herself from whatever he was about to hit her with.

"Today, when you took my picture . . . I lied when I said it was okay for you to take it. The truth is, I was avoiding it."

Her heart deflated slowly. "Why?"

"Because," he said. "I've already told you that I had a close association with someone who probably was wanted in several states. And by that association . . . well, I don't know what might be dragged up. I told you I had a checkered past, Carny. Just like you."

"But if you're not a criminal, they won't have anything on you."

"Not true," he said. "You were with your parents when they pulled some cons. The FBI might have a file on you. That doesn't mean you're a criminal."

"That's true," she admitted. "Although my parents' scams are pretty small-scale. I don't think anybody ever even knows they've been had."

"The thing is, if you send my picture in, and they start dragging up all my past associations, then what do you think will happen to the park? What will happen to all the money that's been invested? This is for real, Carny. I can do this. You just have to trust me."

"I'd like to," she whispered, tears coming to her eyes. "I'd really like to."

"Carny," he whispered, touching her chin with his hand, and pulling her face close to his. "I won't let you down. I've come too far for that. Please, please trust me."

The tears spilling down her cheeks were the only answer she could give, but in her heart, she crossed the threshold from doubt to trust. She did trust him, and she did believe him.

When he kissed her, something burst inside her, something white-hot and fierce, something that she had forgotten was there. He was here, and he wanted her, and she . . . so desperately . . . wanted him.

When he lifted her and carried her back to the bedroom he'd never seen, and laid her gently on the bed, she didn't send him away. She didn't fight, and she didn't dread, and she didn't fear.

Instead, she pulled him down with her.

Their lovemaking was the most fierce, the most frantic, all-consuming, and they held nothing back. Not body, mind, nor soul. Neither of them knew how to compromise.

Afterward, Logan lay beside her in her bed, holding her. But in his eyes, she saw torment rather than joy.

Lifting her head, she looked up at him. "What's wrong? Are you having regrets?"

"No," he said quickly. "Not about being with you."

"Then what?"

His eyes misted, and he turned on his side and looked down at her. "Carny, I've had sex with a lot of women, but I've never felt intimate with one before. Until now."

She smiled.

"No, I mean it. It felt like I belonged right here. With you."

"It felt that way for me, too."

For a moment their eyes held, then finally, he rolled onto his back and fixed his gaze on the ceiling. Slowly, she sat up. "Logan, what is it? What's going on?"

"I don't want lies between us." He swallowed, and made himself look at her. "Carny, what if I told you that you were right about me all this time?"

Something terrible coiled up inside her, and she sat up slowly. "What are you saying?"

There were no barriers in his eyes, no filters, no censors. "What if I told you that I was everything you thought I was, but that something has changed? That there's nothing I want more than to prove you wrong?"

Every muscle in her body grew rigid. For a moment, horror overcame her, the horror of knowing she had been right, but that she had succumbed to him anyway. Grabbing her robe, she got up and went across the room, as far away from him as she could get without walking out entirely. "I . . . I was right about you? About . . . about being a con artist? You were really out to fleece my town?"

"Not anymore, Carny," he said quickly. "The banks and Eric Hart and all the numbers are real. I've worked myself half to death trying to work it all out. But I can't lie to you anymore."

She leaned against the wall, her face still twisted in absolute devastation, and she shook her head. "Why not, Brisco? Why can't you lie to me?"

It was almost a plea that he take back what he'd

confessed, and slip her back into the darkness of his lies. It was almost a plea that he let her feel good just a little while longer.

But he knew better.

"Carny, where were you the day you realized you couldn't live the kind of life your parents did anymore? Do you remember?"

"I was . . . in some little town in Utah. We were driving all night, because we'd almost been caught at something. I don't even remember what."

"And you knew, didn't you, that at some point, you had to jump off the mad merry-go-round you'd been born onto?"

She hugged herself as her eyes glazed over with the memory. "I'd never felt so lonely in my life. Or so scared. Not of getting caught with my parents and going to jail . . . but of trying to stop the cycle. Of escaping it, somehow."

"I've been scared, too, Carny," he said, his luminous blue eyes glistening in the lamplight. "And the closer I've gotten to you, the more terrified I've gotten. But I'm gonna do it, Carny. I'm gonna do it."

Slowly, his words penetrated, and she let the fragile edges of hope work their way back into her heart.

"But it's so hard," he said. He got up, turned his back to her, and looked out the window into the night as he struggled to find the right words. "Carny, it started out to be just another scam. You knew it. You saw it the first day I came to town. But now . . . for the last few weeks I've been trying to make it happen. And I can almost touch it." He turned around, closing his hand into a fist. "I can see it happening, Carny, just like I said. But . . ."

"But what?"

"But it's so much more terrifying, trying to pull off reality. Illusion is a lot easier." He looked her in the eye. "I'm trying to turn my lies into truth, Carny, if that makes any sense. I'm trying like hell."

It was the first time since she'd met him that she didn't find a trace of doubt in her mind. "Why?"

"Because . . ." His voice broke, and he cleared his throat and tried again. "Because for the first time in my life I've found people I want to call my own. In a way, turning this around is just as selfish as what I set out to do. I just want to belong somewhere."

She took a deep, cleansing breath, and let his words sink in. "Selfish or not, it's a lot more honorable, Logan."

He looked at her, helpless, tormented. "You deserve honorable, Carny."

An unexpected sense of peace fell over her, and despite what he'd told her, despite what she knew about him, despite what some part of her had always known, she felt closer to him than she'd ever felt to anyone in her life.

When she walked across the room and stood on tiptoe to slide her arms around his neck, she felt him sink down until his forehead was on her shoulder. She felt the sobs rising up inside him, shaking out of him, years-old, locked-up sobs of a little boy who was too suddenly alone . . . of a man who was suddenly terrified of being alone again.

She held him and cried with him until his emotion had been spent, until hers had been exhausted. And finally, when they made love again, it was sweeter, gentler, and even more cathartic than the first time had been.

Afterward, Carny lay in his arms, and just before she fell asleep, she whispered, "I trust you now, Logan."

She didn't see the tears filling his eyes, or know the thoughts raging through his mind. And she didn't wake when he slipped from her bed.

# 18

*Carny woke to the* sound of Jason banging on the back door, and quickly she turned over to wake Logan.

But he was gone.

Flustered, she grabbed her robe and pulled it on as she ran to the door. On her way, she looked for Logan, hoping he wouldn't stroll out of the bathroom just as she let Jason in.

Jason looked like a rumpled street urchin when she opened the door. "Jason, it's six in the morning," she said, smiling faintly as he shuffled in, dragging his Ninja Turtle sleeping bag behind him.

She bent down and snatched up the bag. "Couldn't you have slept a little later?"

"It was sticky, Mom, and Mr. David snores. I want to get into my own bed."

Pulling him into a hug, she kissed his dirty cheek. "Okay, birthday boy. Sleep tight."

Yawning, Jason kicked off his sneakers and headed for his bedroom. Carny grabbed the shoes and followed him back to his room, glancing toward the bathroom on the way. The door was open, and Logan wasn't there. She went to Jason's bed and tucked the blanket around him. "Night, Mom," he muttered.

"Morning, honey," she said with a grin.

Quietly, she went back into the kitchen and looked around to see if Logan had had coffee or left a note, but nothing had been disturbed. Closing her robe more tightly around her, she stepped outside and looked up her driveway. His car was gone.

Why would he have left so abruptly?

Several possibilities crossed her mind, among them that Jack was alone, or that Jason could possibly come home at any time, or that the neighbors might see his car in the driveway.

Still, he could have told her.

She went back to her room, and sat for a moment on the bed, wishing she'd had the chance to wake up with him and look him in the eye in the morning light, and verify that the feelings they'd shared last night were real. She wanted to see that determination in him again, that vulnerability, that intimacy. And she needed to hear the promises, one more time.

But he hadn't stayed, and now she was confronted with the awkward feeling that the intimacy had been broken, and might be hard to get back.

She thought of showering and busying herself

with housecleaning or mowing the lawn, until she heard from him. But that wasn't her style. Carny had never been a game-player.

So she asked herself what she expected now, and whether she, indeed, had a right to expect anything at all.

Yes, she told herself quickly. She had been closer to him last night than she'd ever been with anyone, and that did give her the right to expect something. She had the right to expect him to keep his word about changing, just as he had the right to expect her to keep what he'd told her confidential.

She had the right to expect to see him again, without awkwardness or their former enmity. She had the right to expect their relationship to move to a new plateau.

But as those rights filed through her heart, she worried that she might not have the final right that she wanted—needed—this morning.

The right to admit she had fallen in love with him.

Maybe she wouldn't have that right until he gave it to her, but she did have all the others. And she wasn't going to cower behind housework waiting for him to make a move.

Opening the drawer in her bedside table, she pulled out the phone book, and thumbed through it for the number of the motel.

When the motel clerk answered, she said, "Doc? This is Carny. I'm sorry to call so early, but would you connect me to Logan's room, please?"

The man hesitated. "I'm sorry, Carny, but he checked out over an hour ago."

Her heart plummeted, and for a moment she couldn't find her voice. "Checked out? What do you mean he checked out?"

"He said he was going to be gone several days, so there was no use keeping the room."

"At five in the morning?" Standing up, she grabbed one of the posts on her bed and tried to steady herself. "Where did he go, Doc?"

"He said to Dallas. Something about his investors."

She covered her face with one hand, and tried to catch her breath, but the air seemed too thin, and her lungs were tight. "Which ones?" she asked. "Which investors? It's Sunday, Doc. The banks are closed on Sunday."

"I'm just telling you what he said, Carny. He wouldn't have said it if he didn't mean it."

Carny felt the room spinning, and she dropped back down on the bed. Slowly, she replaced the phone into its cradle. Staring into space, she let the reality sink in and tried to face what she knew—deep down in her heart—to be true.

*He wouldn't have said it if he didn't mean it.* Wouldn't he? Wasn't saying things without meaning them a way of life for him? What had made her think he'd meant any of what he'd said last night?

Logan had skipped town with everyone's money, after finishing his final con in the town. Getting her into bed. And then, to top it all off, he'd made that big, intimate confession, a final kick in the teeth, just to make sure that all the soft, sweet memories were made into a mockery.

He was probably laughing all the way out of town.

Despair crushed her, but at the same time, she had room in her heart for the rage that coursed through her. She wanted to scream, to cry, to tear something. She wanted to hurt him, to hate him, to *stop* him. For a moment, she thought of going down the list in the phone book, calling everyone in town, and telling them that if they hurried, they might still catch him. But no one would be any more likely to believe her now than they had before.

No one except Joey.

Trembling, she punched out Joey's number, and waited as it rang three times. Finally, on the fourth, he answered in a groggy voice.

"Hello?"

"Joey, I was right," she blurted. "He's gone and he took all the money!"

"Carny?"

"Joey, listen to me. He left about an hour ago. You might be able to stop him."

"Carny, whom are you talking about?"

"Wake up, Joey!" she shouted. "Logan Brisco!"

"Where did he go?"

Without warning, tears assaulted her with brutal force, cracking her voice. "He took off, Joey. Just like I predicted."

She heard bed sheets rustle, then Joey asked, "Carny, are you all right?"

"No!" she screamed. "I'm not. I've been had, just like everybody in this town! Joey, please do something!"

"I'll be right over," he said.

"No," she cried. "You're not listening. Don't come here. Go after him!"

After she slammed down the phone, the sobs took hold of her. How could she have been so stupid? How could she have allowed herself to get caught in his con? How had she managed to fall in love with someone she had known all along was a liar?

The phone rang, and she caught her breath as a fragile hope sprang inside her. Maybe it was Logan, and maybe he had an explanation. . . .

She grabbed the phone. "Hello?"

"Carny, it's Joey."

Her heart sank like a lead weight, and suddenly she hated herself for hoping—even for a moment—that he would call.

"Carny, I just called Doc at the Welcome Inn, and he felt pretty sure that Logan's coming back."

"Then why did he steal out of town at five on a Sunday morning, without telling a soul?"

"He told Doc, Carny. I think you're overreacting a little."

"Overreacting?" she repeated. "You think I'm overreacting? You're not even going to look for him?"

"Carny, there's no proof that he's done anything wrong."

"What do you need, Joey? A written confession?"

"No, but you can't chase a man down just because he checks out of a motel. Maybe he's with a woman or something."

"Well, if he is, he's the busiest stud in town!" she

flung back. Then realizing what she'd said, she covered her face and tried to calm down. "Fine, Joey," she said through her teeth. "Do nothing. But don't forget I tried to warn you. I tried to warn everybody."

She hung up and paced across her bedroom for a moment, struggling to decide what to do now.

The irony of it happening to her—when she had known better than anyone else—smothered her. How could she go to church this morning and look everyone in the eye and tell them they'd been taken? How could she blame them when she'd given Logan more than anyone else had?

The truth was that she was no smarter than any of them, and she supposed that was what Logan's bitter lesson had taught her. He had defeated her in the most personal way—by making her love him and trust him and believe in him, even after he'd told her that she'd been right about him.

Unable to stand the self-recriminations, and certain that she couldn't face the people of Serenity with her own failure, she pulled her suitcase out of her closet and began to pack as fast as she could.

She had to get out of here, she told herself. She had to go where people weren't constantly telling her that she was overreacting, that Logan would never do anything like that, that their money and hearts and souls were safe with him.

After throwing several days' worth of clothes into a bag, she got dressed, then ran into Jason's room.

"Honey, wake up," she said. "We've got to pack."

Jason looked sleepily up at her. "For what?"

She yanked open his drawers and began pulling out clothes. "We're going on a trip."

He sat up, rubbing his eyes. "A trip where?"

"I don't know," she said. "How about New Mexico? We could go to the carnival and see Grandma and Grandpa."

His sleepy eyes lit up. "All right!" he shouted, jumping out of bed. "I haven't seen them in ages! Can I ride the roller coaster, Mom? I'm big enough this time!"

"We'll talk about it on the plane," she said. "I won't be able to breathe until I get out of this town."

A sad melancholy fell over Carny, adding to the despondency she was already nursing, when she came over the hill toward the carnival, and saw the Ferris wheels and roller coasters looming into the afternoon sky. Scratch, the sword-swallower, whom her parents had sent to pick her up at the airfield, fished his pass out of his pocket and prepared to hand it to the gatekeeper to get him onto the fairgrounds.

"Look, Mom! The double Ferris wheel! Nathan went on one at the state fair and said it got stuck, and he had to sit up there for an hour until his dad climbed the wheel and got him down."

Carny breathed a laugh. "I've told you not to believe everything Nathan tells you."

"I'm not scared, though. Can I ride it?"

"We'll see." Already, the scents of cotton candy,

chicken-on-a-stick, fresh taffy, and cinnamon rolls wafted over the area, conjuring up memories of a childhood where almost every meal was eaten with her fingers while walking down the midway, unless it had been a sandwich thrown together in a moving trailer. Still, it smelled vaguely of home, and she felt a small stirring of comfort in knowing that this was where she'd begun. Maybe it wasn't too late to find a few answers here.

When the guard opened the gate for them, Scratch drove straight back, through the infield where the trailers were, to where her parents' trailer was parked. The jalousies were broken on it, and it needed a good bath, and the awning that came out from the side to create a makeshift porch was torn. On the side were the words "Douglas Carnivals Limited."

"Your folks had a meeting with the sheriff," Scratch told them, getting out. "But they said to wait here. Either that, or you can walk around the park."

"A meeting with the sheriff? Are there problems?"

Scratch grinned and hiked one eyebrow. "Nothing a little cash won't fix." Lighting a cigar, he gave a phlegmy laugh.

"What about Ruth?"

"She's working right now. Has a break in about an hour when I take over. But Sas and Peg are over in the Tojo Trailer. Everybody else is working."

"Who are Sas and Peg?" Jason asked.

"They're . . ."

"The kootch girls," Scratch said indelicately.

"What're kootch girls?"

Carny shot Scratch a look that warned him to

shut up. "They're dancers," she said. "We don't need to see them right now. They're probably resting."

"Okay. Is there a bathroom somewhere? I need to go."

"Closest donnicker's by the House of Apes," Scratch said.

"What's a donnicker?"

"It's the bathroom, Jase," Carny said. "Only we can go in Grandma and Grandpa's trailer. The donnickers aren't usually very clean."

"After that can we walk around the park? Please, Mom? I'm hungry, and everything smells so good!"

"Sure," Carny said, taking the key that Scratch proffered and unlocking her parents' door. "We'll just freshen up, and then I'll see how many carbohydrates and buckets of grease I can pour down you."

"All right!"

She opened the door and Jason dashed in. Over her shoulder, she called, "Thanks, Scratch."

"No problem, Carny," he said. "Good to have you back."

Jason had already found the bathroom, and as Carny stepped into the trailer where she had grown up, she was assaulted by a wave of nostalgia. This was home, such as it was. This was where she'd slept, eaten, traveled, studied. This was where she'd dreamed . . . of finding a way out, of settling down, of having a normal family where her children's days weren't filled with longing and disappointment.

"Wow, Mom. This is great! Is this where you used to live?"

"Sure is," she said quietly.

"But where was your room?"

"I slept here, on the couch bed," she said. "Grandma and Grandpa slept in that little room at the back."

Jason's enthusiasm faltered a degree. "Where were your toys? Where did you play?"

"I didn't keep many toys," she said, "but I read a lot. And there was always the carnival. I could ride anything I wanted. And I got to play in the animal truck."

"The what?"

Smiling, Carny hooked a finger for Jason to follow her back outside. "This way," she said, glad she'd finally thought of one charming thing to show Jason about the carnival.

They walked between trailers to the eighteen-wheeler parked at the fringe and stepped up on the rim of the bed. There, she raised the door, revealing the treasures inside.

"Wow!" Jason cried.

In the truck, thousands of stuffed animals lay in soft mountains. Stuffed dolls and dogs and teddy bears all lay waiting to be taken to the midway as prizes to the marks who paid twenty times what they were worth to win them.

Jason grabbed an armful and, giggling, fell back onto a downy mountain of stuffed animals. "Whose are these?"

"The carnival's," she said. "These are all the prizes. I used to play here all the time."

"Really, Mom? They let you?"

"Sure they did. These things only cost a few cents apiece, but the marks will pay a dollar a shot to win them. By the time they walk away with one, the agents have usually scored twenty to thirty dollars."

"What are marks?"

She caught her breath, surprised that she'd used such a word in front of her son. "I meant . . . customers."

"Why'd you call them marks?"

"Because," she said, deciding not to couch it in niceties. "You see, Jason, everybody in the carnival isn't honest. A lot of the people who work here are just trying to find ways to take people's money. And they don't think of them as people . . . or even as customers. They think of them as marks."

"Did you think of them as marks?"

She sighed. "Yeah, I'm afraid I did. I grew up calling them that."

"Then I'll call them that. Heck, I'll even *be* one!"

"Not if I can help it," she said, sitting down on a pile of teddy bears and leaning back against the wall. "I hope I can teach you not to get taken, Jason. I hope you'll grow up knowing better."

"Like you?"

Tears sprang to her eyes, tears she hadn't seen coming. She shook her head. "Jase, I'm just as big a mark as anyone, if you can just get me on the right gaff." Her gaze drifted out of the truck to the midway just beyond the trailers. Coming here was tantamount to moving backward, she thought, and yet she'd had to. These were her roots. They were what made her who she was. Now and then everybody needed to go home.

She wondered where Logan went when he was at his rope's end. Where was he now? Was he in Tahiti, counting his money and ranking her lovemaking on a scale of one to ten? Did she get extra points for being such a challenge? Was there a bonus for her trust, and another for her love?

"Mom, I don't understand. What's a gaff?"

Carny glanced back at her son, who had burrowed down under a pile of stuffed animals and stuck his head out as if he was one of them.

She smiled and blinked back her tears. "A gaff is a con, but don't worry about it. There's just something about being home that makes you slip back into your old vocabulary, no matter how hard you worked to lose it. I guess no matter how far you run, you can't ever escape who you were when you started." It was a startling realization, one that she could have done without. And that it paralleled her more closely with Logan disturbed her more than she wanted to admit.

"Hey, do you think Grandpa would let me have one of these?"

Jason's question shook her out of her reverie, and she took a minute to reorient herself. "I'm sure he would."

"But I'd rather win one. That's more fun."

She thought of a nice way to tell him that the games were rigged, but there were things she wasn't ready to let him know just yet. It was like telling your child there was no Santa Claus. Part of you knew he couldn't go on believing forever, but another part hated to destroy his wonderment. Maybe she still knew some of the agents at the games Jason was interested in, and could talk them into letting him win something.

"Carny, my baby!" Carny turned at her mother's shriek across the infield and saw the little lady with platinum-dyed hair bounding toward her.

"Mama!" Jumping down from the truck, she intersected with her mother and allowed Lila to spin her around.

"You look like one of those cultured ladies," her mother said, setting her back and looking her over. "Like you've been spending all your time in a beauty shop getting your nails done. Is that what you've been doing, Carny? Are you a lady of leisure?"

"Of course not, Mama," she said. "You know I'm a pilot. And I haven't painted my nails in three years."

"Then you must be eating healthily. Where's my grandbaby?"

"On the truck. Under a pile of animals. You'll recognize him right away, since he's the only one who's not purple."

"The same place I always found you," her mother said. "Jason? Jason, come here and give your grandma a big hug!"

Jason raised his head from a mountain of stuffed animals and looked out at her. "Huh?"

"Oh, my God!" her mother shrieked. "He's a little man. Jason, when did you get so big?"

Jason got to his feet and tried to step over the stuffed animals. "Um . . . I don't know."

"How old are you now?" she asked, holding up her arms to catch him when he jumped down. "Five, six?"

"I'm eight," he said, lifting his chin with indignation. "My birthday was yesterday."

"Eight? My heavens, Carny, has it been that long?"

"Yeah, Mama. It has."

"Well, we have lost time to make up for, don't we? Not to mention birthday presents. Come with me, Jason. I'll show you around the park. Maybe even put you to work, if you're interested."

"That'd be great! Can I, Mom?"

Carny touched Lila's arm, stopping her. "Mama, no. I'll just keep him with me."

"For heaven's sake, Carny, I'm his grandmother. What are you afraid of?"

Carny's face reddened, and she wished she didn't have to fight this battle so soon. "You sometimes . . . get distracted. You might forget him."

"I won't forget you, will I, Jason?"

"And I don't want him being put to work."

"Well, for heaven's sake, what did you think I meant? I only thought that maybe he could stand on the bally of the House of Wonders and make like an announcer. How would you like that, Jason? We'll give you a microphone and you can pantomime the recording."

Carny thought of the freak shows inside the House of Wonders. That was where Ruth, the fat lady, sat most of her day while people paid to ogle her, and Scratch did his sword-swallowing trick, and Bounce, the contortionist, bent his body into virtual knots. That was where Allesandro, the half-man, half-woman did his act, and where Georgie Jingles practiced his illusion of being half-man, half-horse. It was where Snake disrobed to show the scales he'd had tattooed all over his body, and where Burt set himself on fire.

It was the core of the worst part of the carnival, yet it was the stuff that fascinated little boys.

"Please, Mom. Let me go!"

"Mama, I promised him I'd take him on the double Ferris wheel. Don't you want to do that, Jase?"

"Sure I do!" Jason shouted. "Then can I go with Grandma?"

"We'll see," she said, taking his hand.

Her mother set her hands on her hips and looked disgusted. "Your mother's afraid you'll like it too much, and want to be a carny when you grow up," Lila said. "And there wouldn't be a thing in the world wrong with that."

"Jason's going to be president, aren't you, Jase?"

"No," he argued. "I'm going to be an astronaut. Either that or a baseball player."

Carny smiled. "He's given this a lot of thought."

"Or maybe a sultan like Logan!" Jason blurted as an afterthought.

"A what?" Lila asked. "He knows a sultan?"

"No." Carny frowned down at her son. "Do you mean a consultant, Jason?"

"Yeah, that's what I want to be. Somebody who plans big fun stuff like Logan, and gets everybody to invest."

Carny's smile fell, and her dismal gaze met her mother's. "Well, I guess that's not so far from being a carny, is it, Mama?"

"Who's this Logan fellow? The amusement park guy? Did you talk to him about our retiring, Carny?"

Before Carny had the chance to answer she heard a familiar voice behind her. Swinging around, she saw her oldest friend, her dearest confidante, her teacher and mentor, and her personal philosopher, riding toward her on a golf cart. "Ruth!"

Letting go of Jason, Carny ran and threw herself into the massive woman's arms. When she'd last seen her, Ruth was five hundred pounds, but Carny suspected she was even bigger now. Ruth's hug was tight and warm, and her body shook as she laughed out loud. "You look beautiful, baby! Look at you."

Carny pulled back and saw that Ruth's eyes were moist. "And the baby . . . is that little Jason?"

Jason stretched to his full height, and extending a hand, he said, "I'm Jason Sullivan."

"You can call me Ruth," Ruth said, pulling him into a hug and sobbing as if she'd found her own long-lost child. "Oh, you feel so good! And Carny, you look gorgeous. Like a fairy princess or something. Oh, lands, it's so good to see you."

Carny couldn't help the tears pushing to her

eyes. Of all the people she'd grown up with in the carnival, her parents included, Ruth was the one she had missed the most. "Jason, Ruth is the lady I told you about. The one who taught me practically everything I know."

"The computer lady?"

"Yes," Carny said. "She's the one with the computers all over her trailer."

Ruth wiped at her eyes. "Well, that's a switch. I'm usually called the fat lady. That's what I am, Jason, in the House of Wonders."

Jason looked embarrassed, for he didn't know how to respond to that without hurting Ruth's feelings. "Mom talks about you all the time."

"And I talk about her," Ruth said, sniffing. "A day doesn't go by that I don't think about you two."

"Maybe she'll listen to you, Ruth," Lila said. "I was just trying to talk Carny into letting Jason go around with me for a little while, but she's convinced I'm going to turn him into a delinquent while he's with me."

"We're going on the double Ferris wheel," Carny said, stroking Jason's hair. "Aren't we, Jase?"

"Now, Mom? Can we go now?"

"Sure we can." She leaned over and hugged Ruth again. "I'll be back in a little while, and we can catch up, okay?"

"You know where I'll be," Ruth told her. "You hold on to his hand, now. The crowd has gotten rougher than it used to be, and it's easy to get lost around here."

"Good lord," Lila said, waving them off. "It's the same as it's always been, and Carny grew up just fine. Just look at her now." She leaned over and kissed Jason's cheek. "Make her stop by the Ring Toss to see Grandpa Dooley, Jason. He's filling in for the agent there while he takes lunch. He can't wait to see you."

Jason bounced with anticipation. "Now, Mom? Can we go now?"

"All right," Carny said, laughing. Waving back at Ruth and her mother, she let Jason pull her off toward the midway.

Jason's eyes danced with excitement as they got off the Ferris wheel, and he looked up at her as he cried, "Can we go again, Mom? Please?"

"Later, Jason. There are a lot of other rides, too."

"You were so lucky when you were a little girl! Did you really get to ride anytime you wanted?"

"Pretty much. But it didn't seem so lucky at the time."

"Why? How could you ever want anything else?"

She took his hand, and they began to stroll up the midway. "I wanted the things you have, Jase. A real house with a backyard, friends I could play with, school . . . "

"But those things are boring."

"Only to those who have them." Sadly, she glanced up the row of game booths, and saw a little girl with stringy blonde hair and a dirty face sitting on the steps leading to the booth door. She didn't know the agent—he was probably one of the newer ones—but she recognized the waiflike look on the child's face, and knew without a doubt that she was a carny's kid. "See that little girl over there, Jase?"

He looked in the direction she nodded, and said, "Yeah."

"She's probably traveling with the carnival."

"How do you know?"

"The way she's sitting on the steps, like she belongs there. The way her eyes are scanning the crowd. You know what she's thinking, Jason?"

"What?"

"She's thinking about the children she sees. The ones who are holding their parents' hands, like you. The ones who are excited to be here, the ones who see it as a treat. She's wondering what kind of houses they live in, and if they take ballet, and if they play softball. She's wondering if their parents take them to church or how many kids they have in their classes at school. She's wondering if they have birthday parties."

"Didn't you ever have birthday parties, Mom?"

"Well, yeah, sometimes some of the carnies would get together and get me a cake, and sing happy birthday. But I always had dreams of having lots of little girls over, all dressed in fancy dresses. . . ." Her eyes took on that longing that she thought she'd discarded long ago. "Only I never knew many little girls."

"But you knew the sword-swallower, and the magician, and the kootch girls."

"Yeah, I did," she said, chuckling softly. "I sure did."

"Hey, kid, did your mama put a bowl on your head to cut your hair or did you cut it yourself?"

Jason swung around and saw Tojo the Clown sitting in his dunking booth, targeting him. "Is he talking to me, Mom?"

"I'm afraid so," she said. "His gaff is to insult people until they get so mad they want to pay money to dunk him."

"Can I?"

"Hey, kid, you can't dunk me. You'd have to let go of Mommy's hand first."

Jason dropped her hand as if it had burned him. "I bet I can."

Carny recognized the agent taking the money and passing out baseballs to be thrown at the plate that would dunk Tojo. "Jello? Is that you?"

The old man chuckled. "Carny?" Laughing, he stretched his arms wide, and she hugged him. "Your folks said you'd be coming today. How the hell are you?"

"Great. Jello, this is my son, Jason. . . . "

"So are you gonna stand there scratching yourself, kid, or are you gonna make a fool out of yourself with that baseball?" the clown shouted.

Jason eyed the dunking booth. "Mom, I've got to dunk him."

Carny laughed. "You sure do. Look out, Tojo," she shouted to the clown. "He's pretty good."

"Is that you, Carny?" the clown shouted back. "What swamp did they drag you out of? I heard your husband ran off with a beautician. Did you come back here to find another one?"

Undaunted by the rueful chants she'd heard all her life—though she had to admit they stung a little more when they were true—she paid Jello for the privilege of drowning the clown, got her three balls, and gave them to Jason. Knowing they were weighted and rarely hit the plate, she said, "Aim high, Jase. These aren't regular balls."

Jason threw the ball with all his might and missed. "You haven't lost your spark, have you, Carny? Letting your kid take your shots for you?"

"Try again, Jason," she said. "Aim higher this time."

"Hey, Carny, we could use you back in the carnival. They need another kootch girl. You don't mind wearing tassels, do you?"

Jason shot and missed again. "You do this one, Mom. Please, we've got to dunk him."

"I've imagined you in tassels, Carny. Did you dance for your Texan husband? Did you use what Peg and Sas taught you?"

Taking the ball, she mentally eyed the plate and tried to concentrate. "You're gonna need a dozen more to get me down, Carny."

"Just one will be fine, Tojo!" she shouted.

With one rip of her arm, she threw the ball, hit the plate, and sent the clown into the cold water beneath him. Jason jumped up and down, whooping. "You did it, Mom! You did it!"

"Somebody had to." Dusting off her hands, she

took Jason's hand again and started away. "See you later, Jello."

"Later, Carny," the old man said, chuckling.

"You can't do it twice," Tojo sputtered, climbing back onto his swing. "I'll bet you a night like you've never had before that you can't come back here and do it again."

"I can be conned," Carny said under her breath, "but it takes a heck of a lot more than some wet clown shouting insults at me."

Jason looked up at her, bewildered.

She sighed. It took someone as slick as Logan Brisco, someone who deserved an Oscar for his work, someone who didn't stop until he'd conned everybody in his way. Someone a world smarter than Tojo the Clown, though he didn't have any more scruples.

They came closer to the booth where her father was substituting, and she heard his laughter over the crowd. Something about that laugh made her chest tighten. It wasn't his usual laugh . . . it was his con laugh . . . the one that set people off guard and enabled him to take them.

"There's your grandfather," she said.

"Let's go talk to him!"

"Not yet," she said, holding back. "Wait until that customer leaves."

They watched while the young man laid down the last of his money for a few more rings to toss, missed, and then looked longingly at the stuffed animal he'd been trying to win for his date. "I'm out of money," the young man said. "You wouldn't take a check, would you?"

Her father seemed to consider that for a moment. "Well, we don't normally, but . . . well, okay. In this case . . ."

Anxiously, the man wrote out his check, tore it out, then handed it to Carny's father. "Twenty-five dollars worth, huh? You're pretty serious about this, aren't you?"

He gave the mark enough rings to win every animal hanging from the ceiling, if only the game wasn't rigged. Of all the rings he tossed, he hit only one on a winning peg.

The young man's date looked crestfallen, and he looked humiliated as they started to walk away. "Look," Carny's father said, stopping them. "Everybody has a bad day now and then." Taking down a stuffed dog, he tossed it into the man's hands. "And as for the check, just don't worry about it." Quickly, he tore it up, and let the pieces fall to the floor at his feet.

"Thanks, sir," the young man said. "I appreciate it."

"Yeah, well, you were probably going to stop payment on it tomorrow, anyway, weren't you?"

With a laugh that said he'd been caught, the man shrugged, handed the dog to his girlfriend, and strolled away.

As Carny and Jason stepped up to the booth, she saw her father pull the real check out of his sleeve, and chuckle as he put it in the cash box. The one he'd torn up had been fake.

"Hi, Pop," she said.

He looked up at her. "Carny! I thought you were probably here by now!" Quickly, he ran out the door of the booth and embraced her. "Have you grown taller?"

"No, Pop, I don't think so."

"Well, you sure haven't put on any weight. Where's the boy?"

"Right here," she said, exasperated that he had looked right past him.

"No!" Her father looked down at Jason, and shook his head in disbelief. "That can't be him. This boy's at least ten years old. My grandson couldn't be more than four."

Jason frowned, as if he didn't know whether to be flattered or insulted. "I'm eight. My birthday was yesterday."

"Eight! That can't be."

Carny tried not to laugh. "It is, Pop."

"Well, I think maybe we'd better take him over to the age booth and let Morris see if he can guess his age. He's bound to win something. Well, he's big enough to play linebacker for Notre Dame!"

Slowly, Jason began to smile. "I am?"

"Well, practically. Within another year or two, you'll be a number-one draft choice." Taking Jason's hand, he said, "Come with me now. I'll show you. If Morris guesses your age, I'll swallow that sword of Scratch's."

Smiling almost reluctantly, Carny followed her father and her son, and she watched Jason win another stuffed animal for fooling Morris about his age.

\* \* \*

Carny spent as much time taking Jason around that day as she could, not because she wanted to ride everything in sight, but because she didn't want to give her parents the opportunity to be alone with him. By the time night had fallen and they'd ridden the roller coaster, Jason was feeling a little woozy, and his feet dragged as he walked.

"Where are we gonna sleep tonight, Mom?"

"With Grandma and Grandpa. It'll be a tight fit, but—"

"In the trailer? That'll be cool." But his voice didn't have its usual fervor. The little boy was exhausted, and Carny had to admit that she was, as well.

Still, the thoughts that had raced after her all day kept flitting through her mind. She hadn't come here to ride the rides and rekindle old memories. She had come home to nurse her wounds. To find some sense in the fact that she, who thought she was immune, had been conned.

It wasn't as if she hadn't been warned. Logan laid the bet with her at the very beginning. Winner take all. And he had won.

Jason was asleep within five minutes of lying down, and Carny found herself sitting alone at the table that had served as her dining table, her desk, her dollhouse, her ironing board, and a million other things as she was growing up. Her father sipped a beer he'd gotten before the carnival had closed down, while her mother nursed the customary hot toddy she had every night before bed.

"So tell us how plans for the park are shaping up," her father said, not bothering to keep his voice low for Jason's sake.

"I told you, Pop. It's not going to happen."

"But you didn't say why."

She leaned back in her chair and wished she had never brought up the subject of Logan with her parents. It had never been easy for her to discuss feelings with them. Her father was a stick-to-the-facts kind of guy. His main interest was the bottom line. And as much as she hated to admit it, the bottom line usually had to do with how much money it could make him.

"He was a grifter, Pop. It was all a scam."

"Hmmm." Her father tossed back the last of his beer and set the glass in the same wet ring he'd taken it from. "Too bad. It was a terrific idea. So where'd he go?"

"If I knew that, it wouldn't be a scam. I'd go get everybody's money back."

"Do you think he's trying it in another town?" her mother asked.

A sick feeling came over her. "I hope not. But I guess he probably is. Unless he's just lying low for a while, waiting until everything blows over. He's real smart. He's probably left the country."

"So what was his line again?" her father asked, frowning intently and leaning forward onto the table. "He picked out a town that was down in its luck, but still had money, and convinced everybody that he was going to make it a tourist town and make everybody rich?"

"Yeah," she said softly. "Even got bankers involved, and Eric Hart, the country singer. Conned them all."

"He must be damn good. I wish you'd introduced him to us."

Something about Dooley's attitude brought back all her old bitterness about their lifestyle. "Why, Pop? So you could get in on the action? Trust me. He would have conned you, too."

"I doubt it," her father said, chuckling. "You can't con a man who doesn't want to be conned."

Carny leaned forward on the table, facing off with her father, and whispered, "That's bullshit, and you know it."

"Carny!" Lila admonished. "I won't have that language from your lips!"

Carny started to chuckle, but there was no mirth in the sound. "That's funny, Mama. All these years, you didn't mind my wallowing in the mud with you, or watching you rip people off, or being part of your stings. You didn't mind my learning to pick people's pockets, or listening to the stories that the agents told about their sexual exploits with townies. But you were always real firm about the words I used."

"I didn't want you sounding like a . . . a . . ."

"A what, Mama? A gypsy? A carny? A piece of trash?"

"Wait a minute!" Dooley slapped his hand down on the table. "Don't you talk to your mother like that!"

Tears came to Carny's eyes, and she tried to

hold them back. "I don't know why I came back here. I just wanted to come home for a little while."

Her mother took her hand, a rare, affectionate gesture that took Carny by surprise. "Honey, this isn't your home anymore. You've grown so far away from it, you don't even recognize it now. And it seems to me like you have nothing but contempt for it."

Carny sniffed and wiped her eyes. "It's funny that no matter how far you go, you've still got one foot tangled up in your roots. And that's the foot that'll trip you up no matter what you do."

"Did you give him money, Carny? Is that why this Logan character has bothered you so?"

She breathed a laugh and wiped her eyes. "No, Pop. I didn't give him money. I did know better than that."

But she couldn't tell her father that what she'd given him was more personal than money—and that he had flung it back in her face.

"Then it shouldn't matter what he took from everybody else. They probably deserved it."

For a moment, she stared at her father, seeing the picture of the man to whom she'd been so loyal all her life. "Pop, I've defended you for years and told myself that you did have a conscience. That you weren't just out for yourself. I've even fooled myself into believing you did it for me. To feed your family. To survive. And I started letting myself think that about Brisco, too. But you know what, Pop? We pros can con *ourselves* better than anybody. All the alibis and excuses and justifications . . . They're nothing but scams we turn on ourselves."

"You don't believe that, Carny." Her father got up and went to the small refrigerator.

"Yes, I do, Pop. The truth is that *nobody* deserves to have their pride trampled, or their trust destroyed, or their innocence mocked. Nobody deserves to wake up one day and find out that they've been nothing but a sick punch line in a greedy power game!"

"So that's it," Dooley said. "He stung you, so you came home to take it out on us."

Lila touched his arm to calm him. "It's all right. That's what parents are for."

Carny wanted to laugh, but it wasn't funny. Instead, the tears fell faster. "I didn't come home to take anything out on you. I came because I needed a time-out. But I'm so tired of all the lies, Pop. Aren't you tired of them?"

"I told you we're trying to retire, Carny. We're doing the best we can. We always have."

But it was just another lie, and Carny realized that nothing was going to change.

Slowly, she came to her feet, and went to cover Jason on the little bed she had slept on as a child. Then wiping her face, she said, "I'm gonna go over and say good night to Ruth. I'll be back in a little while."

"We'll have your pallet ready," her mother said quietly, almost as if relieved that they could let go of this uncomfortable conversation. Lila had never liked for Carny to make a scene, unless it had been rehearsed.

Solemnly, Carny left the trailer and trekked across the fairgrounds to where Ruth's trailer was parked. The lights were still on, and she knew Ruth was probably working on her computers.

She knocked softly, and heard a voice say, "Come in."

As she stepped inside, a truer sense of home confronted her. The familiarity was welcoming. All the computers were in place, exactly as she remembered, though Ruth had added a few extra pieces since she'd been here last. This was where Carny had gotten her education, where she'd spent so many hours as a child, where she'd found someone to confide in, where she'd felt most accepted and welcomed. She wondered if that little girl she'd seen sitting on the steps of the Duck Shoot was one of Ruth's students now. She hoped so. The child looked like she needed someone like Ruth in her life.

"Hi, baby," Ruth said from the love seat that her huge body filled. "I was hoping you'd stop by. Are you ready to tell me what's bothering you now?"

Carny smiled and wiped at the fresh tears under her eyes. "What makes you think anything's bothering me?"

"Oh, I don't know. Call me psychic. I sense that those tears mean something. Besides, you wouldn't have brought your baby here if you hadn't really needed to come home."

Carny dropped opposite her onto Ruth's couch, and pulled her knees up.

"Your heart is broken, girl," Ruth said. "I can see it. Don't forget, I'm the one whose lap you used to sit on, when you were shorter than a yardstick, crying and not knowing why. But I always knew."

"You did, didn't you, Ruth?"

Ruth chuckled, the sweet sound warming Carny's heart. "Don't blame your folks, child. They do the best they can."

"So they say," she whispered. "But the truth is, they should have never had a child."

"Probably not. But I'm awfully glad they did."

Getting up, Carny went to sit on the arm of the love seat and hug the woman who seemed to grow bigger with each year. This was where she'd found comfort most of her life, and understanding. This was the real reason she had come home.

"I always wished you were my mother," she said.

"Imagine me as a mother." Ruth laughed. "Wouldn't that be a hoot?"

"No," Carny said seriously. "Not at all. You were probably the only one I really missed when I left the carnival."

"And I missed you like crazy, too," Ruth said, "but I was awfully happy for you. I had big hopes for your happiness. You haven't let me down, have you?"

"No," she said. "I've been happy. Really happy. It's just lately . . ."

"You fell in love with him, didn't you, baby?"

Carny's shoulders slumped, and wearily, she went to sit on the couch. Hugging her knees, she said, "Yeah, I guess I did, but it was all just a con to him. It's got to be one of the stupidest things I've ever done. Besides marrying Abe."

"I didn't blame you for marrying Abe," Ruth told her. "You never were happy here. Your soul was too pure for this kind of life, and he was your escape. You were nothing but a child then, but you're grown now. To fall in love with a flimflam man, when you found such happiness there with decent folk . . . I don't know, Carny. It doesn't sound like you."

"Of course it doesn't," Carny said. "Ruth, I've thought this all out. Did I fall in love with him because he's so much like Pop? Would my subconscious deliberately seek out someone who led the very lifestyle I hated?"

"Maybe you've been bored in that little town, child. There's a lot of gypsy in you. Maybe part of you misses the excitement. Maybe that's what he represented to you."

Carny found that explanation unsettling. "Then that would mean I deserved what just happened to me. That I invited it. Just like Pop said."

"Dooley told you that?"

"Well, not about Brisco. But that's his general contention about all marks. And that's just what I am. Brisco's mark. Only I *didn't* ask for it, Ruth. I can't believe I did."

"Are you saying that you don't still have a wanderlust? A need for excitement?" When Carny hesitated, Ruth went on, "Then explain the plane you fly, and the bungee-jumping you wrote me about, and the motorcycle you ride around town. I remember you as a little girl, child. I know you."

"But that doesn't mean I haven't put the lies and deceit and all the ugliness behind me, Ruth. And it doesn't mean that I'd go looking for it again. I've made a good life for Jason and me."

"Then why did you let yourself get conned? You're too smart for that, girl. Something about him made you want to believe. Something inside you needed what he had."

"Then what does that say about me?"

"It says that you're just as human as anybody else, child. And that you're not so tough. That's why people like Dooley and Lila keep getting away with the same scams. They paint pictures of hopes and dreams. They make hard people trust."

"And then they take them for everything they're worth."

"But they teach good lessons, girl. There's always a lesson."

"Some lessons are better not learned," Carny whispered. Dropping her feet, she leaned forward. "The crazy thing is, when I think of last night, I don't see signs of the lies I saw before. He was sincere. He told me what he really was, confessed everything. He said he wanted to change. Ruth, he had tears in his eyes, and . . . and there was the dog he adopted, and really, really loved. And he was so gentle with Jason, and he got him to come home after he ran away. And he said that I deserved better than him, but that he was going to *be* better." The tears made a second assault, and her face reddened as she dropped it into her hand. "Ruth, I really believed him."

She caught her breath on a sob. "But it doesn't matter what I believed. He's gone. With all that money, and all those hopes and dreams. I tried to tell everybody, but they wouldn't listen. And why should they, when I was eating out of his hand, too?"

Ruth watched her for a long moment, processing everything she'd told her. "Maybe he'll come back."

"What?"

"If you believed him that much, and if all you say about him is true, I can't help thinking that maybe it's not over. It's just hard for me to believe you could be taken that way, girl. Maybe you weren't wrong about him. Maybe it's not over yet."

She sniffed back the pain that threatened to smother her, and whispered, "No, I'm sure it's over. Why else would he have taken everything and slipped out in the wee hours?"

"I don't know, child. I wish I had the answers."

But no one had the answers, she thought as she went back to her parents' trailer and tried to get comfortable on her pallet. No one but Logan Brisco, and for the life of her, she wished she could find him, corner him, and make him tell her what pleasure he got in breaking her heart. She had never seen that kind of cruelty in his eyes, not even in the beginning when she'd least trusted him. She hadn't believed that he could be capable of hurting someone so deeply.

But that, she supposed, was what made him so good at what he did.

She wondered if the folks of Serenity had started to worry yet. She wondered if Joey had contacted the FBI. She wondered if they'd picked up his trail at all.

These thoughts kept her awake that night, and she realized as she lay awake on the floor of the trailer she had been so eager to leave years ago, with her sweet innocent little boy lying beside her, that it didn't matter who she had been, or who she'd become. The bottom line was that she could look herself in the mirror each morning and know that she did the best she could. She was strong, and she had survived before. She'd get over this, just like the town would. It wouldn't be easy, and it would take time for her to heal. But she had too much going for her to let someone like Logan Brisco rob her of her spirit.

As dawn peeked into the room, lighting the old trailer with gray tones, she asked herself the final question that kept eating at her.

Why couldn't she hate him?

That was the ultimate conclusion of his con, she thought. That no matter what he did to her, she couldn't hate him. And the most awful part of all was that she was in love with him. He was the first person since Abe who had made her that vulnerable. And that part wouldn't be easy to get over.

Jason woke then and turned over. "Mom? Can we ride the roller coaster today?"

Smiling, she told herself she would get by as long as she had Jason. "Sure, honey."

"Can we stay here a long time?"

"Maybe a couple more days," she said. "Until they tear down."

"Really? We don't have to rush back home?"

"No," she whispered. "I'm in no hurry to get back home."

# 19

*They had been with the* carnival for three days, when Carny began to sense something in her father that she hadn't seen in a long time. It was the integrity of a grandfather, and the dignity that came from an older, and supposedly wiser, man, trying to pass some of his experience onto a third generation.

Finally feeling as if Jason would be safe with her parents, she allowed them to take him around the carnival with them, so he could watch them take care of the myriad details that had to be attended to each day before the gates opened. She saw her parents revel in the chance to entertain Jason, and for the first time, she realized that the lessons he could learn here might not be so bad.

She also discovered that, despite their lifestyle,

she had been loyal to them for one reason: because she loved them. And in their own peculiar way, they loved her.

"Do you think a man who lies for a living can ever be trusted?" she asked Ruth one day as she watched Jason drive her parents off behind the wheel of the golf cart.

"Do you mean Logan?"

"I guess," she said. "Although I was kind of thinking of Pop."

"Oh, come on," Ruth said. "You trust your father. You know he'd never do anything to hurt you or Jason. He does love you, and so does your mother."

"I know," she said. "And that's what makes me wonder about Logan. Do you think that maybe Logan loved me, too, in his way?"

"I've been giving it a lot of thought," Ruth said, "and I think he did. And leaving probably caused him as much grief as it caused you."

"How do you figure that?"

Ruth shrugged her wide shoulders. "Well, honey, if a man couldn't change, if he only knew the kind of life where you had to cheat and lie to get by, maybe the last thing on earth he'd want to do is fall in love. Maybe that's why he left."

Carny fought back the tears threatening her again, and said, "He told me, 'You deserve honorable, Carny.'" Swallowing, she said, "I felt in my soul that he meant it."

"Then I'm sure he did, honey. Maybe he's more noble than you think. Maybe he left because he knows you do deserve better. And maybe he just didn't have it in him to *be* better."

Later, when Ruth had gone to the House of Wonders, Carny went to the Ferris wheel. She rode it alone, and when it lingered at the top, giving her a view of the world of her childhood, a view that should have made things clear to her, she remembered Logan's words again. *You deserve honorable, Carny.*

He *had* meant it. She knew he had. And as crooked as he might have been when he'd come to town, something had changed. But it wasn't enough.

And as the sun set, she wept in her lonesome seat in the double Ferris wheel. She wept for all the dreams she'd had as a child, walking alone down a midway teaming with families. She wept for the broken heart she kept having to mend, even after vowing it would never be exposed again. She wept for the hopes that Logan had tricked her into embracing, when she'd known better all along. She wept for the night of bliss they had shared together, when the world had seemed so perfectly in tune, as if every disappointment and hurt in her life had been specifically designed to bring her to that moment. But the moment had been so short.

And now, in spite of herself, she couldn't say she regretted that moment.

The Ferris wheel came to a stop while the jockey let off some passengers, and she looked down at the lights blinking beneath her. She listened to the clashing sounds of the rock music at the Himalayan, and the twangy country music at the Bucking-

Bronco-Bull ride, and the dubbed voice at the House of Wonders. It all reminded her of a childhood full of chaos and longing. A temporary childhood, where roots weren't allowed to grow and friendships were never planted. A youth where trust was never cultivated, and life was an endless pursuit of something that never really existed.

That night, when she was back in Ruth's trailer, listening to the sound of the fat woman's fingers clicking across the keyboard as she worked on a program she'd been designing for years, Carny came to a sudden realization that she had needed to find.

"He did give me something I needed," she whispered.

Ruth's fingers stopped. "What would that be, baby?"

"He reminded me that I could fall in love. And that I'm not invincible. That, after all these years of standing on my own, of insisting that I didn't need anyone, maybe I really did, after all."

"You don't *need* anyone, Carny. But there's nothing wrong with wanting someone." Ruth turned her body around on the bench she sat on. "Look at me, honey. I weigh more than anybody I've ever met. I can hardly get up to walk across the room. I make a living getting stared at all day. But at night, when it's late and dark and cold in this trailer, I sometimes wish . . ."

Carny waited, but Ruth didn't seem able to say the words.

"What, Ruth? What do you wish?"

Ruth's eyes filled with tears, and she blinked them away. "Oh, baby, I want more for you than I have. And you do have more. You have that little boy. But you should have even more. Logan was right. You deserve so much. And there's not one thing wrong with your wanting someone to hold you at night."

Carny wiped the tear stealing down her face. "It makes me feel weak. It sets me up to fall."

"I don't know what's worse, baby. Never getting off the ground at all, or setting yourself up and falling. Personally, I think I'd choose to make the memories."

"Memories," Carny whispered. "Why do they always turn out disappointing?"

"Maybe there's an ending you haven't predicted yet, child. Maybe the ending is a happy one."

"No, Ruth. I don't think so. How can I ever let myself fall again?"

"I believe you will, Carny. And when you do, it'll be all right."

But Carny couldn't put much hope in that as she went back to her parents' trailer, climbed onto the small bed with her son, and held him close as she slept that night.

When a week had passed, and the carnies were tearing down, preparing to head to California, Carny faced the fact that it was time to go back. Time to confront the horror in the faces of her friends. Time to admit that she'd been as big a fool as they'd been, and when all the losses were tallied, she had probably lost more than any of them.

They waited until all the rides had been dismembered, until all the booths had been loaded onto their trailers, until there was nothing left but concrete and tar. Finally, Carny saw the look of disillusionment on Jason's young face. "It's all gone," he said softly. "And it happened so fast. Like magic. Only in reverse."

"What do you mean?" she asked.

"The best part came first. And then there was . . . just nothing."

Her heart responded to his words, someplace deep inside, and she almost wished she had taken him home yesterday, before he'd had the chance to see the magic go up in smoke. But there was a wise poignance in his words, an understanding that she too had possessed at his age. And despite her wish to protect Jason's innocence, there were things he needed to know. Stroking his hair, she said, "Sometimes it happens that way."

Jason was pensive as their plane left the ground later that day, and finally, he looked at his mother. "Mom, can I call Logan when we get home, and tell him we're back?"

Carny hadn't spoken of Logan to Jason since they'd left, and for a moment, she pretended to be intent on flying the plane. Jason prompted her to answer.

"Mom?"

"No, honey," she said, finally. "Logan . . . Logan is gone. He took off the night before we left."

"On my birthday? But . . . why?"

She struggled to find the right words, but failed. "It's kind of like the carnival, Jason. The magic comes first, and then there's nothing."

"Logan's not like that."

She bit her lip, wishing she could tell him he was right. But he wasn't, and she wouldn't lie to him. "He is, baby. He's just like that."

"He'll be back," Jason said. "He has to. He's my friend."

Carny didn't answer, and again, Jason waited. Her face reddened, and tears came to her eyes. "Honey, I don't think we're going to see Logan again."

He caught his breath, and when she looked at him, she saw anger rather than surprise. "But what about the park?"

"Honey, the park was just made up—"

"No!" He screamed out the word, startling her, and she realized that she'd never seen more rage on her son's face. Not even the night he had run away. "That's not true! Logan wasn't lying. He'll be back! You'll see!"

Swallowing the tears in her throat, she didn't answer.

She watched as Jason looked out the window, hiding the tears pushing into his eyes. When she reached over to touch his hand, he jerked it away.

"You still think he lies, don't you? After all he's done!"

"Jason . . ."

"Well, he doesn't!" he shouted. "You'll see. Logan's gonna do everything he promised!"

For the rest of the trip, Jason cried quietly in his seat, staring out his window. Carny couldn't seem to fight her own tears, and by the time they landed, she was exhausted from the tension in the plane.

When they finally pulled onto the tarmac at Carny's hangar, she tried to reach her son again. "Jason, you know I love you, and I would have done anything to keep you from getting hurt. I'm so sorry."

"You're wrong, Mom," he said. "I know you are."

And before she'd killed the engine, Jason was out the door, running to their truck.

The Texas sun was directly overhead as Carny reached her house. The grass had grown taller than she liked it, since she hadn't mowed it before she left. Next door, she saw Janice out working in her garden, who abandoned her hoe and ran across the empty lot between them when she saw Carny. Before she'd even gotten out of the truck, Janice called through the window, "Carny, where have you been? Everybody's been looking for you. You had us scared to death!"

Carny got out of the truck. "We went to see my folks. I'm sorry you were worried."

"Why didn't you tell someone? J. R. and Bev are worried sick! People don't just disappear without an explanation."

"Some do," Carny said, pulling their suitcases out of the back of the truck. But she wasn't going to ask about Logan now, not in front of Jason.

Handing the smaller suitcase to her brooding son, she said, "Take your stuff in, Jason, and I'll call J. R. and Bev to let them know we're back before I unpack."

"Then I'm going to Nathan's." Jerking up the bag, Jason took it into the house.

"Go ahead and call them," Janice said, breaking into a soft smile. "Then come over and I'll update you on things." She started to walk away, then turned back. "I'm so glad you're all right."

Carny smiled. "I'm sorry I didn't leave word. It was pretty thoughtless of me."

"Yeah, well. It all worked out." Waving, Janice cut back across the yard.

Carny got her suitcase and went into the house as Jason shot back out. The curtains were still drawn and the lights were out, and it was hot, since she had turned the thermostat off before she'd left.

It was the first time since Carny had bought the house that she hadn't been happy to come home to it.

She took her suitcase to her bedroom and confronted the unmade bed. Logan had slept in it the last night she had, and she hadn't bothered to make it up. The dent of his head still crumpled her pillow, and the sheets were still flung back from where he'd gotten out of bed.

What had he been thinking? That he'd made a mistake, sleeping with her? Or that he'd finally won?

Tears assaulted her again, and she dropped her head, and sat down on the side of the bed.

Taking a deep breath and trying to sniff back her tears, she grabbed the phone and punched out her in-laws' number.

"Hello?"

"Bev, it's me. We're back."

"Carny, where on earth have you been? We've been worried sick...."

Outside, Carny heard Jason's shouts, and standing up, she looked out the window. He was running with Nathan on his heels, heading for the house with a smile the size of the state on his face.

"It just isn't like you to go off without even filing a flight plan. Where did you go?"

"Uh . . . Bev, let me call you right back, okay?"

"Carny!"

"In just a minute," Carny said.

Hanging up the phone, Carny raced to the door and caught Jason as he burst through. "Jason, what happened? What is it?"

"Mom, Mom! It's started! I told you it would!"

"What has?"

"The park!" He tried to catch his breath. "Nathan said there were bulldozers and cranes, and they're clearing all the land!"

"What?" She turned to Nathan, who was bent over, trying to catch his breath. "Nathan, that can't be. There's no money."

"Sure there is," Nathan said. "Logan's got all the money. Our money, and the bankers', and some other investors he got. It's gonna be so great! My dad took me out there to see the work this morning. They've been working for three days...."

Carny felt the color draining from her face. "Are you sure?"

"I'm positive, Carny. Dad said they're clearing all the trees, but the ground-cutting ceremony is next week."

"Ground-cutting? You mean ground-*breaking*?"

"Yeah, that. The governor is coming and everything!"

She brought her hand to her forehead and released a shaky breath. "This is unbelievable."

"I *told* you, Mom! I told you!"

"Get in the truck, Jason," she said, grabbing her keys. "We're going to see."

"All *right!*"

Together, they climbed into the truck, and Carny screeched out of her driveway and sped toward the site.

"Isn't it great, Mom? Logan did just what he said he'd do. Now aren't you sorry for what you—"

"Jason, please!" she snapped. "Just . . . just let me think for a minute. I have to think."

Jason got quiet, and Carny tried to sort out the thoughts spinning through her mind. If what Nathan said was true, then all the conclusions she'd drawn in the last week were wrong. And maybe . . . just maybe . . .

But she couldn't entertain the "maybes." Not yet. Not until she had proof.

She drove fast up the highway until she came near the site, then slowed down.

"Mom! Hurry up! You're slowing down."

Swallowing, she forced herself to step on the

accelerator again. And as they passed a cluster of trees, she held her breath.

"Mom, look! A bulldozer!"

Jason began jumping up and down on the seat, and Carny brought her hand to her mouth. Across the horizon, she saw bulldozers and bush hogs and other machinery clearing the land. Teams of men worked on various parts of the site.

"This can't be!" she whispered.

"I told you, Mom! I told you!"

"But . . . where's Logan?"

"He's not far, Mom. You'll see!" Jason jumped out of the truck, and slowly, she got out, too, and scanned the grounds for someone with authority. A man with a hard hat and a clipboard stood near them, talking into a walkie-talkie, and with great effort, she went toward him. "Excuse me," she said. "Who do you work for?"

The man took off his hat and wiped his tanned face with the back of his arm. "Logan Brisco and the town of Serenity, ma'am. We're clearing for the amusement park."

Still amazed, Carny looked around. "Are you sure? I mean . . . did he pay you? With money?"

The man set the hat back on his head and laughed. "Well, I sure wouldn't be out here in this heat if he hadn't paid a good portion, lady. And MidSouth of Houston and the FSB of Dallas guaranteed the rest. I've done a lot of work for them, ma'am." He looked her over, then glanced back at her truck. "Are you from the zoning board?"

Her breath seemed to come harder, and her

brain spun with possibilities, and her heart hammered . . . but whether it was with hope or dread, she wasn't sure. "No. Uh . . . where is Mr. Brisco?"

"Last I heard he was still in Dallas. But he's supposed to be flying in sometime today. We have a meeting at three, so it'll have to be pretty soon now."

The fragile hope growing in Carny's heart frightened her as she took the jubilant Jason back to Nathan's, then headed for the airstrip. As she drove, she had the dizzying feeling of teetering on the edge of a cliff, waiting to fall off with the slightest breeze. That she had been wrong, that he hadn't left town with the money, that their night together had not been a sham was too much to hope. Yet she did hope.

The airstrip was quiet when she got there, and she went straight to the radio and sat in front of it, wondering who would be flying him in, where he'd gotten the plane. . . .

But from the back of her mind came the nagging voice that had tormented her for the past week. What if it was just more of the same scam? What if the town had only *assumed* he was going ahead with things? What if Logan still intended to fleece them?

"This is XRT821C, to ZZX432B."

Carny gasped and grabbed the radio mike.

"Come in, Carny. Are you there?"

Stunned by the sound of the voice she had, only a few hours ago, believed she'd never hear again, she said, "Brisco?"

"Oh, thank God." She heard a long pause, then in a raspy whisper, he asked, "Where have you been?"

Tears filled her eyes. "Where have *I* been? You're the one who took off in the middle of the night—" Catching herself, for fear that someone might be listening on the same frequency, she tried again. "I thought you had left for good. Over."

Again, a long pause. "I told you I wouldn't, Carny. I wanted you to trust me. Over."

"I did, until you disappeared!"

"I called you from the road around ten that morning, after I was sure you'd be awake. But you were gone, and nobody knew where you were."

"What was I supposed to think?" she asked. "You couldn't have any meetings with bankers on a Sunday, and you hadn't mentioned going the night before. Over."

"I didn't sleep that night, Carny, and I made the decision because I was so eager to tie things up. I went when I did so I could spend the day in the Dallas library, researching the final things I needed to get the investors to commit. And I knew Eric Hart was in Dallas that day because he'd had that charity concert the night before. I was hoping to set up a meeting with him. Over."

She couldn't think, for the answers were reeling through her mind, answers she hadn't believed she'd ever hear. And now here they were, and they made sense, and she believed. . . .

Closing her eyes, she leaned her forehead against the mike. All that grief. All that misery. All that soul-searching. And all because she had been so sure he was going to let her down.

"You know, Carny, you're not the only one who can change and make it stick."

A tear rolled down her cheek, and trying to steady her voice, she whispered, "Where are you, Brisco?"

"About fifteen miles from Serenity," he said. "I'll be landing in a few minutes."

She laughed, a soft laugh that held volumes of relief. "In what?"

"I'm in Eric Hart's plane," he said with a chuckle. "He's in for three million dollars, Carny. I convinced him last Sunday, and he stayed over in Dallas Monday and visited the bankers there with me. We've gotten approval to call the park Hartland."

"You're amazing, Brisco."

"I have a lot to tell you. Are you ready to talk me down? I'm still not sure about these landings."

Collapsing back in her seat, Carny wiped her eyes. "Are you by any chance alone in that plane, Brisco?"

"Except for Jack," he said. "For some reason, Eric's under the impression that I'm a longtime pilot. So he loaned me the plane for a few days. Only thing is . . . I forgot to tell him my landings are a little shaky."

She wondered if he'd forgotten to mention that he hadn't logged a single solo hour, much less gotten his license. "Did you tell him you were behind on your paperwork, Brisco?"

Logan knew exactly what she meant. "I'll get it later, Carny. Don't worry."

He paused for a moment, and the timbre of his voice dropped. "I missed you, Carny. I tried to call you a hundred times. I knew what you must be thinking."

For a moment, she stared at the mike, then finally whispered, "I'm sorry, Brisco."

"No, *I'm* sorry," he said. "Funny thing is, when I let people down it's usually planned. This is the first time I've been so desperate not to, that it happened anyway. But it's the last time. I swear it, Carny. Over."

Too overwhelmed to answer, she looked out the window until she could see his plane coming into view.

"So what do you think?" he asked. "Fifty bucks says I can land this pup as smooth as butter."

"No bet, Logan," she said. "You've been flying by the seat of your pants all your life. Something tells me you'll land the plane just fine."

She heard him laughing across the radio waves, and standing up, she watched him come in for his landing. He had landed smoothly the last few times they'd flown, and she was confident that he could do it. Logan could do anything.

It was as if he'd done it a thousand times, and as he came in with the finesse of a veteran pilot, she abandoned the mike and went out to the tarmac to meet him.

Her heart hammered, and tears flooded her eyes again. Idly, she wondered if she'd ever again be that stoic, free spirit who never cried. So much had changed since Logan blew into her life. And for the first time, she began to let herself think that the changes were good ones.

She watched him taxi up her small runway and pull onto the tarmac, and as she wiped her tears, she gave in to the relief and unadulterated joy merging in her heart now. He was here. He'd had the chance to run away, but he had chosen not to.

She could hardly breathe as the plane came to a stop, and he opened the door and let Jack out first. When she couldn't stand still any longer, she broke into a run as he came toward her, and soon he was running, too, his face a fragile mask of new, unexplained emotions. He swept her into his arms as they met, and crushed her against him.

"God, you scared me," he said in a fierce whisper. "What if I'd never seen you again?"

Before she could answer, he kissed her, a desperate, ravenous kiss salty with her tears.

When he was able to speak again, he whispered, "There's so much I have to tell you."

"Tell me."

He leaned back against the building, and pulled her close. Wiping her wet cheek with his thumb, he said, "Well, let's start with the way I had my bags packed—more than once—to leave town with the money, and I couldn't go. Or the way I kept fantasizing about being the kind of person you deserved and living here for the rest of my life. Or the way I started wanting like hell to make the park a reality . . . for you . . . for Jason . . . and for everyone here in Serenity."

His voice broke, and he looked out over the runway. "But the past is so powerful, Carny, and when nothing's ever come easy except a scam . . . when the only people who ever gave a damn were grifters themselves . . . when the only accomplishments that amounted to anything were the stings you pulled . . . "

"You start thinking that's who you are, who you'll always be," she whispered. "I know. I've been there."

"And shaking that life loose is the riskiest thing I've ever done, Carny. It's scarier than sneaking out of town with a lynch mob waiting to catch me. It's scarier than dodging gunfire while I try to find an escape out the back door of a hotel. Hell, it's scarier than having your best friend die on you."

His gaze was soft and honest as she stared at him. "Then why did you do it?"

His eyes misted over. "Because I'm in love with you," he said, "and all of a sudden, the most important thing in the world to me is being the kind of man you deserve. But I've thought about the possibility that you might have left because you didn't want me—" His voice broke, and he pulled in a shaky breath and went on.

"You just can't imagine what's been going through my mind. That you saw things clearer in the morning and realized you didn't need to be involved with a lowlife like me, that you were disgusted by what I'd told you, that you'd hate me . . . "

He lifted his chin defiantly. "But then I decided that you'd have to come back eventually, and when you did, I'd be here, spending the rest of my life proving to you that I could be decent. Even if you didn't want me here, I'd stay, Carny. Because I can do this. I can bring Serenity back with this park. I can make something out of all this. And maybe not now, but someday, I can make you love me."

"It's too late," she whispered as tears streamed down her face.

For a moment, he only gave her a dismal, longing look. "Are you sure, Carny?"

She smiled through her tears. "Yeah, Brisco. You see, someday is now. And my loving you is already a done deal."

He leaned into her arms then, burying his face against her neck, and she held him like he'd never been held, like he'd never even dreamed. For one couldn't dream of a joy one had never been exposed to.

"I don't suppose you would marry me," he said finally, pulling back to look at her.

She smiled and wiped the tear traveling down his cheek. "Oh, I might be persuaded, if you asked at the right time and place."

"And what would that time and place be?"

"Anytime, anyplace," she said. "From this second on."

Laughing, he lifted her in his arms, and carried her into the hangar, as Jack followed behind them.

Logan used his persuasive talents to talk Hugh Berkstrom, the town's biggest investor, and the man who bragged that he was the first to see the brilliance in Logan Brisco's plan, into "throwing" the wedding of the century on the back lawn of his estate.

After they had been pronounced man and wife, Carny's parents wasted no time cornering Logan and trying to persuade him of the genius of their own plan to set up a string of games at the back end of the park. "And if you'll listen to me, son," Dooley said, "I can give you a thousand ideas on how to turn a profit in other ways. We really need to talk, son."

Logan nodded toward Carny, who was dancing with Joey across the room. "You'll have to talk to Carny," he said. "The town just appointed her park commissioner. She's going to be in charge of keeping Hartland clean and legitimate. And she'll even oversee the hiring . . . you know, just to make sure that everything's kept aboveboard."

Lila's face fell. "Well, she won't have time for that. Not with the airport expanding. She'll need help."

"Oh, Carny can handle a lot more than you think. And she'll *have* help."

"But she doesn't trust anyone," her father said. "If you leave it up to her, the only people that get hired will be inexperienced townies who don't have a clue how to make money."

"We'll have some good, wholesome, decent people working in Hartland," Logan said. "There's nobody better qualified to do this job, or more passionate about doing it right. She's fair," he added with a chuckle. "Submit her your proposals. She'll let you know."

Dooley and Lila were crestfallen as he left them standing there. He saw Ruth sitting in her golf cart with Jason on her huge lap, watching Carny dance with a brilliant smile on her face. Strolling toward them, he watched his bride with soft eyes. "She's really beautiful, isn't she, Ruth?"

"She's stunning," Ruth said. "You'd better be good to my baby, Logan."

"How could I be anything else? Don't worry, Ruth. I'll spend the rest of my life making her happy."

Ruth took his hand. "Somehow I think you will."

Cutting through the dancers, Logan tapped Joey on the shoulder, and when the brooding deputy stepped aside, Logan took his wife in his arms. "I thought I'd never get you back," he said with a sigh.

She smiled. "So what were my parents talking to you about?"

"Working for the park. I referred them to you."

"You didn't! No wonder they looked so upset. They know they don't stand a chance with me."

Logan caught sight of her father across the lawn, animated as he talked to a group of guests who'd gathered around him. "Tell me something. Does your father make bets on card tricks?"

"Only if they're rigged."

"Well, he's liable to rack up at this reception."

Carny looked over her shoulder and saw him engaging in the same tricks he'd used for years. "Oh, lord. He never quits. We'd better break up the reception before he takes everybody here for whatever they've got left."

They left in Carny's truck—decorated with shaving cream, toilet paper, and tin cans—and headed for the airstrip, where Logan had filled Carny's plane earlier with white roses.

"Nassau, here we come!" Logan said, carrying her, wedding dress and all, to the plane. "Imagine Serenity raising the honeymoon money for our wedding gift. And I didn't con a single one of them."

"No, you didn't," she said. "They did it for you, so you could rest. With the pace you've been keeping, they were afraid you'd collapse before the park is finished."

"Oh, I have plenty of energy," he said. "And rest is the last thing I've planned for our honeymoon."

She laughed as he put her into her seat and dropped a handful of white rose petals into her lap. Breathing the aroma of the roses, she closed her eyes and smiled. Logan went down the pre-flight checklist, as she had taught him, then took off into the sunny sky. "So what exactly *are* we going to do in Nassau?"

A wicked grin crept across his face. "Oh, I don't know. I hear there's a lot of money there, Carny. Montague always had this dream of hitting that place. And I had this great idea. . . . "

Her smile collapsed. "Don't you even think about it."

Throwing back his head, he laughed. "Had you going for a minute, didn't I?"

She moved closer to him and grinned up into his face. "I can see right through you, Logan Brisco. You know that, don't you?"

"And you married me anyway. Whoever said you can't con a con?" Slipping his fingers through her hair, he pulled her face closer. "Don't worry, baby. The only scams I'm going to pull from now on are the ones to get you into bed."

"A hundred bucks says I'll fall for it every time."

That wicked grin returned, and setting the plane on autopilot, he began unbuttoning her dress. "You're on," he said with a chuckle. "Winner take all."

## AVAILABLE NOW

### *Winner Take All* by **Terri Herrington**

Logan Brisco is the smoothest, slickest, handsomest man ever to grace the small town of Serenity, Texas. Carny Sullivan is the only one who sees the con man behind that winning smile, and she vows to save the town from his clutches. But saving herself from the man who steals her heart is going to be the greatest challenge of all.

### *The Honeymoon* by **Elizabeth Bevarly**

Newlyweds Nick and Natalie Brannon are wildly in love, starry-eyed about the future...and in for a rude awakening. Suddenly relocated from their midwestern hometown to San Juan, Puerto Rico, where Nick is posted with the U.S. Coast Guard, Natalie hopes for the best. But can true love survive the trials and tribulations of a not-so-perfect paradise?

### *Ride the Night Wind* by **Jo Ann Ferguson**

As the only surviving member of a powerful family, Lady Audra fought to hold on to her vast manor lands against ruthless warlords. But from the moonlit moment when she encountered the mysterious masked outlaw known as Lynx, she was plunged into an even more desperate battle for the fate of her heart.

### *To Dream Again* by **Laura Lee Guhrke**

Beautiful widow Mara Elliot had little time for shining promises or impractical dreams. But when dashing inventor Nathaniel Chase became her unwanted business partner, Mara found his optimism and reckless determination igniting a passion in her that suddenly put everything she treasured at risk.

### *Reckless Angel* by **Susan Kay Law**

Angelina Winchester's dream led her to a new city, a new life, and a reckless bargain with Jeremiah Johnston, owner of the most notorious saloon in San Francisco. Falling in love was never part of their deal. But soon they would discover that the last thing they ever wanted was exactly what they needed most.

### *A Slender Thread* by **Lee Scofield**

Once the center of Philadelphia's worst scandal, Jennifer Hastings was determined to rebuild her life as a schoolteacher in Kansas. She was touched when handsome and aloof Gil Prescott entrusted her with the care of his newborn son while he went to fight in the Civil War. When Gil's return unleashed a passion they had ignored for too long, they thought they had found happiness—until a man from Jennifer's past threatened to destroy it.

## COMING SOON

### *Alone in a Crowd* by Georgia Bockoven

After a terrible accident, country music sensation Cole Webster must undergo reconstructive surgery which gives him temporary anonymity. Before he can reveal his true identity, Cole loses his heart to Holly, a beautiful woman who values her privacy above all else. Cole must come to terms with who he is and what he's looking for in life before he can find love and true happiness.

### *Destiny Awaits* by Suzanne Elizabeth

When wealthy and spoiled Tess Harper was transported back in time to Kansas, 1885, it didn't take her long to find trouble. Captivating farmer Joseph Maguire agreed to bail her out on one condition–that she live with him and care for his two orphaned nieces. Despite the hardships of prairie life, Tess soon realized that this love of a lifetime was to be her destiny.

### *Broken Vows* by Donna Grove

To Rachel Girard, nothing was more important than her family's cattle ranch, which would one day be hers. But when her father declared she must take a husband or lose her birthright, Rachel offered footloose bounty hunter Caleb Delaney a fortune if he'd marry her–then leave her! Cal knew he'd be a fool to refuse, but he would soon wonder if a life without Rachel was worth anything at all.

### *Lady in Blue* by Lynn Kerstan

A delightful, sexy romance set in the Regency period. Wealthy and powerful Brynmore Talgarth never wanted a wife, despite pressure to restore the family's reputation by marrying well. But once he met young, destitute, and beautiful Clare Easton, an indecent proposal led the way to a love neither knew could exist.

### *The Long Road Home* by Mary Alice Monroe

Bankrupt and alone after her financier husband dies, Nora MacKenzie's life is shattered. After fleeing to a sheep farm in Vermont, she meets up with the mysterious C. W. Friendship soon blossoms into love, but C. W. is keeping some dangerous secrets that could destroy them both.

### *Winter Bride* by Teresa Southwick

Wyoming rancher Matt Decker needed a wife. His mother sent him Eliza Jones, the young woman who had adored Matt when they were children. Eliza was anxious to start a new life out west, but the last thing Matt wanted was to marry someone to whom he might become emotionally attached.

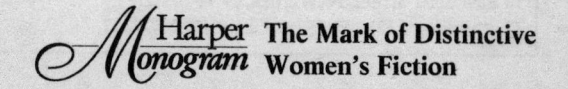

**Harper Monogram   The Mark of Distinctive Women's Fiction**

**ATTENTION: ORGANIZATIONS AND CORPORATIONS**

Most HarperPaperbacks are available at special quantity discounts for bulk purchases for sales promotions, premiums, or fund-raising. For information, please call or write:
**Special Markets Department, HarperCollins Publishers,
10 East 53rd Street, New York, N.Y. 10022.**
**Telephone: (212) 207-7528. Fax: (212) 207-7222.**